A DISORDER PECULIAR ★ TO THE ★ COUNTRY

a novel

A DISORDER PECULIAR TO THE COUNTRY

★ TO THE ★

COUNTRY

a novel

Ken Kalfus

**SIMON &
SCHUSTER**

London · New York · Sydney · Toronto

A CBS COMPANY

First published in the United States by HarperCollins, 2006
First published in Great Britain by Simon & Schuster UK Ltd, 2006
A CBS COMPANY

Copyright © Ken Kalfus, 2006

Portions of this book have appeared, in slightly different form, in the
Philadelphia Inquirer Magazine and *Tin House*

1 3 5 7 9 10 8 6 4 2

Simon & Schuster UK Ltd
Africa House
64–78 Kingsway
London WC2B 6AH

www.simonsays.co.uk

Simon & Schuster Australia
Sydney

A CIP catalogue record for this book is available from the British Library

Hardback ISBN: 0-7432-8608-1
EAN: 9780743286084

Trade Paperback ISBN: 0-7432-8621-9
EAN: 9780743286213

Printed and bound in Great Britain by
The Bath Press, Bath

For Bobby,
and for Lauren

... there is a disorder peculiar to the country, which every season makes strange ravages among them ...

—OLIVER GOLDSMITH
The Citizen of the World, 1760

CONTENTS

A
DISORDER
PECULIAR
★ TO THE ★
COUNTRY

a novel

SEPTEMBER

O N THE WAY to Newark Joyce received a call: the talks in Berkeley had collapsed, conclusively. She closed her eyes for a few moments and then asked the driver to turn around and head back through the tunnel. It was still early morning. She went directly to her office on Hudson Street to sort out the repercussions from the negotiations' failure—and especially how to evade blame for their failure. About an hour later colleagues were trickling in, passing by her open door, and Joyce thought she heard someone say that a plane had flown into the World Trade Center. The World Trade Center: the words provoked a thought like a small underground animal to dash from its burrow into the light before promptly scuttling back in retreat. She wasn't sure she had heard the news correctly; perhaps she had simply imagined it, or had even dozed off and dreamed it after less than five hours of sleep the night before. Fighting distraction, she pondered the phrasing of her report, resolved not to be defensive; at the same time she wondered whether something had just happened that would dominate the news for months to come, until everyone was sick of it. In that case there would be plenty of time to find out what it was. She presumed the plane had been a small one, causing localized damage, if it was a plane at all, if the World Trade Center had been involved at all. The towers weren't visible from her office window, but she could see several of the company slackers in the adjacent roof garden, smoking cigarettes and looking downtown. She worked for a few minutes and then suddenly she heard screaming and shouts. She thought someone had fallen off the roof.

Even now Joyce moved without hurrying, careful first to save what was on her screen. If someone had fallen she would shortly learn who, and the consequences would play out either with or without her. But as she stepped through the door to the roof she understood from their continuing shrieks what her colleagues had just witnessed: a *second* plane striking the World Trade Center. Every face of every man and woman on the roof was twisted by fear and shock. One belonged to the unyielding, taciturn company director, who had never before been seen to express emotion; now his mouth dangled open and blood rushed to his face as if he were being choked. Among her colleagues tears had begun to flow only a moment earlier. Women buried their faces in the chests of coworkers with whom they were hardly friendly. "No, no, no, no," someone murmured.

Joyce turned and saw the two pillars, one with a fiery red gash in its midsection, the other with its upper stories sheathed in heavy gray smoke. Sirens keened below. She could hear the crackle and chuffing of the burning buildings more than a mile away.

Nearly everyone in the firm had now come onto the roof, crowding shoulder to shoulder. Joyce stood among her colleagues rapt and numb and yet also acutely aware of the late summer morning's clear blue skies that mocked the city below. A portable radio was brought out. Joyce's colleagues haltingly speculated about what had happened, the size of the planes, how *two* planes could possibly have crashed in the same place at the same time. Their conversations withered in the heated confusion and terror spilling from the radio.

After a while one of the towers, the one farther south, appeared to exhale a terrific sigh of combustion products. They swirled away and half the building, about fifty or sixty stories, bowed forward on a newly manufactured hinge. And then the building fell in on itself in what seemed to be a single graceful motion, as if its solidity had been a mirage, as if the structure had been liquid all these years since it was built. Smoke and debris in all the possible shades of black, gray, and white billowed upward, flooding out around the neighboring buildings. You had to make an effort to keep before you the thought that thousands of people were losing their lives at precisely this moment.

Many of the roofs in the neighborhood were occupied, mostly by office workers. They had their hands to their faces, either at their mouths or at their temples, but none covered their eyes. They were unable to turn away. Joyce heard gasps and groans and appeals to God's absent mercy. A woman beside her sobbed without restraint. But Joyce felt something erupt inside her, something warm, very much like, yes it was, a pang of pleasure, so intense it was nearly like the appeasement of hunger. It was a giddiness, an elation. The deep-bellied roar of the tower's collapse finally reached her and went on for minutes, it seemed, followed by an unnaturally warm gust that pushed back her hair and ruffled her blouse. The building turned into a rising mushroom-shaped column of smoke, dust, and perished life, and she felt a great gladness.

"Joyce, oh my God!" cried a colleague. "I just remembered. Doesn't your husband work there?"

She nodded slowly. His office was on the eighty-sixth floor of the south tower, which had just been removed whole from the face of the earth. She covered the lower part of her face to hide her fierce, protracted struggle against the emergence of a smile.

THEY HAD BEEN INSTRUCTED to communicate with each other only through their lawyers, an injunction impossible to obey since Joyce and Marshall still shared a two-bedroom apartment with their two small children and a yapping, emotionally needy, razor-nailed springer spaniel Marshall had recently brought home without consulting anyone, not even his lawyer. (The children had been delighted.) In the year since they had begun divorcing, the couple had developed a conversation-independent system for their day-to-day lives, mostly centered on who would deposit the kids at day care (usually Joyce) and who would collect them (usually Marshall), and also who would make their lunches, talk to the caregivers about which particular problems, buy the groceries, do the laundry, make dinner for the kids, be with the kids on which weekend, and so on. Whenever something disrupted this system—and something would disrupt it several times a day: either a borderline fever, or an evening business appointment, or some toilet-training backsliding, or the inexplicable consumption of a completely full half gallon of milk purchased the day before—Joyce and Marshall were forced to speak to each other, and even the most trivial discussion was likely to escalate into a blistering argument encompassing all the issues that had brought them to divorce in the first place.

It was in a previous decade, another century, that this had started out civilly, as an agreement reached almost affectionately, that their marriage was not as warm as it had been. In the six months of therapy in which they were encouraged to break down the barriers that prevented them from speaking frankly, Joyce and Marshall discovered that they hated each other. Issues that had never before come up—money, sex, children, vacation destinations, Joyce's weight gain, and wildly differing estimates of Marshall's contribution to the child-rearing enterprise—now misted the air blue within the counselor's office, which had already been made stale by the arguments from the previous couple's appointment. The counselor finally urged them to make the break nonadversarial and referred them to divorce arbitration. Now all the arguments fell away or were subsumed by a single point of disagreement: money. Marshall's salary was substantially larger than the salary earned by Joyce, who had twice changed careers and had twice interrupted them to give birth. She demanded the apartment and that he should continue paying half the mortgage and child support as well as some to-be-determined maintenance. Once they reached this impasse, and after returning to it every week for several months, they gave up on arbitration and hired individual lawyers, a woman for Joyce, a man for Marshall. The lawyers turned out to be friends and kissed each other hello when they met.

Even before Joyce and Marshall stepped together onto the path meant to separate them, their two salaries had been insufficient. Two-thirds of their total take-home pay was consumed by the mortgage and maintenance on their ill-lit, inadequately maintained, brilliantly located co-op in Brooklyn Heights. They both cherished the apartment and the surrounding streets, their painfully won toehold in New York. Their front window faced another apartment building, but beyond it lay Manhattan, of which they could see the very top floors of the World Trade Center. It would have been impossible for Marshall to continue paying *any* part of the mortgage and at the same time rent elsewhere in the neighborhood, or in any half-safe neighborhood within the city—a conundrum that satisfied Joyce in the same way she might have been satisfied by some classic philosophical puzzle. She wanted to ruin him, not only financially but personally, and not just for now, but forever.

How *he* hated *her*. He could have written sonnets of hatred, made vows on his hatred, performed daring, heroic feats of physical labor to prove his hatred. Late at night he would sometimes glimpse her sleeping form on the couch—he had refused to give up the bedroom; Viola, their four-year-old daughter, persisted in the belief that her mother fell asleep watching TV every night— and Marshall would be seized by such passionate loathing that he would lie awake for hours, clenching and unclenching his fists. It was probably just as well that he couldn't sleep, because when he did he ground his teeth, according to his dentist, who said that he could tell from the marks in his enamel that he was getting divorced. Some repairs that he couldn't afford were recommended. Either in bed or in the dentist's chair with his damaged, doomed mouth hanging open, he thought again of what Joyce had done to him. Her pettiness and irrationality had brought the entire structure of their lives down on their heads, down on the heads of their kids. He was humiliated by his inability to expunge the memory of having loved her once as romantically as he hated her now.

He plotted; she knew it. Marshall worked stealthily, finding allies among distant acquaintances and family; he passed damaging gossip untraceably; he undermined Joyce's resolve by preempting her complaints with mirror-image accusations. Nothing in her life was beyond his reach: even her father had made an obliquely critical comment that suggested he had heard something somehow unfavorable to her, but the presumed charge was too vague to be contested. Marshall spoke rudely to her colleagues when they telephoned with important messages, which he never passed on. He resumed leaving the toilet seat up, his straight razor soapy and wet at the edge of the basin, and his underwear on the bathroom floor: all habits she had exorcised from the household years ago. He was making remarks to the kids; she heard their echoes in their questions at bedtime: Why do you look so old? Why don't you like Snuffles? Snuffles was the dog, a slobbering, stinking, slacks-tearing instrument in Marshall's campaign against her, a war fought in the shadows.

The divorcing transpired within a universe in which time was an elusive, shadowed quantity. Joyce swore that she'd have him out by the end of the year; with the year left unspecified, Marshall defied the oath. He countered that she would need to file a motion; his lawyer filed an opposing brief; this took an entire winter. Holidays intervened. The apartment had to be appraised, another process profligate of Joyce's office-desk Joke-a-Day Calendar; they hired competing appraisers, jinn and sorcerers who turned gold into lead and vice versa. Marshall's fine arts degree, which he had earned during some of their time together and therefore supported her claim to his future earnings even though it had no bearing on his current career, also had to be appraised, twice. Legal fees rapidly depleted their savings accounts, which were not only divided and separated, but had been placed in competing banks, located in nonadjacent boroughs. Feelings between Joyce and Marshall acquired the intensity of something historic, tribal, and ethnic, and when they watched news of wars on TV, reports from the Balkans or the West Bank, they would think, yes, yes, yes, that's how I feel about *you*.

Meanwhile their two children—products of their former love, their marriage's fatal complications, their divorce's civilian casualties—had to be raised. Joyce and Marshall watched them on alternate weekends, but Marshall believed that to maintain his moral right to the residence he should remain in the apartment on Joyce's weekends. He occupied most of these in the bedroom, with the door closed provocatively, ominously, without even the hum of his television audible. He left it only to feed and walk Snuffles, which Joyce refused to do, even when Marshall wasn't home and the dog was frantic. He had been forced to subscribe to a dog-care service.

Something seemed to stress, fault, and shift these two impacted continental plates one Sunday afternoon at the end of August. Joyce had just arrived at the playground with the children; two-year-old Victor sat on the asphalt by the park bench examining a piece of foil while Viola climbed on the playground equipment. Suddenly Viola rushed to her mother, laughing. She had a very sweet smile and could be a tender, affectionate child; sometimes her parents gazed into her bright brown eyes and completely forgot that they had ever been unhappy. "Poop!" she announced. It ran wet down her legs. The girl was already four; Joyce swore bitterly. Viola laughed at that too. Fortunately, Joyce had brought changes of clothes with her. She grabbed several baby wipes from her bag and tried to clean Viola's legs, but the girl's overalls were full of it and the stream was too intense: she was still pooping, willfully. "Stop it," Joyce said. "Stop it right now." Joyce wanted to drop the wipes, lie facedown on the bench, cradle her face in her arms, and quietly cry herself to sleep, floating away from this life on a river of tears. Other mothers and caregivers, no one she knew, watched coldly; even some kids with a basketball, usually oblivious to anything but the basketball, observed her. She lifted Viola by the arms and carried her around the locked toilets to a garbage receptacle, trying to keep the girl's body away from hers. She unfastened the snaps of the overalls and let the whole shitty mess drop into the trash. Viola would have outgrown them anyway. With one hand suspending the girl over the garbage, Joyce used wipes in the other to remove the turds. It took about a minute, maybe two. The girl was still filthy. Joyce swung her bare-assed and giggling back to their things—but she saw that at their bench by the stroller something was horribly wrong. Her stomach pitched. Vic was bawling, bawling furiously, in the arms of a crazy man, a disheveled, wild-eyed, gesticulating, spitting man: her husband. He was with the dog.

"Where." Marshall could hardly speak. He was shaking, he was vibrating, he looked like he was about to launch himself into space. He gasped after every word. "Were. You?"

"Viola pooped in her pants."

"You abandoned him!"

"Fuck you. I was cleaning her off."

Snuffles must have thought they were talking about dinner. Wagging his tail and barking, he lunged at Joyce and gleefully stabbed the nails of his front paws into Joyce's legs. Joyce teetered back, Viola fell wetly against her blouse, and she saw that the leash was being held by Marshall's very close friend Roger, husband of her former very close friend Linda; in fact, she had once been her best friend. A year ago, before they agreed to tell their friends about their marital difficulties, Marshall had confessed them to Roger and Linda in one long night of tears, hugs, and vows of everlasting friendship. Now Roger looked away, embarrassed to see her again.

"For how long?" Marshall cried. "You didn't come back for five minutes *after* we got here! We timed it. A baby-snatcher would have been over the bridge by now! This is it, Joyce. You're finished. My lawyer's going to question your fitness as a mother."

Marshall's promise was kept: the incident was brought up at their meeting the following Friday. Roger would testify, if need be. Joyce's lawyer told her not to worry, she would have to do much worse to lose primary residential custody, that he had no case, that custody hadn't even been an issue before now. Joyce knew that Marshall didn't even *want* custody, but the threat would be potent enough to persuade her eventually, wretchedly, tearfully, inevitably, to scale back or fully eliminate her mortgage demands—and there was no way she could afford the apartment on her own. She was being beaten and crushed, suffocated and abandoned. The force of Marshall's hatred was nearly self-validating: after all, how could a man believe with such fervor and be wrong? How could she have left Victor like that? Everything was going against her now: she had gained another three pounds, the Berkeley deal was stalled, her annual review was coming up.

Afterward she sought refuge in Connecticut with her parents, who were visibly disappointed that she came without the children, even though they knew it wasn't her weekend with them. Back in Brooklyn peace reigned. With Joyce gone, Marshall was suddenly more optimistic, more free, more alive. He sang show tunes. He wrestled with the kids. He took them out for pizza. They walked Snuffles along the promenade over the harbor, where Viola named for Victor all the important buildings in the Manhattan skyline. On Saturday night Vic fell asleep on Marshall's chest. The boy's weight comforted the man, who had begun to feel himself hollow and insubstantial. The boy's mass was real and truthful and loving. For the first time since they lit the fuse to their divorce, Marshall believed that he could succeed as a single father.

Marshall's golden weekend was extended through Monday. Joyce went to her office from her parents' and after work ate dinner out. Marshall cheerfully brought the kids home from day care, fed them, and put them in front of the TV so that he could review some company reports. The phone interrupted him twice, both times on Joyce's behalf. The first call was from some dickhead in California who had been trying to reach her on her cell. Breathy and agitated, and clearly clueless about their family situation, he told Marshall at length that such and such negotiations now appeared to be moving forward but desperately required Joyce's presence the next day. The second was from a woman at her corporate travel office, who at the dickhead's request had booked Joyce's flight from Newark and made the other arrangements.

LaGuardia would have been more convenient, but Marshall stayed silent. As a matter of principle he was reluctant to help Joyce at all. He doodled the information into his workbook, unsure whether he would pass it on—any message could be seen as weakness, or a peace feeler, or an apology for not passing on messages before, or even an expression of forgiveness for all the messages *she* hadn't passed on to *him*. On the other hand, here was an opportunity to get her out of the apartment perhaps for the rest of the week. He contemplated the semiotics. Still brooding, he finally copied the flight number and the name of the hotel onto another sheet of paper, without salutation or closing, as tersely and as barely legibly as possible, and placed it on the kitchen counter below the microwave, where she would very likely miss it.

But Joyce was hungry when she came home. Compelled against her better judgment to put a frozen pastry into the microwave, she found the message. She was relieved that Marshall's bedroom door was closed because she feared the slightest possibility that she might blurt a word of gratitude. She recharged her cell phone and packed. The next morning her taxi came so early that Marshall had to take the kids to preschool, which dictated a vein-bulging, door-slamming argument just as she left.

He dressed the kids in their sleep.

"Where's Mommy?" Viola mumbled.

"Berkeley. It's near San Francisco, in California. She's left you to go to California."

"Before breakfast?"

With no time to walk Snuffles, Marshall urged himself to remember to call the dog-care service. They finally made it to school, where he fell into a prolonged and subjectless but immensely amiable conversation with Viola's bouncy, curly-haired teacher. She was probably just out of college, with cheeks no less ruddy than those of her charges. Marshall dug her and— and this was not entirely confirmed and it might have been wishful thinking, like his self-conscious optimism about single parenthood, intended to counteract his desperate emotional state, which comprised sentiments of worthlessness, unattractiveness, failure, and mortality—she appeared to dig him digging her. But now he was late for work.

AN HOUR LATER Marshall was sprawled across some debris that he had fallen over in the dark, in a place that he could not precisely identify, after a series of events that he could neither order nor fully signify. There had been panic in the elevator lobbies, explosions, contradictory emergency announcements, pandemonium in the stairwell. He had never made it to his office. Now, in the smoke and dust-choked gloom, men and women were moaning and crying and calling in pitiful voices for help. Breathing was difficult. Water ran someplace, plashing and tinkling as if in an alpine glade. Parts of the ceiling and walls had collapsed, and something had either fallen on him or he had run hard into it. People had struggled up the paralyzed escalator with him, perhaps even following him. *Up* had seemed wrong, but that's where he thought the cop at the bottom of the stairwell had directed him. Now they were lost.

He came to his feet and brought his hand to his head. The side of his head felt wet, probably with blood, but Marshall told himself that he was all right and that his mind remained clear, unbearably so. Nothing that had happened earlier this morning—the argument with Joyce, the flirting with Miss Naomi—had subsided or grown distant in his recollection. A portion of his consciousness recognized that these were proba- bly the last moments of his life and that he would never again see Viola and Vic; also, that he would never again be permitted to think of them. Yet he also remembered that he had to call the dog-walking service, or the dog would piss on the rug in the entrance foyer. It had already ruined the afghan. Drywall dust pitted his face and he could taste, without explanation, the odor of gasoline on an airport runway.

"Police! Police! We're trapped!" The shouts echoed. No re- ply was made, but he could hear the sirens outside. They seemed close.

Marshall ran his hands against some debris and pulled away when he touched a jagged shard from a broken window. He was aware now that the fabric of the darkness was more tenuous up ahead, and he moved toward the faint glow, his hands directly in front of his face in case he encountered more glass. He understood that he was stepping through the window. His hands led him around some kind of support column.

He turned and called behind him, "I see daylight!"

He bumped into more debris and passed around it, and then abruptly found himself at the edge of the plaza between the twin towers—another planet's landscape, lightning-charged, caustically lit, inimical. He recoiled. Ashy flakes fell on a carpet of ash inches deep, covering fleeing footprints. Objects burned in the ash, pieces of industrial-like machinery, pieces of concrete that had fallen from the towers, and some other things that required another moment to be identified. They were human body parts, yes, and with them whole bodies scattered on the slate pavement blocks. Charred memos, reports, printouts, balance sheets, and Post-its eddied around them like departing spirits. Men and women ran from the building, some shrieking, their briefcases on their heads, though the things that fell into the plaza were much larger than briefcases. Taffies of molten steel spilled from the upper floors of the towers, fragmenting into gorgeous sparks of blazing shrapnel when they hit the cold ground.

"Here we are!" he shouted back inside the building, against an outpouring of gray smoke. "C'mon, let's go!" He thought of a joke. "Ladies and gentlemen, this way to the egress!"

But people were already coming out, led by a trembling middle-aged woman whose white blouse was streaked with grime and tears. She wasn't wearing shoes. She blinked against the light and then against what she saw in the plaza, flinching just as he had.

The precipitation was becoming heavier every minute.

Pelted by small, stinging objects, Marshall shrank against the sheer wall of the tower. The middle-aged woman took off toward an abandoned line of ash-rimmed sandwich carts at the far edge of the plaza, running in her stockinged feet, nimbly avoiding the most obvious pieces of sharp debris in her path. Men and women were still falling from the upper stories, possibly even from his own office: colleagues and friends.

Shadows continued to emerge from the tower, materializing halfheartedly into substance, coughing and wiping their eyes. Shocked by the plaza's carnage, the survivors didn't see Marshall. They immediately ran off, one couple holding hands. The sirens were tremendous now, their voices filling the sky. Marshall knew he should go, but he hung back. He wondered about this reluctance, this sudden loss of instinct for his own preservation. It was the divorce, the fucking divorce—he had been beaten down so badly. He called into the building, "Hey, anybody left?"

There was no response. He took a few steps back in under a sagging window frame through a dark, rubble-strewn passage. Smoke and dust seared his eyes. He thought he could feel the building shudder. He told himself that he would go no deeper than the next step, but he pushed on. Something was here at the edge of the passage, some wraith. He could hear its breathing and smell its fear, which was hardly distinct from his own.

"Hey," Marshall said. "Come. Let's go."

Marshall found a sleeve and tugged on it, surprised by its tangibility. The creature to which it was attached moved without speaking. Marshall led him back through the passageway, probably a distance of no more than ten yards, but the exit seemed much farther now, like a journey or transition to a new world. A damp, cold confidence had enveloped him. What he was doing seemed right, just as everything that had gone on between him and Joyce during the past two years had seemed so terribly wrong. In his struggle with Joyce, even when defending his most fundamental interests, he had doubted that what he was doing was either right or good—it had been only necessary. Now... in these moments of peril, decision, and action... something was being revealed. He could discern hope. He could, at this instant, glimpse a vision of the man he could yet be.

They reached the lip of the plaza, where Marshall turned and briefly examined his captive. He was older than Marshall, with gray around his temples. His thick mustache appeared matted by blood. The man's eyes were inflamed and the blank expression on his face made Marshall wonder if he could see anything at all. Marshall said, "Okay, we're almost out of here."

The man crumpled into a sitting position against the side of the tower. He stared out across the plaza's wastes for a moment and then bowed his head toward the ground. He might have been praying. Marshall thoughtfully bit his lip and tasted what seemed like plaster. Finally, he said, "Hey, my name's Marshall, what's yours?"

The man didn't stir.

"What's your name?" Marshall said. For the moment the plaza had become quiet, with no one fleeing the towers and only a drizzle of gray particles. He lightly touched the man's shoulder, and when that had no effect, he shook him roughly. He recalled that in an emergency the usual urban strictures against body contact with strangers didn't apply. The man's head bounced as if it were on a spring. "Tell me your name."

Startled, the man raised his head and whispered, "Lloyd."

"Lloyd," Marshall repeated. "I'm Marshall. Look, this is a bad place to rest. Everything's falling. What do you say we get out of here, huh? C'mon, you go, I go, maybe we'll get a skim latte or something. You have to stand, Lloyd. You have to stand and come with me right now. Up, now. Otherwise we're going to get hurt. Do you have a kid? I've got two, Victor and Viola, a real handful. What's your kid's name?"

Lloyd looked at Marshall for the first time. The edges of his eyelids seemed crusted with something and the whites were red and heavily veined. Marshall didn't want to look at them, didn't want to see what had happened to them, but he knew that it was important to hold the man's gaze. "Sarah," Lloyd mumbled.

"That's sweet. How old is she?"

"Six."

"Great age, I'm sure. My girl's four, still has going-to-the-bathroom accidents. Drives us crazy. C'mon, up we go."

Saying *us* felt false, though it was technically true, since Viola's incontinence tortured Joyce as well as Marshall, but separately, not as a concern they shared. Marshall had Lloyd by the arm. If he let go, he'd fall. He wondered if Lloyd was married, and if so, how happily; also whether he could possibly explain to him his ambivalence about *us*. He tried to orient Lloyd in the direction of Church Street. The man staggered like a drunk. Just as they were about to make their run, an object that was recognizably a woman in a navy business suit, possibly a suit that could be described in regard to its cut and weave, and possibly even its likely provenance if you knew about such things, thumped hard less than twenty feet away, and bounced and burst. Her shoes had come off in mid-fall and clattered emptily against the pavement a moment later. "Don't look," Marshall said. "For God's sake don't look." He pushed him into the plaza. Crazily, both men still had their attachés; Marshall's was on a shoulder strap, but Lloyd clutched his in both hands, as if the morning's escape were part of his regular commute. The ash crunched and blood was slicked black around the bodies. Sickly sweet gas fumes tinted the air. Pounding across the plaza, their shoes swirled up ash. Small objects were still falling and something hit Marshall on the shoulder. Whatever happened today was terrible and historic. He kept his eyes fixed on the far side of the plaza and wondered about the date. He knew that Friday would be September 14, because a once-important meeting had been scheduled for that day, and he knew that today was Tuesday, but he could not from this knowledge make any further calculation.

Something spectacular happened in front of them, involving something the size of a car. Marshall covered his face and the blast, its fire and noise infernal, passed right through him. He dodged to the right, shoving Lloyd, who was sliding out of Marshall's grip. Marshall squeezed his sleeve hard and felt the fabric start to give way.

"We're almost there," but he saw that Lloyd wasn't listening, that half his head—Marshall couldn't tell which half—had been ripped away.

Lloyd's attaché fell and ejected its suddenly irrelevant contents, papers, reports, and a sandwich wrapped in Saran. Marshall knew what he had to do then. He had to lay the man in the ash, gently but swiftly. He had to try not to look at his head and he would have to will himself to forget whatever he saw. Smoke lifted from the man's body as Marshall pulled away.

HE DESCENDED from the plaza into a street of abandoned cars, some of them on fire. Men and women were running between them. By now none of this seemed unusual; for all he knew, all over the world men and women were in flight from their own local cataclysms. *The kids*—he couldn't complete the thought. At Chambers Street he heard an explosive crack and then a long crashing sound behind him: one of the towers was falling. The mob responded with a collective gasp and then a cascade of screams. Cops up the block waved them on, windmilling their arms. The falling building's roar was like the break of the surf and it seemed to lift him from the street. Debris rained down on his back and chalky dust filled his mouth and nose. He sprinted without strain or fatigue, weightless now, his briefcase banging against his side. When he finally slowed and looked back down Church, men and women like seraphs and nymphs were emerging from the huge gray-white cloud that on this still-dazzling late summer unnumbered day obscured the whole of lower Manhattan.

Marshall had to get back to Brooklyn, to the preschool, but for now he joined the great march north, its legions mostly speechless. Around Canal an EMS worker came into the middle of the street, tenderly took his arm, and led him to a triage station next to a parked ambulance, where his forehead was cleaned and bandaged. The medics had a small radio tuned to the news. The radio reported that two hijacked jetliners flying from Boston had struck each tower of the World Trade Center—shocked, Marshall jerked his head and looked downtown for confirmation—and added that the Pentagon had been attacked as well.

Marshall didn't know Lloyd's last name or the name of the firm that had employed him. At this moment the absence of the man from his future was like an enormous hole in the sky, yet he had somehow forgotten the name of Lloyd's little girl. The sentiment that had embraced him in the plaza and which had promised him so much now vanished, leaving him with a not-unfamiliar despair. The extent of the tragedy was becoming evident. Real people lay under the rubble, men and women he had worked with or ridden elevators with nearly every weekday for years.

When the north tower collapsed, the evacuees began running again and Marshall was sent off. With many others he tried to head for one of the East River bridges, but Kevlar-wrapped police officers at the main intersections shouted at them to move uptown, warning of bombs and asbestos dust. His cell was dead and long lines snaked from the pay phones. He worked his way down side streets. After a while, fatigued and confused, he stopped outside a Chinatown pastry shop that was taken up by a crowd watching a television hung from the ceiling above the cash register.

The audience spilled from the shop, conveying news into the street. Air traffic in the U.S. had been grounded, but some planes were still flying and more attacks were expected. At least one other jetliner had crashed, somewhere in Pennsylvania. The president was being taken to a secret location.

Marshall turned to a young man wearing a CNN T-shirt. "Are we at war or something? Did they say a plane hit the Pentagon?"

The young man couldn't see the TV either, but he spoke with authority. "Destroyed half the building. American Flight 77, out of Dulles. And the plane that crashed in Pennsylvania left from Newark. No one knows what they were aiming for. Hey, you're some sight. Were you there?" He gestured in the former direction of the towers.

Marshall said, "Tell me something: the Newark plane, where was it flying to? Do they have the flight number?"

The fellow shrugged, but he asked the people standing in front of him and the request was passed into the pastry shop. It took some time to echo back. Meanwhile Marshall sat on the curb and opened his briefcase, which was now encrusted with history like an antique portfolio. He rooted inside for his workbook. He flipped through it until he found the page with the notes he had been studying the night before when the phone rang.

"Ninety-three," the young man announced. "They say it was United, to San Francisco."

Marshall nodded grimly and closed the workbook. He returned it to his briefcase and stood. As if his pants weren't already ruined, he unhurriedly brushed them off. He touched the bandage on his scalp. It had become moist. The medics had said he would need stitches. On the street the curbs could barely contain the flood of refugees: filthy, dazed, grieved, bereft. Many still masked their mouths and noses. Women limped in bare feet. A few people supported each other. Many wept, but most of their faces had gone as blank as the indifferent sky. Marshall went among them and headed for the bridge, nearly skipping.

OCTOBER

JOYCE HAD ALWAYS known that New York cops and firemen were more attractive than those employed by other municipalities: it was their sharp haircuts, their exotic ethnicities, their well-spokenness, their vivacity. But now they had taken on the graces of classical heroes, clear-eyed and broad-chested, manly and kind, applauded as they strode down the avenues and into delis, tragedy etched on their faces. Even now those faces were innocent and beautiful. The firemen, especially, presided over the city's September 11 sorrows. They spoke softly. They admitted to insomnia and loss of appetite. They visibly scorned that autumn's unnaturally prolonged run of transparent skies. Each of them in the five boroughs had lost at least one "brother" from his firehouse or a friend from another; quite a few mourned actual brothers, fathers, and sons. Now at any moment anywhere in the city a fireman might appear and civilians would stand back as he passed among them, his big-boy body beneath his protective black denim overalls moving like the parts of an antique engine. Every step in his rubber waders was profoundly deliberate.

Two of the young women in Joyce's office worked nights at a volunteer kitchen near Ground Zero, feeding the rescue workers when they came off their shifts. Dora and Alicia would arrive at the office late, weary and drained, yet also with the kind of glow usually associated with pregnancy. They'd talk about Ground Zero the rest of the day to whatever small congregations assembled around their cubicles. No one saw the point to their jobs right now. Alicia had been escorted into the excavation pit early this morning wearing a hard hat and a bright yellow fireman's slicker that was much too big for her—under the two-thousand-watt halide lamps she must have been impossibly fetching. She was seeing one of the firemen, an Italian guy from Bay Ridge, half his company lost in Tower Two, a married guy, and she spoke of his pain and brokenness, and she herself had assumed some of his suffering. The descent into the pit had somehow brought her closer to all the men at the site; also, closer to her real self, she said. And making love to her fireman was like nothing she had ever known before: "He's so strong and he needs me so much. I don't know where this is going. But right now, at this moment, I have to be with him. *I* need *him*."

Joyce's coworkers, many of whom were unmarried and younger than Joyce, knew exactly what Alicia meant. The awfulness of the terrorist attacks had kindled desperation in every life; either the stakes had been raised or they had been made irrelevant. Last week Dora found herself necking furiously with a casual friend she had known for years. In a quiet voice, so that the men in the office wouldn't hear, she spoke of another friend's string of one-night stands. The sex had been unprotected; her partners had been guys she met in bars and in one case on the subway steps at Spring Street. Dora's friend had never done anything like this before. She had come up out of the station, Dora said, and had absentmindedly looked for the towers to orient herself, but they weren't there and the man was and he understood her confusion at once. The other women nodded grimly. They called it terror sex. Everyone needed

something now, some release or payback or just acknowledgment that their lives had been changed. Joyce turned away
from the conversation and gazed absently from the window
looking south at the mutilated skyline. She had narrowly
escaped destruction and had seen the towers come down, but
so far she hadn't had any terror sex, just terror Cherry Garcia.

Joyce hadn't made love once in the past two years, approxi-
mately: she couldn't pinpoint the actual date of her final sexual
relations with Marshall. On the last several occasions on which
they had attempted sex, or something like sex, something physical and almost tender that might possibly have gone some
small way toward restoring their intimacy, they had only deepened their anger with each other—anger about the sex, but
also anger about the laundry and the squalling babies and the
AmEx bill and the spilled milk. Pointlessly they had wrestled
across the sheets. These struggles usually ended with tears and
slammed doors and before any penetration could be accomplished. Joyce couldn't recall the ultimate half- or quarter-
hearted attempt that had preceded their determination, a
consensus reached without words, that lovemaking was no longer worth the effort. So it had been at least two years. She was
thirty-five. After Alicia and Dora told their stories, Joyce realized that she wanted something too: she wanted one of these
men they spoke about to throw her onto a bed and fuck her as
if there would be no tomorrow. She wanted some terror sex.
After everything that had happened, to her city and to her marriage, she deserved it.

AND PERHAPS there would be no tomorrow. On her way back
from the ladies' room, Joyce was crossing the central open area
of the office where the clerks and junior associates were installed when one of the temps, a middle-aged woman named
Anne-Marie, began to shriek. She held in her hands a white

legal-sized envelope that had been torn open. Even before they had seen what had fallen onto her desk, everyone in the office knew what the shriek was about, what it had to be.

In the last few days similar envelopes dosed with fatally poisonous anthrax bacteria had been arriving up and down the East Coast. First there had been a mysterious death at the offices of the *National Enquirer* in Florida, and then the bacteria—the deadliest known to science—was found at the U.S. Senate and the headquarters of several news organizations in New York. Several people had died, including people who were not in these offices, apparently people who had contact only with mail that might have had contact with other mail that might have had contact with anthrax. The mail had become another kind of unsafe sex. Everyone was trying to get a prescription for Cipro. A welfare-to-work trainee, Anne-Marie was opening mail today because the person whose job it was had abruptly taken her personal days this week, all of them, for this year and the next. Anne-Marie wore rubber gloves and a surgical mask, but she knew they were useless against the uncountable number of malevolent white grains that had just spilled from the tear in the envelope. The grains had already gone airborne. She and everyone around her had been exposed.

Joyce turned, went down the elevator, and immediately left the building, leaving her things in her office. She had two children to raise. Living in New York and trying to get a divorce: she had taken too many chances with her kids' welfare already. She held her breath until she reached the street. She kept walking, uptown, away from her office and the concatenation of evil forces that had met at Ground Zero in September and continued to possess it and haunt the city. She felt ridiculous. It was ten-thirty in the morning, she was about to receive a crucial phone call from a client, and she was wearing four-inch Dolce & Gabbana slingbacks in which she could barely stand. They had been an impulse purchase. And right now the fatal microorganism was possibly boring into her lungs. A fleet of police cars screamed past her.

She had gone about four blocks before she realized that she wasn't carrying money, not even a MetroCard, and that the keys to her apartment were back in the office in her bag. So what was she supposed to do? How would she get home? Why was it that her entire life had become totally impossible? Was she supposed to call *Marshall*? She hadn't even tried to call him last month when there was a distinct possibility that a 600,000-ton building had fallen on top of him. He had arrived home that afternoon with stitches in his scalp and his suit shredded, and she had said, "So you made it out?" He had looked away, into the air, and replied, "So you weren't on the plane?" He added, his voice leaden, "We're such fortunate people." Now she stood on the corner of Charles Street, unable to walk farther or make a single decision about anything. This was her life today: frozen-solid, shut-down, dead. Pedestrians walked around her as if she were an inconveniently placed newspaper box. There was nothing she could do but return for her pocketbook.

By the time she walked back the entire building was nearly evacuated. The entrance was being cleared by the police, and spectators massed across the street. Joyce noted with grave dissatisfaction that the others in her office had remembered to take their bags and jackets. Except for Anne-Marie, who was bawling without respite and was being lifted into an ambulance, her colleagues remained calm. They spoke among themselves and smoked cigarettes. Police were coming in and out of the building and none of them had masks. Joyce's flight had been overly hasty. She stood apart, watching. She needed her bag. She couldn't do anything without her bag. Breathing shallowly, she followed one of the officers inside the building and into the elevator. The cop didn't look at her twice, but when they exited at the fourth floor she was stopped by another policeman.

"Turn around, lady," he said. He was young and dark, a handsome kid with a bobbing Adam's apple. He barely looked at her. "We've got a call about a suspicious package here."

"It wasn't a package," she snapped. "It was an envelope. I work here. I need my pocketbook." Joyce's speech was clipped and strained by her effort to minimize the amount of contaminated air she inhaled.

The cop shook his head and turned away. He was speaking to the policeman who had come up in the elevator with her about why they couldn't seal the outer offices with masking tape—the tape they had brought with them wasn't wide enough to cover the doorframes. The elevator door remained open, uncharacteristically patient as it waited for Joyce to return. Her eyes stung. She was going to cry. She was appalled by the prospect: only last week, at the end of another bellowing, kid-terrifying, tear-filled, completely humiliating argument with Marshall (about *what*? she couldn't remember), she had vowed that she would never cry in front of a man again.

"I need my keys!" she insisted. "I have to go home! I have kids!" And here came the tears. No, not yet, she was fighting them, the tears were gushing *to* her tear ducts but not from them yet. Meanwhile she was trying not to breathe. She must have had a very peculiar expression on her face, because the policemen had interrupted their conversation to look at her. But she wouldn't cry.

The young cop said, "Look, lady, we don't know what we have here. Maybe it's anthrax, maybe it's baby powder. But you're being evacuated, that's orders." The other cop, aware now that he had been careless to allow her into the elevator with him, glared menace at her.

"Officers!" Now someone else was angry, a squat guy in a suit, hurriedly coming down the hall. "What's this, a tea party? We have to clear the building."

"We told her," the second cop said sullenly.

Not even looking at Joyce, the new man took her elbow and pulled her toward the elevator. The motion sloshed the tears swelling in her eyes and they nearly spilled over. She jerked her arm away.

"Who are you?"

"FBI."

He said it almost mournfully—indeed, his tone was entirely mournful. For good reason. His agency had been disgraced. It had ignored evidence that terrorists were planning the September 11 attacks. It had been warned about specific individuals entering the country and about followers of Osama bin Laden attending American flight schools. It had lost track of thousands of Muslim fundamentalists who had violated their immigration visas. Now the FBI was being derided for its response to the anthrax crisis, its personnel rushing from site to site without the proper equipment or consistent procedures. The bureau had been at first slow to identify the anthrax, and its warnings to the public had been vague and contradictory. And this bureau representative hardly inspired confidence. He was short and out of shape, jowly and heavy-browed, and he was perspiring heavily even though the building was cool. The air-conditioning was still running, dispersing the bacteria. No one had a mask yet.

The agent added, an unattractive pleading element in his voice, "Please cooperate. You can be arrested if you don't."

"I need my keys!" she repeated. "You're going to close us down for the day, maybe for the rest of the month! I have to pick up my kids. How am I going to bring them home if I don't have keys?"

"Doesn't your husband have keys?"

"We're separated," she said. The agent gazed at her with his jaw set hard, his eyes cold. He was listening, judging her words as carefully as he would have appraised the words of a suspected terrorist. Something seemed to pass across her body, similar to what she imagined she felt when she went through a metal detector. She observed that the agent's hair was thin, but he had a great haircut that mitigated the deficiency. In New York even the middle-aged FBI schlepps had great haircuts. She qualified her testimony in a rush: "We're getting divorced, but actually we're not technically separated according to state law since he insists on living in the apartment, but we have lawyers and a court date. I've filed a suit demanding that he leave. He's contesting. I never know where he is at any given moment, I just know that I have to pick up the kids from day care today. The main thing is that I can't ask him for a favor."

The cops exchanged skeptical pouts. She felt herself blushing and the tears gathering again like a thundercloud, and also that she was taking suicidally full breaths. Even this explanation wasn't fully accurate: certain details, caveats, extenuations, and implications had been left unexpressed. The agent made no immediate response. He was thinking over her words. She wished she had brought her lipstick with her when she had gone to the ladies' room, but then of course she would have had her bag.

His mournfulness didn't dissipate when, finally, he said, "Where are the keys?"

"In my pocketbook," she blurted. "In my office, the third on the left. My nameplate's next to the door. Joyce Harriman. The bag's right on the windowsill."

The agent muttered to the cops, "It's not like the place is sealed off. They can't even bring the right goddamn masking tape." He said to Joyce, "Wait here."

Joyce resumed holding her breath as he disappeared through the doorway. Neither of the cops looked at her. One of them went off. The other turned away and said into his radio something unintelligible that was answered unintelligibly. A new cop came into the hallway and eyed her suspiciously. He left without speaking. Another arrived at last with a handful of surgical masks. He didn't offer one to Joyce. The air-conditioning was *still* running; they had probably evacuated the only person who knew how to shut it off. She was being bathed in deadly bacteria. After everything that had happened, after all the grief and mortifications of the past year, this would be a fitting end to her life as a woman, wife, and mother.

"Is this your bag, miss? You'll have to show some ID."

The FBI man was coming into the hallway. He carried her pocketbook on his shoulder, one hand resting on the clasp. It was a Fendi Baguette, with a beige leather strap and a large buckle. The agent was carrying in the other hand her commuter shoes. One of the cops snorted. Men carrying women's accessories rarely amused Joyce, but she was stricken now by a terrible seizure that had some of the characteristics of laughter. And this did it: the tears broke through every firewall she had erected against them. She gushed, mascara probably streaking her face, and she was laughing at the same time in all the ways and in the historical sequence in which she had learned to laugh: first a giggle, then an innocent crystalline chuckle; then, from her adolescence, a kind of strangled chuffing sound that she knew was unpleasant and had eliminated from her range of responses long before she left high school; then, a mean snigger; then, a big, chortling guffaw; then, subsiding, an adult *heh-heh*. Her nose was running too. The mascara would ruin her blouse and she didn't even have a tissue: they were in her bag. The cops and the FBI agent were amazed. They stared, unaware that she had been laughing at all.

MARSHALL WAS ABSENT when she finally returned home; he left every morning as if he were going to work, despite the destruction of his company's offices at the World Trade Center, and came back in the early evening. She presumed he had another job somewhere. Her lawyer would find out, eventually. Snuffles bounded across the foyer to greet her. Joyce grabbed the dog by the collar and pushed it into the children's bedroom. She closed the door hard. The dog scratched the door and whined. Joyce steeled her heart against the animal: it was Marshall's pet. Now, if she could ignore the dog's entreaties for company, she had the apartment to herself until she fetched the kids from day care. She turned on the television and was immediately tuned to a live special report about the suspicious letter that had arrived at her company's offices. The reporter, who was virtually shouting the news, stood in the middle of Hudson Street, which had been closed to traffic, and behind him Joyce's building was blocked off by emergency vehicles and ribbons of yellow tape. The report showed film of Anne-Marie being wrestled into the back of the ambulance. When the news went back to the live feed, Joyce looked for colleagues among the onlookers, but they had left. She was disappointed not to see the FBI man or the cops she had met among the people coming in and out of the building.

As if this would wash away the anthrax, she took an extremely long, very hot shower. She washed her hair for the second time that day, deeply massaging her scalp. She let the water hit her full in the face until her skin was raw and puffy. She tried to lose every sense of herself now: the jet would scour away the memory of her sad, constricted daily life.

She usually dressed in the bathroom, away from Marshall, but this afternoon she celebrated her solitude by coming into the living room with her plumpish pinkish body lightly wrapped in a towel. Another towel was wound around her head. The heat of the shower had made her languid and achy. This mood, of course, was precisely conducive to sex. She thought again of Alicia's fireman. The thought didn't arouse her, but she believed she could be aroused by it, with a little effort. It had been years since she had been sexually aroused, years since she had even masturbated. She felt the rush of an idea. Almost anything now had the possibility of changing her life for the better.

She arranged the towel on the couch evenly and lay on her stomach. Asking herself whether she really wanted to do this, she worked her hand between her legs and felt for the right place and was surprised by a shudder when she found it. The TV was still on, unfortunately; the breaking news had given way to some soap opera—*One Life to Live,* to be exact—and the dog was whimpering now, its snout at the bottom of the door. She tried to force these sounds from her consciousness. She worked at the place and, sure enough, as if an arcane scientific theory were being practically demonstrated, a once-familiar fluid warmth spread down her thighs and legs. Her behind was bare and still damp from the shower, but the chill on her skin was good, intensifying her reception to the heat swelling around her upper thighs. Use it, she whispered, use it, her mouth tightening as she reached deeper into the place. Her nipples hardened. She felt the towel's fabric against them. She reminded herself how great her breasts were. She had gained some weight in her legs and tummy, but after nursing two children she still had terrific breasts, exquisitely round and high, probably nicer than Alicia's. A man would like to touch them. She tried to think of a fireman she might have seen in the street, or in the television reports or newspapers. He was blond and young, his white-and-blue baseball shirt snug against his chest, the outline of his chest muscles... She came down hard against her finger, grinding her pelvis into the couch. The couch squeaked, she heard herself grunt, and Snuffles launched a series of high-pitched yaps. She worked more and it felt like something under there was about to turn over. Turn over, turn *over.* Perhaps the fireman had a mustache. No mustache. Mustache. She had met him on the corner of Charles Street when she fled the building. He had seen that she was lost and terrified. Big arms. Soft hands. She had fallen into him, against his chest, and he had enclosed her with his big arms and soft hands. He took her home (no keys? forget that), to this couch, and they hardly spoke. He needed her as much as she needed him. But the image shimmered. No mustache. Mustache. Forget his face, don't look there. But she did look there, and the fireman had Marshall's face. He had Marshall's eyes and Marshall's lips. Look away, she insisted, working her pelvis with greater force, trying to make that thing turn over, reaching harder, grinding harder, as it slid away. Fireman with a mustache. No mustache. She groaned, almost there, not quite there, never there. But now she could see only Marshall's face, scowling.

Fuck.

She was sick. Sick, sick, sick. She was hopeless.

THE MOOD WAS LOST; she doubted the mood had ever really been there; it had been an invention, some kind of romance about who she was and what she wanted. She wanted to make love to a fireman? She felt foolish now and wished she had time for another shower. She dressed, went out, and brought Victor and Viola home from preschool. While she was making them dinner, her boss called to tell her that the mysterious white powder that had spilled from the envelope had been tested. It was talc: a hoax. He sounded as if he had been distraught and was now very relieved, even intoxicated. He said the office would be closed for the next several days as the FBI conducted further environmental tests. Also, the FBI wanted the staff to come to the agency's New York headquarters in Foley Square for interviews the next morning. The agency was desperate in its search for clues that would lead to the source of the real anthrax.

But Joyce wasn't relieved. If this time the anthrax wasn't real, then why not the next? She resented her former belief that their lives in America had been secure. Someone had lied to them as shamelessly as a spouse. All over the planet people wanted to kill Americans; here too nutjobs acquired automatic weapons, deadly bacteria and viruses, nuclear material and explosive fertilizer. How could she have brought her kids into this world, a world even more sinister than her marriage? Their future was chilled by a lethal, indelible shadow.

Marshall arrived while the kids were finishing their dinners. As always he offered the children a fully engaging smile and sweet, tender kisses. He asked them warmly about their day's trivia, his voice a singsong, and he dispensed the most perfect small presents that he had picked up on his way home. He didn't once glance in Joyce's direction. He had it down to a science. Joyce didn't look his way either, but in her avoidance, she felt, she expended the greater effort. He dropped his attaché in his bedroom and took the dog for a walk.

The door slammed, and at that moment, just as the network news came on, Viola knocked over her milk, a full glass that had never been sipped. The milk streaked across the dining room table toward Joyce's pocketbook like a tsunami. The little girl giggled. Joyce nearly tripped as she swooped low to save the bag. Milk poured onto a chair, splattering onto the floor. It was then that she realized that Peter Jennings was talking about her office, mentioning her company by name. Joyce went quickly to the kitchen counter to tear off a paper towel, then ran back to get the whole roll and saw from across the room a network news report filmed in front of her building. She hurriedly dabbed at the puddle. Alicia was being interviewed, seen from her size 2 waist up. She smiled demurely and thanked the NYPD for the courage and professionalism with which its officers had evacuated their building. Next a deep-voiced spokesman for the FBI in Washington, standing at a podium before a bouquet of microphones, concluded that the mysterious substance was in fact ordinary baby powder. He showed the camera a picture of the handwritten envelope in which it had been delivered.

Joyce let the milk drip and rushed to the television, the sopping towels in hand.

"Mommy, she hit me," Victor announced triumphantly.

The envelope was on-screen perhaps fifteen seconds—long enough for Joyce to see and understand and to see again and to reflect on the abruptness with which everything could change, again. The envelope lingered in view, even after the reporter stopped speaking about it. Anne-Marie had made an excruciatingly neat incision with her letter opener. The envelope carried a LOVE stamp, and the FBI said the faint, smudged cancellation mark revealed that it had been mailed from near Trenton, New Jersey, as were several of the real anthrax letters. The primitive cursive hand-lettering, which wandered northward across each line of the address, could have been characterized as babyish, or retarded, or lunatic. It was also immediately recognizable. Although every character was distinctive, it was the two lowercase *g*'s in her company's name that gave away their author. In each *g* the descending loop was an isosceles triangle and the rest of the letter was angular and elongated. The damn thing looked like a mutilated paper clip. No one made *g*'s like that, no one but her husband Marshall.

She knew his hand as well as she knew his dick. In their early courtship, which had taken place long ago, in the pre-Cambrian, Marshall had sent her a lengthy series of importunate and passionate letters handwritten on loose-leaf paper. Even on lined paper, the script had ascended as it flew to the right. Over the years Marshall's unique penmanship had marked innumerable holiday cards, shopping lists, and telephone messages. And now, when they weren't communicating through their lawyers, their principal means of communicating with each other, besides shouting, was through handwritten notes, so that copies could be saved for their lawyers. She knew all the distortions in his penmanship that occurred when he was tired or angry, or trying to be extra careful or trying not to be readable at all. She could even recognize, in her brief glimpse of the envelope on network television, the efforts he had made to disguise his penmanship.

Joyce was elated: now she had him. The Justice Department was investigating anthrax hoaxes as seriously as it was investigating the real anthrax mailings, promising to prosecute them as acts of terrorism. After years of careful, relentless, hard-assed maneuvering, legal and personal, Marshall had blundered catastrophically. Forget Joyce's wimpy, pearls-and-twin-set, eager-to-be-reasonable divorce lawyer: Marshall could deal with John Ashcroft now. Let them put him in jail. Let them send him to Guantánamo. She would keep the apartment.

She stole a look when he returned with the dog. Marshall turned away, his complexion darkening and his cowlick flopping down around his eyes. He went to his room and shut the door. Joyce almost smiled, but then stopped to wonder if the hoax anthrax could possibly, in actual fact, have been sent by her husband. Was he capable of doing something so wrong and so criminal? She told herself yes, citing all the malicious actions he had taken against her since they had begun getting divorced, and all the deadly infighting and all the lies and slander he had broadcast to the world, but she wasn't persuaded. Although she hated him with every cell in her body, she didn't believe he was a bad man, not really. She had loved him once, and the memory was a little traitor sabotaging her every effort to survive this divorce. He had nursed her through a month of meningitis before they were married, bringing her wonton soup and a single red rose every night after work. At Viola's birth he had gently lifted the girl from the bloody sheet and laid her on Joyce's chest. But don't forget the g's—was she living with a dangerous crackpot? It was true that he had always enjoyed practical jokes—the FBI would discover that he had been arrested for a fraternity prank in college—yet he had never done anything as dangerous, or as sick, as this before. Was he suffering from some kind of post-traumatic stress syndrome? What had happened to him on September 11? He had never told her or anyone she knew. He had never explained how he had escaped the World Trade Center when his entire office had been destroyed. He had lost friends and colleagues. But he had said nothing. It was bottled up within him, with all the strains of the divorce war, and he had simply lost his mind. If he was capable of sending baby powder to her office as a practical joke (and perhaps he wasn't, not really), what could he do to her and their children right here in their apartment?

Nothing was heard from behind the door. How did he spend his hours in his shadowed bedroom? Was he putting more baby powder in envelopes or doing something worse? She had to take the children away, right now, tonight. She couldn't risk keeping them in this apartment—but *could* she take them, without court permission? The lawyers were still arguing over custody terms. Any precipitous action could be used against her. She was sharply wounded by this gross unfairness—she just wanted to protect her babies! Again, for the second time that day, she had been put in an impossible position. What could she do?

Joyce lay on her couch that night anxious and frustrated. In the morning she would be going to the FBI. She wondered if she should tell them about the envelope. It was crazy to think that you could identify someone's handwriting from a brief glimpse of it on television. Perhaps she had been the one who had lost reason and perspective after September 11. Or perhaps not. She listened for stirrings in the bedroom, or for footsteps, or for the hissing release of poisonous gas. She pondered the ways in which Marshall's mind might have become deranged.

YES, MARSHALL *was* disturbed; even, he would admit, a bit deranged that autumn. Thousands of photographs had been taken near Ground Zero on the eleventh of September and he had not appeared in a single one. In his bedroom's perfect solitude he had studied the papers, the magazines, and the special commemorative issues that had been published in the past month. He looked for himself and for people he might have encountered during the evacuation. He carefully passed a magnifying glass over the pictures, especially those taken of the office workers fleeing the site after the south tower collapsed. He found no documentary evidence that he had been at the World Trade Center that morning, nor evidence that he had survived.

He looked too for photos of Lloyd among the few that had been taken in the plaza before the buildings fell, but they were from another part of the plaza or he was simply unable to recognize the body. He could barely remember the man's face, which had in any case been obscured by dust, grime, and shock. In the published lists of the dead appeared several men whose first names were Lloyd. Every morning Marshall checked the "Portraits of Grief" in the *Times*. Some of the entries included head shots. So far he hadn't recognized Lloyd among them, and none of those Lloyds whose obituaries had appeared had fathered a daughter named Sarah or Sofia or anything like that.

Marshall had searched for Lloyd's face on the "Person Missing" posters that had been attached to lampposts and advertising hoardings throughout the city in the days after the attack. He had hoped to contact his widow and daughter, to offer them some words of comfort, though what these words would have been he didn't know. He wouldn't even have been able to explain his strong attachment to Lloyd. All he had was that odd, ambiguous moment in the plaza. How would he have explained what happened? It could be argued—by Joyce, for example— that Marshall was indirectly responsible for Lloyd's death: if he had pulled him from the building at another moment, or perhaps had let him come out on his own, Lloyd wouldn't have been killed. Marshall imagined himself arguing back: no, regardless of what happened two minutes later, through no fault of his own, at the moment he reached Lloyd inside the building, he had been performing heroically. *Can't you see that! Damn you, can't you see that!*

He stared at the bedroom ceiling in the dim evening light, looking to read something in the faint patterns that had been left by the paint rollers years ago: elegant spirals and coils, labyrinths of kinks and vortices, the entire ceiling in a heavenly gyre. He thought he might read something within these convolutions. He thought he might learn from them, as he had nearly learned when the buildings fell, the exact lines and patterns that connected him occultly to every stranger in the world.

JOYCE DOZED for a few hours before daybreak, but rose early to get the children ready for preschool and to dress herself for the FBI. Pulling clothes from the hall closet, she moved with an alert, muscular determination, as if she had already consumed several cups of coffee. The third outfit she tried on was a gray-black suit she often wore to the office. It was a bit severe, but these were severe times she lived in: post-9/11, the papers said, fashion would be held in abeyance. No spectacle, nothing ironic. Marshall remained in his bedroom, or had already left the apartment or even fled the country. She brought the kids to school and continued on to the City Hall subway stop in Manhattan.

Emerging from the station, Joyce followed the signs to the federal buildings at Foley Square. Although it was morning rush hour, the neighborhood seemed oddly hushed. She was only a few blocks from Ground Zero. There was hardly any traffic except for emergency vehicles. A police car was parked at an intersection, its roof lights flashing. The way ahead was defended by a formation of black Humvees and a gray army tank. Concrete barriers lined the sidewalks, and sandbags were piled high at certain mysteriously strategic positions. Policemen crisply ordered civilians onto the sidewalks or off them according to unknown distinctions, while soldiers stood by with their rifles raised. It was all very thrilling. At the checkpoints pedestrians displayed their driver's licenses for identification and passed through metal detectors. A soldier ordered Joyce to stand in a line that stretched halfway down the block. She was about to explain that she had important information about the anthrax attacks, but another soldier, swarthy and intense, came up and stared into her face as if to remember it and she remained silent. She wondered where Marshall was now and what he would do next.

"Mrs. Harriman?"

She turned, surprised and eager: her name had been spoken by the agent who had rescued her pocketbook the day before, and she realized that since then, whenever she had contemplated the FBI, she had been thinking of him. He had just come from around the corner with a cup of coffee in a paper bag. Evidently his night hadn't been any more restful than hers. Perhaps he had never gone home. His skin hung loosely from his face; the haircut seemed a single day less stylish. He hadn't smiled yesterday when he brought out her handbag. After waiting for her sobs to subside, he had asked again for a photo ID.

Now Joyce explained, "They said we should come in for interviews."

The agent frowned. "Yeah, yeah. Don't just stand there, look busy."

"It won't be useful?"

"Come with me," he said, pulling her from the line. Several people had already joined it behind her. They watched her go with fierce interest. The agent's light tap on her shoulder echoed up and down her arm. "We have a bioterrorist out

there and no leads at all," he said. "So we're checking everything, including pranks. They do enough damage anyway and
we'll press felony charges. But you're absolutely right, this is a
total waste of time."

They walked along the curb on the other side of the barriers. The queuing office workers gave Joyce dirty looks, but she
stared ahead. At the first checkpoint the police waved them
through. It was like being taken past the velvet ropes at a
nightclub.

She felt emboldened. "I don't even know your name."

He didn't respond at first, as if considering this declaration
a piece of evidence. He replied reluctantly, "Special Agent Nathaniel Robbins. I'll give you my card when we get inside. Now,
please, Mrs. Harriman, can you tell me what's your position in
the company?"

"Please call me Joyce," she said.

"Right," he said. He asked the question again, and also for
the name of her immediate supervisor and who she in turn
supervised. She was definitely being interrogated, but he was
distracted. The cover to his coffee cup had come loose and the
bottom of the bag was wet. He kept it away from his body like
a ticking bomb. He asked her who their main competitors
were, who might benefit from the company's temporary shut-
down, and if she knew of any individual who might bear a
grudge against the firm. She paused significantly before she
answered the last question, inviting further interrogation, even
though she feared it. He didn't follow up. As they approached
the last checkpoint, Joyce saw Alicia waiting to be wanded. Her
bare, lathe-turned arms were up. She too was wearing black, an
above-the-knees crepe sheath. She looked impatient. She
turned at just the right moment to view Joyce glide past. Joyce
had assumed a very serious, collegial expression. When they
entered the building, Agent Robbins gently took her elbow,
guiding her through the door.

"Am I under arrest?"

He laughed, briefly but easily, and his face shed years. A toothy, crooked smile remained there. At the elevator lobby he disposed of the paper bag, letting it drop from the cup into the trash. He refastened the cover, still chuckling. The success of her remark gave Joyce a surge of warmth. And then Agent Robbins said, "Not yet." That was thrilling too.

His office was a medium-sized cubicle with very few personal items: no pictures of children. Joyce had noticed that he didn't wear a wedding band—she had noticed it *yesterday*, in fact; observing it was a kind of reflex. The observation didn't necessarily encourage her: she had yet to formulate, at this fairly hopeless point in her life, what it meant for her to be interested in a man. But she wondered if there was something wrong with him if he'd never had children or didn't keep their relics. She knew Marshall had at least displayed pictures of Victor and Viola on his desk. The desk assigned to Agent Robbins was mostly occupied by piles of green-and-white computer printouts that sloshed over the keyboard of a new-looking PC. The only object hanging on the movable orange-fabric wall was a map of the New York metropolitan area. Circles radiated from the still-locatable World Trade Center at progressive intervals, starting at a tenth of a mile.

He pointed to a black vinyl-covered chair and said, "Please. This will take a minute."

"Do you want me to repeat what I said? You didn't take notes."

"I don't believe in taking notes," he murmured, half to himself. He put down the cup. "Too much information jams the system."

He opened his desk and removed a ziplock bag that contained an empty glass bottle and several long Q-tips. On a filing cabinet beneath the map rested a large jar with a clear liquid inside it. He unscrewed the cover and dipped two of the swab sticks. He held them in front of his body as he came around to the front of his desk.

"This is all I have to do," he said, abruptly dropping to his knees by Joyce's chair, so that their heads were level and very close. "We're collecting as many samples as possible."

"You're taking samples?" she asked anxiously. He was wielding one of the swabs between them.

"Inhaled anthrax spores. In case the hoaxer has a link with the bad guys. Who knows."

He reached out and gently cupped his hand around the side of her face. *Oh!* He brought her to him. His fingertips carried the aroma of coffee. In a single fluid movement he raised one of the swabs to her nose and pressed it against the inside of her lower right nostril. She had nowhere to look but into his eyes, which were focused on her nose. The swab was wet and oddly warm, and his touch was sure. The swab did a half turn inside her nostril, pulling at the short hairs before he removed it. He dropped the stick into the empty bottle and applied the second swab to her left nostril. He seemed to hold this one a moment longer and in that moment he looked up and caught her gaze. There was nothing wrong with him, Joyce saw, nothing at all. She could feel his pulse transmitted through the swab stick. The swab was withdrawn, again with a lingering half rotation.

"Don't worry about this," he said, handing her a tissue as he got up from his knees. "We won't find anything. But thanks for coming in."

She was rooted to the chair. "Thank *you*," she said, idiotically.

He nodded. Getting to his feet had brought a soft blush to his face.

"I can go?"

Agent Robbins himself seemed disappointed. Then he smiled. "That's it. No rubber hoses. If we suspend habeas corpus, you'll be notified."

"I hope you find the guy."

Using a thick felt-tip pen and big block letters, he was printing her name on a sticker attached to the ziplock bag. "Yeah, me too. Let me have your number."

"By all means," she said, but he wrote the digits on the sticker and disposed of the bag in an open canvas satchel next to his desk. The satchel was stitched with the letters *FBI*.

Joyce contemplated her next move as she collected her pocketbook. This was her last chance. She looked as if she were strategizing how to get out of the chair. Halfway up, she reversed her ascent and dropped back.

"Are you sure it wasn't anthrax?"

"What wasn't?"

"The powder sent to our office."

"It's been ionized, fluoroscoped, and put under an electron microscope. It's talc, Johnson and Johnson's. We know the lot number, we know where and when it was manufactured. But it doesn't get us any closer to the killer."

She wondered if she should leave now and forget the whole thing. Once she spoke events would spin beyond her control. The Q-tips had left her unsettled. She wanted to go to a bathroom and vigorously blow her nose.

"Agent Robbins," she began, and wondered if she could go on. She thought for a moment and decided she could. "You asked if there was anyone who might have a grudge against our company. And I can't think of anyone who does. But I know who has a grudge against *me*: my husband. I told you yesterday, we're getting divorced, it's an ugly situation. He was in the World Trade Center September 11 and survived, but, I don't know, he's seemed a bit disturbed since then. I thought he was disturbed before September 11—what he's put me through—but now...September 11 may have sent him over the edge. He may have done this to get back at me somehow."

The FBI man looked away, as if eager to move on to the

next interview. She regretted the phrase *what he's put me through*.
It made her sound like a whiner. "Yeah," he said.

"And that envelope shown on the news last night...Do you
have a copy? I know my husband's handwriting and, I swear,
it's the same exact penmanship. They're his *g*'s, for one
thing..."

Robbins grimaced, removing an enlarged copy of the hoax
anthrax envelope from under some printouts.

He asked, "*Would* you swear it?"

It took her a moment to understand the question, and then
she wasn't sure what her answer should be. Would she *swear* it?
Did she really believe Marshall had sent the baby powder? On
the enlarged copy, the handwriting didn't seem as similar to
Marshall's as she had first thought. The ascending loops of the
cursive *h*'s and *l*'s were too round; the crossbars of the *f*'s were
too long. She opened her bag and pulled out the sheet of paper
on which Marshall had scrawled last month, *Newark–SF Un. 93
8:02 Berk Best West*. There were no *g*'s.

"This is a sample," she said.

She passed it over to Agent Robbins. He handled the gift of
actual physical evidence as if it were a strand of pearls. He
turned it one way and then the other and then lined it up
against the photocopy.

"I'll give it to forensics. It's close, all right."

"My God."

"What's his name and where can we find him?"

"Are you going to arrest him?"

Now he didn't laugh. He hadn't looked at her like this before, not even yesterday when she had explained about her
keys. His gaze was as attentive as a predator's. He was noting
every aspect of her dress and bearing, every mannerism, every
parsing of her accusation. "Would you like me to?"

"No," she said hurriedly. He was frightening her. "Not unless you think it's necessary."

"We'll see. What's his name?"

"Marshall Harriman. I don't know where he spends his days, but he still lives with us. I have his cell phone, his lawyer's number…"

Agent Robbins wrote the numbers in a spiral notebook and slowly read them back to her. Now Joyce felt like an informer. She wanted to leave.

"Has he done anything like this before?"

"No. I mean, in college he was a bit of a goofball, but not like this…"

"Tell me about your marriage."

"My marriage," she said. The specter of her marriage rose up before her, a tower one hundred stories high. So high, you can't get over it. So low, you can't get under it. She didn't know where to begin. That had been the problem with counseling: neither of them could decide what to tell the therapist first. So wide, you can't get around it. "That's personal," she concluded.

He scowled. "I'm the FBI."

"Right. Well," she started again, trying not to hear herself speak. "My marriage—"

"We'll do tests," he said, suddenly relaxing his posture. He smiled and gave her his card. He had decided that he didn't want to hear. "Call me if you think of anything else, or if something happens."

She studied the card without comprehension. "What could happen?"

"Nothing," he said, unreassuringly. "Nothing can happen. This is probably nothing, Mrs. Harriman. If I need anything, I'll call."

EVERY WEEKDAY Marshall rose at his usual time, put on a suit, and left the apartment with the kids, if it was his day to bring them to preschool, or without them, if it wasn't. He went to Borough Hall and took whatever train into Manhattan was running. He exited with the other passengers at the first stop downtown, walked over to Ground Zero, and looked in at the cleanup. He wasn't sure why he was there: he was drawn to the spectacle, he supposed, the cranes and the trucks, or perhaps he was simply attached to the habits of his morning commute. His usual coffee and bagel guy, who had lost his truck in the rubble, had come back with a new truck. Marshall would have his breakfast alongside the firemen and construction workers. The mornings were uniformly, monotonously fine. And then he would spend the rest of the day in the streets, looking hard into other people's faces.

He had no plan nor specific direction. Some days he remained downtown, shuffling along the shadowed, narrow streets, which even in this straitened time a month after the attacks churned with people. They churned too with commerce and history. Other days he walked to midtown. He spent hours in Barneys without buying anything. He went into bookstores and ran his fingertips along the spines of books he would never read. Sometimes he crossed back into Brooklyn over the bridge. One day he discovered that simply walking east, through neighborhoods as foreign as Mazar-e Sharif, you could reach Nassau County by late afternoon.

In some of these hours, on some of these days, he was so consumed by grief he could barely take another step forward. He would stand on a randomly selected street corner and think of Joyce and how thoroughly their lives had been ruined. What had he done to her? Why did he deserve this? Why did she hate him so?

But these questions occupied only a few hours, hours in which the events of September 11 had vanished from human memory. In other hours he was keenly aware that he was living in October 2001, under a wartime regime, traversing a battle-field terrain, in a city that bore the standard of one civilization under attack by another. *This* civilization comprised Barneys, the *Times*, MetroCards, a raven-haired woman in tears standing in the street hailing a cab, yellow cabs, mojitos, divorce lawyers, and Derek Jeter, the elements in constant commotion and collision with each other. It was a civilization defined by the phenomenon of collision and consequent phenomena: he was in collision too, with every unfamiliar face and sight that presented itself on the sidewalk, each encounter generating another observation, thought, or idea about something or other. That autumn Marshall was buffeted within a maelstrom of ideas. Yes, it was a very fine autumn, this was a very fine day, the sky a pulsing, lucid membrane and beyond it something too wonderful to even speak about. He bought himself a midmorning lunch, a hot dog with mustard and relish.

Marshall had lived in New York for years and had never by chance met on the street, beyond the immediate surroundings of his home and office, a single person he knew. The city was too large, its citizens' movements too unpredictable: here, another distinguishing characteristic of *this* civilization. Marshall didn't doubt the cultural richness of rural, traditional societies, but he knew that the ideas generated within, say, an Afghan village involved interactions between families, or between cousins and longtime acquaintances, or between an individual and his predictably seasonal natural environment. Those ideas were rooted in history and familiarity. In the city of New York the content of human consciousness was usually drawn from strangeness, the chaotic interplay of individuals: a young man in a wrinkled black tux came down Third Avenue; two teenagers emerged from a cloud of steam alongside an open manhole blocked off by Con Ed trucks; policemen on horseback; a woman in a tight ankle-length skirt, on her cell phone discussing some dangerous male. She announced that she was taking the week off.

At the corner, chewing the frankfurter, whose oily, gamy

texture he barely noticed, Marshall reflected on this promiscuity that threatened the society on which it thrived. He could be killed. His *children*—. Somebody was at work right now. Bacterial grains were being milled and coated with silica to minimize their electrostatic properties. Pentaerythritol tetranitrate was being molded into the bottoms of running shoes. Turbaned men were even now double-clicking obscure, awesome icons.

And yet we lived hardly aware of our connections with each other. We maintained elaborate fantasies of our autonomy, the idiotic belief that we created meaning in ourselves. He understood very well now. The automobile traffic, the subways, the telephone, e-mail, the fuel-laden jetliners dangling above our heads, the U.S. Postal Service: all this held us in a fragile, shimmering, spidery web of meaning. A single act of malice could rip it apart. We held each other's significance in our hands.

AGAIN JOYCE TOOK a long shower when she arrived home. She was worried by her encounter with the Federal Bureau of Investigation, of course, but also intrigued, and she was also consumed by a roaring, elemental avidity that she had not yet explained to herself. Again the heat from the shower was delicious, both soothing and arousing, but the mood it conjured didn't promote another attempt at masturbation. She uncharacteristically investigated her true sentiments; it was a rare moment in which she had the opportunity to ask herself what she wanted to do. The answer came to her: what she was most in the mood to do this long, empty, anxious day—it was just past noon—was to paint her nails. Yes, she would paint her nails. She finished toweling off and opened the medicine cabinet. From the top shelf, spinning end-over-end, a container of baby powder dropped into her hands.

She captured it cleanly. She *never* bought baby powder; she had read once that talc was suspected of being carcinogenic. She never caught things in midair either. This meant something, she thought. *Johnson and Johnson's*: well of course it was Johnson and Johnson's, everyone bought Johnson and Johnson's, but still—

She heard the door to the apartment open. She immediately turned the lock to the bathroom door, hoping he wouldn't hear it click.

"Joyce? Are you home?"

Marshall had seen the closed door. Joyce was struck by a bolt of terror, almost knocked down on the tiles by it. She looked at her towel-wrapped self in the half-steamed bathroom mirror, holding the baby powder in her hand. Her mouth was dry and she was dizzy. Shit, her clothes were in the living room. The dog began to howl.

"Joyce?" Marshall repeated.

"Yeah," she said at last.

"What are you doing home?"

"I'm taking a shower."

"Now?"

"Free country."

Thank God! Thank God! She had brought her pocketbook into the bathroom, with her cell phone and her BlackBerry. How long before he guessed she had discovered the baby powder? Agent Robbins' card was in her wallet. Marshall was too near for her to use the phone, but the card offered the agent's e-mail address in the lower left-hand corner. Hardly able to breathe, she listened for Marshall to step away from the door. She didn't want him to hear her punch the keys.

Snuffles was howling. *Walk him,* she prayed. Marshall moved away from the door. Clicking the BlackBerry with her thumbnail, she wrote in the subject line: "urgent anthrax."

dear agent robbins,

  i found talc in our bathroom. we never buy talc. lot 141b,
man may 01. he's here. can't talk, locked myself in the
bathroom. what should i do?

  it was a pleasure meeting you. please reply asap.

joyce harriman

The dog had stopped howling, but Joyce was sure that Snuffles and Marshall were still in the apartment. She held the baby
powder in one hand and the BlackBerry in the other, staring at
both before placing them carefully on the vanity. She closed the
lid to the toilet and sat on it. She wondered if Marshall was
suspicious. He shouldn't have left the baby powder in the medicine cabinet; he should have thrown it in the trash—in the
street, in the Bronx. He was possibly realizing his mistake at
this very moment. At the same time, Agent Robbins was very
possibly not at his computer, not checking his e-mail. He could
be eating lunch. She imagined him in the FBI cafeteria, his
laminated identification badge swinging from his jacket as,
sighing, he placed on his tray a bowl of vegetable soup. He took
a piece of bread with it and would finish neither. He was anxious, he was frustrated. He was probably not thinking of her.
He must have done a dozen swabs that morning. But they had
made some kind of connection. It was not necessarily a romantic connection; very likely he was attached, or too dedicated to
his work to get attached. But it would not be useless right now,
not useless at all, for her to have a friend. And it *could* have been
a romantic connection, there had been heat in those dark eyes,
anything was possible. And meanwhile she *needed* him, right
now. He needed her to break this case, and she needed him to
get her out of the bathroom. How often did he check his mail?
She checked hers. There was nothing.

She heard Marshall and Snuffles moving through the living
room and Marshall's low murmurs to the dog. They weren't

going out. She would have heard the rustle of the leash and Snuffles' four-legged tap dance of expectation on the parquet. A plastic dish scraped against the slate-tiled kitchen floor; even through the closed door the sound irritated her. Marshall was feeding the dog.

How long could she remain in the bathroom? Joyce tried to calm herself and prepare for a long wait. Marshall had gone away. Good. She stood to rearrange the towel and left it off for a moment to view herself in the mirror, which was still obscured by steam in parts. It wasn't a bad body, no, not for a thirty-five-year-old mother of two, especially above the waist. Lovely breasts. Nice, soft skin; slender ankles. Now she looked at herself hard, but from an imaginative distance. She willed herself to see her naked body through Agent Robbins' eyes. His eyes were by turns mournful, lonely, thoughtful, generous, and predatory.

She heard Marshall's steps. She checked the lock again. He said, "Joyce, are you coming out? I have to use the john."

That was what her marriage was like: this bathroom. She had been locked in this tiny, humid, windowless room for years, trying to protect herself from a madman.

She said, "Go to Roger and Linda's."

It was a poisonous remark. She recalled—and now so would he—the evening years ago when their entire apartment building had lost its water supply for several hours and they had gone to Roger and Linda's new, just-painted, unfurnished co-op three blocks away to brush their teeth and wash. It had been a weekday night and they all had work the following morning. So what: this was before kids. They consumed two packs of cigarettes and several bottles of wine that night, ordered in pizza, and sat on the floor in a circle, talking nearly all the way to dawn. Their eight feet and legs had knocked against each other from time to time. Joyce remembered the paint's lingering aroma. At one point she had stretched out on her back, stared at the ceiling, and allowed the conversation to wash over her. At that moment she had thought how lucky she was to have these stylish and witty friends and such a clever, go-getting husband, and to be young and bright and living in New York. And then these friends had betrayed her, persuaded by Marshall to take his side against her.

"Joyce?" Marshall's voice was hardly inflected. He was restraining himself. Because he knew she had found the baby powder or because he didn't?

"Go to Roger and Linda's," she repeated. She grabbed one of the towels and covered her face with it, pressing hard against her eyes so that she wouldn't start sobbing. Marshall went away again.

She checked her mail again, and there it was, Re: urgent anthrax, from Robbins, Agent Nathaniel. She clicked on it but only a blank screen came up. She scrolled down and found a lengthy legal admonishment warning against unauthorized use of the message. She returned to the menu and tried calling up the message once more. It was still without text.

Marshall came back. She heard him pacing near the door.

"C'mon, Joyce," Marshall said, his voice both pleading and exasperated. "I need to use the john. Badly. Very badly. Okay? Joyce?"

Joyce stared at the BlackBerry. Another message arrived from Agent Robbins. It too was blank. Shit. The third message had text, finally, but consisted of a single letter:

H

"Joyce?"

"Go away," she said.

"Joyce?"

"What?"

He didn't respond. She wasn't sure he was still there. She leaned forward, listening. And then he said:

"Joyce, are you all right?"

Her mouth fell open and she stared at the place in the door from where the question had originated. He thought she was sick. Perhaps he thought she was even suicidal, and perhaps that was true, she was. She had thought more than once about cutting her wrists in the bath. There was genuine concern in his voice. It was like recognizing an old friend in a crowd.

"I'm fine," she said. It came out harder than she intended.

She heard him stay in place. He didn't speak. She could picture him now: his lips pursed, his fingers snagged at his front pockets. He too was staring at the door. She regretted her tone. The question had been asked sincerely and she wished to be civil. Maybe she was wrong about the baby powder; maybe she was wrong about everything.

His next question was asked in evident pain:

"Is there someone with you?"

"Yeah," she snapped. "A fireman."

"Joyce—"

"Go away."

He did go away; she hadn't expected him to. She put her ear to the door. He was doing something in the kitchen, moving a chair, laying out dishes on the counter. Then there was a series of explosive, hydraulic sounds. With a start, she realized what they were: he was defecating into the kitchen sink. She fell back to her place on the closed toilet seat and closed her eyes. How did they get here, to this shameful point? Had this moment been predetermined by the inborn flaws in their characters? Or had their marriage been destroyed by chance, by external events and fortuities that had reconfigured their personalities and made them profoundly, ridiculously, disgustingly incompatible? They didn't even have a garbage disposal. She heard him running water.

After a while he came back.

"Come out, Joyce," he said. He sounded exhausted. He might have been in tears. "Come out now. Do you want me to bring you your clothes?"

"Don't touch my clothes."

"What do you want then?"

"I want you to go away. What do *you* want?"

He said, "I want to know what you're doing in the bathroom. You've been in there more than an hour."

"Go away."

"Open it. Open it *now*."

He was trying the knob. It was an old door, with a loose, rust-spattered lock. It was probably one of the few prewar artifacts left in the apartment. They had never replaced it because they had supposed—without actually talking about it—that the kids would eventually contrive to lock themselves in. They had assumed they would have to force it open, but now the mechanism held. Marshall began pulling and pushing the door violently, rattling the screws. Joyce shrieked.

"Come out!" he bellowed. He gave the door a powerful punch. Everything in the bathroom was shaken by the blow. The container of baby powder tumbled off the vanity onto the tile, spilling and testifying to its anomalous presence in the household. Of course those *g*'s were his. Everything in Marshall's sad, twisted life pointed to his guilt. Had the container's clatter reached him?

"Leave me alone!" she cried. She picked up the container, twisted it shut, and put it in her bag.

He pounded against the door again. He was certain to break the lock or the entire door. This was a man who had just crapped in the kitchen sink.

"Joyce!"

"You'll be sorry."

"I can't be any sorrier than I am now," he said.

He was working the knob back and forth. It was coming loose. She desperately checked her messages. There was another from Agent Robbins. She opened it—and this one had a full text:

ELLO, ARE YOUGETTING THIS EXCUSE ME
WEHAVNT HAD OUR TRAIBNING YET CANT
"CALL UP" YOUR EMAIL ANYWAY WE HAVE A
SUSPECTA PRANKSTER IN NJ HEEWALKED
HIMSELF INTHABNK YOUFOR YOURHELP

"I swear, Joyce," Marshall was yelling. "I'm calling my lawyer. The agreement calls for each of us to have full access to the bathroom, the kitchen, and the TV. Do you hear me?"

"Go away!"

"Don't think I'm going to forget this!"

She said, "That would never have occurred to me."

A screw fell from one of the hinges. She stared at the screen, not even hearing Marshall. She ran her thumb feverishly over the BlackBerry's keys. She wrote back:

agent robbins, i'm glad that worked out. nice to meet you. by
the way, do you ever see your potential felony witnesses
socially? :)

Marshall started banging on the door again—a steady drumbeat. Joyce ignored it and launched the message into the ether. She calmly rewrapped her towel, taking care to make it as neat and prim as possible. She looked at her face in the mirror and brushed away the signs of upset. One of her contacts had slid off-center and she blinked a few times to put it right.

"Joyce, I'm calling my lawyer! I have the phone in my hand! I'm dialing!"

She breathed deeply and forced a smile at the mirror, only to reassure herself, and then she just as forcefully took it away.

"Okay, okay," she said.

She opened the door. Marshall did indeed have his phone, holding it in the air like a loaded pistol. His face was flushed and he had allowed his shirt to come halfway out of his pants. He looked perfectly capable of terrorizing the city.

"Can't a person have some privacy?" she said quietly. "I'm going to ask my lawyer about *that*."

And then she scooped her clothes from the couch and went into the kids' room to change.

NOVEMBER

BACK WHEN JOKES were made, a running joke in their household was that neither Marshall nor Joyce could properly pronounce or spell the vowel-packed name of their doctor, a burly sad-eyed general practitioner from some mysterious country of the East. "I'm going for a checkup with Dr. Mouiwawaa—" Marshall would begin, and Joyce would giggle. Before she had children Joyce had come down with bronchitis three winters in a row, but otherwise they saw him only once every several years, when he would take their blood pressure, check their urine, and listen to their hearts, which had not yet shown signs of breaking, and write scrips for blood tests that they often put off until the week before their next checkups. The doctor hardly ever spoke to either. They were unsure whether he recognized them from one visit to the next.

The surgical thread in Marshall's scalp had been stitched and removed at the local emergency room, but he felt compelled to see his own physician when a strange condition inflamed the right side of his body, running all the way from mid-thigh to his lower abdomen. The skin had become painfully tender and the center of the rash was moist and scaly. The doctor's examination was brief.

"How long have you had it?"

"About a week and a half. It started three days after September 11." The doctor looked at him blankly and Marshall was embarrassed. Everyone was dating everything now from September 11, regardless of whether they or anyone they knew had been at Ground Zero—when was that going to stop? Marshall explained, "I was there. In the World Trade Center. I escaped."

The doctor bunched his eyebrows and frowned. "Really?" he said, momentarily disbelieving. "How did you escape?"

Marshall preferred not to speak about the terrorist attacks and had spoken very little about them with other people, but he understood that September 11 was now part of his medical history. He told the doctor everything that had happened from the moment the first plane hit the twin towers, omitting only the mention of Lloyd, the man who had fled the buildings with him and been killed. That little incident, of no significance to anyone, he kept to himself as a secret part of himself. Marshall parceled out the rest of his account in small, concise pieces, in case he was giving too much detail, while the doctor interrupted from time to time, his interest growing: "Where was that?" "And then what?" "And what did that feel like?" In the waiting room patients were accumulating.

When he was finished, the doctor shook his head. "Well, that was something terrible, Mr. Harriman. Now you know what it's like to live in history."

Marshall wondered if he could put his pants back on. He was sitting on an examination table with a paper sheet over his privates. "Do you think the rash has something to do with it?"

The doctor rubbed his face thoughtfully. "All sorts of debris products were put in the air when the towers came down: asbestos, PCBs, dioxin...Toxic material, or something you may be allergic to. Perhaps it's an infection. I'll write you a prescription for an antibiotic. Come back in a week. Give it air and don't let it chafe. If it gets worse, call me. Here's my service number."

"Could it be contagious?"

He shrugged. "Does your wife have symptoms?"

"I was thinking about my kids. I have two, four and two years old. They seem fine."

The doctor nodded his big, bald head. "That's right, I remember: a girl and a boy." Marshall smiled, gratified that he remembered. "No, I wouldn't worry unless you see something. And if your wife's okay—"

"I don't know," Marshall blurted. "I wouldn't know. We're not talking, we're not sleeping together. We're getting divorced. We're virtually separated except I'm still living in the apartment. She wants to force me out and then charge me with abandonment, or something like that. It's been the worst year of my life."

He threw up his hands, stricken by bewilderment. This was even more painful to speak about than September 11. His gaze was imploring.

"Well," the doctor said gravely. His forehead darkened like a thundercloud. "She always seemed a bit high-strung."

Marshall bobbed his head in agreement, but he was so surprised by the doctor's remark he could hardly speak. Commenting on the personality of another patient must have been against every principle of professional ethics. This lapse, by a distinguished physician with a Clinton Street brownstone and a wall of degrees, could have been provoked only by the most extreme and obvious circumstances. *High-strung?* Of course Joyce was high-strung. Marshall had always known it. Now he had received expert confirmation.

He had never before left a medical office feeling so satisfied. He closed the door behind him and, standing on the top step of the hall stairway, turned to look at the doctor's nameplate. The letters in the name swam in front of his eyes, a hydra of vowels in a pool of murky consonants. There was what seemed to be a mid-syllable hyphen and two *q*'s flagrantly *u*-less. Marshall put his lips together, accomplishing the name's initial *m*-sound. He made a soft, feminine moan, trying to breathe life into the characters that followed. It was impossible. Nor would he ever succeed in recalling this specific arrangement of letters. He frowned and went on his way.

The inflammation didn't respond to the antibiotics and within a few days its edges had become painfully itchy. "Don't scratch," the doctor warned at their next appointment, prescribing an ointment. Over the next month they tried several treatments on the rash, which hardly diminished. They talked, mostly about September 11; Marshall waited for the doctor to issue another observation about his wife. None came, as if the word "high-strung" had adequately dispatched her. The doctor's limping, doe-eyed assistant—his daughter, it turned out—often brought the two men small sweet cups of tea, a regular service at the doctor's first medical clinic, in Kunduz, Afghanistan, before the Soviet invasion. While they sipped, the doctor described his family's terrifying yearlong passage to America, through Iran and Pakistan. The girl had been hurt by a land mine. After being told this, Marshall would have been embarrassed to ask him how to pronounce his name.

Looking for razor blades in the drugstore one afternoon, he impulsively purchased a container of baby powder. He doused himself with the talc every morning for a week and the rash finally disappeared. He returned for another follow-up visit anyway. He found ease in the brownstone and its muted, dimly lit waiting room. The doctor impressed him with his sobriety and quiet heroism. The daughter smiled shyly. He was congratulated for his pink and healthy skin.

"I wish talc would work on my other problems," Marshall said sourly.

The doctor made a clucking sound. He was very much a New Yorker in dress and comportment. His accent was mid-Atlantic. The clucking sound, however, was unmistakably foreign. "No resolution yet?"

"I'm afraid not."

"Be strong, my friend," he said, smiling more warmly than he ever had before in Marshall's company. "You've survived worse."

The doctor put his hand firmly on Marshall's shoulder. Marshall had hoped his remark would elicit a personal comment. He could have remained there, sitting on the examination table, for the rest of the day.

THIS WAS the month the U.S. pressed its military campaign against the Taliban, using intense aerial bombardment and its special forces to assist the Northern Alliance, which, after some initial hesitation, began its march toward Kabul and laid siege to Kunduz and Kandahar. Every day brought news of another U.S. raid; also, of missed targets and slain civilians. Joyce studied the maps in the *Times* intently, so that she soon knew the country's arid, high-relief terrain, swept by an ocher Martian dust, and how its ethnic groups, the Pashtuns, Tajiks, Hazaras, and Uzbeks, were distributed across it. She located the big cities, as well as the Taliban and anti-Taliban strongholds outside and within them. She attended the warfare's fits and starts, which were dependent on shifting alliances, treachery, and the question of whether the U.S. would need to commit ground troops. She savored the beauty of the Afghan people who stared into the cameras: blue-eyed, dark-browed, sultry, fierce. The women wrapped themselves in purple and maroon robes, gold-threaded kerchiefs, and lacy paisley scrims. One evening when Marshall had the kids Joyce went through her jewelry box and found an old Middle Eastern bracelet, inlaid with lapis lazuli, which she had often worn until her first pregnancy, when her wrists had swelled. Now she fastened it to her right ankle and took herself to a local Afghan restaurant for dinner. She ordered a fragrant yellow rice and lamb dish, *qabili*. It was delicious. A large American flag hung above the entrance to the kitchen and red, white, and blue car-dealer pennants garlanded the front door, but she felt continents away, and also exotic and gritty-real.

She was fascinated by the Afghan warlords and the inconstancy of their allegiances. No militia was immune to betrayal or an invitation to a new alliance; the blood-oath affiliations of entire families and clans were shifted without their members' awareness. Great sums of cash—American dollars, in twenties—were airlifted into the mountains. Top-of-the-line military equipment and transport were liberally dispensed. But the militias never made it to their appointed posts, or if they did, they refused to fire their weapons. Their chiefs fingered their opponents as Taliban only to settle old scores, directing the U.S. military to bomb civilian convoys, schools, and, just this week, a wedding party. The bride, the groom, their brothers, a sister, and several family elders had been killed, eliciting oaths from the grieving, seething survivors: blood for blood, forever. Real Taliban and al-Qaeda melted into the population. To ensure the Afghans' cooperation in liberating their own country, the Americans were forced to look the other way as opium production soared; they knew that the same Afghans would eventually have to be paid off to curtail it.

As Joyce became aware of the particularities of Afghan life through newspaper and television reports, she saw that Afghans hardly related to each other as individual men and women.

They were each more significantly part of a clan, and each clan's relations with other clans operated through fundamental calculi of conflict. Entire decades of Afghan history were explained by simple communitive equations like "the friend of my friend is my friend," "the enemy of my enemy is my friend," "the friend of my enemy is my enemy," and so on. She took note of the position of Afghan women, observing that they were not merely property, but valuable objects with mystic attributes. The Afghan woman's sexuality, for example, was a vessel that retained the honor of her father, brothers, and husband. It was handled gingerly, swathed and cushioned in the bubble wrap of tradition. A man could be ruined by a female relative's behavior or even by another man's behavior toward her. In Faryab province earlier this month, Pashtun raiding parties had attacked several Tajik villages only to rape, the forced sex act (perhaps performed, she thought, not much less romantically than among Tajik husbands and wives) promising to disgrace marriages, families, and clans for generations. In Afghanistan sex wasn't "fun" or an expression of "love"; it was a weapon.

Yet Joyce felt increasingly drawn to the Afghan people, for their beauty and primitive dignity, even if that dignity seemed contradicted by their brutality, untrustworthiness, and venality. It was commonly held that September 11 had changed America forever. Joyce wondered if the real transformation would come now, in America's close embrace with warlords and peasants, fundamentalists and mercenaries. Would American wealth and the expediencies of its foreign policy corrupt the Afghan people? Or were we being corrupted by their demands for cash, their infidelities, and their contempt for democratic ideals?

Meanwhile her life hadn't changed. She was still not divorced and she had lost hope of ever being divorced; or, more precisely, her marriage was a contest governed by one of

Zeno's paradoxes, in which divorce was approached in half steps and never reached. After the long post-9/11 interregnum, Joyce and Marshall had resumed meeting with the lawyers, who themselves seemed wearied by their disputes despite the cornucopia of billable hours. Now Marshall had come up with a new tactic: worry for the children, as if his previous concern for the children had ever been sufficient to allow him to spend time alone with them without putting on the TV, or to remember to bring home milk for them without being specifically asked, or to take them for a walk while she cleaned the apartment, or to ask his company for a raise so that they could save a little money in advance of the financial Armageddon of private school, or to be a good husband, or to be a good person. Marshall claimed now that Joyce's intransigence was damaging the kids. Before she could deny that she was being intransigent—after all, for her to be intransigent required an exactly equal and opposite intransigence on his part, a slightly complicated thought that she wasn't able to fully articulate at the moment—the lawyers had moved on to the question of how they would establish how much damage she had done.

The phone rang. The kids were on the floor, playing, in their fashion. Viola was trying to get Victor to give her a truck he was using mostly to drive up and down a bump in the rug. Victor had refused; Viola had complained; viewing this as an instructive moment, Joyce had told them to resolve the issue between themselves. She clicked down the live television report from behind the Northern Alliance lines and picked up the receiver.

"Mrs. Harriman!"

It was a friendly voice, a familiar voice. It belonged to a man and he sounded delighted to be speaking with her.

"Yes?"

"It's Jerry Boyd!"

Jerry Boyd. The name fell into a well, but there was no

identifying echo in response. It sounded like somebody she should have known. Clients, colleagues, old friends...She flipped her mental Rolodex. His voice was optimistic and smoothly modulated.

"Jerry Boyd," she repeated, trying to recall whether she had ever spoken the name before.

"Yes, from Headhunters Transnational! How are you this evening? I hope I'm not catching you in the middle of dinner."

No, she didn't know him—but he was a headhunter! Immediately everything that was wrong with her job became obvious: the salary, the declining prospects of advancement, the people, the fact that they had all learned that her marriage had failed. She would do anything to change her life, even if it meant relocating and giving up the co-op. Accomplishing that without benefiting Marshall, however, would be tricky.

"No, not yet," she said. She hadn't even figured out what to make for dinner.

"Great! I don't want to inconvenience you."

As Joyce waited for the man to explain himself, the compilation of her list of professional dissatisfactions was running out of control.

"Well, how can I help you?"

"Is Mr. Harriman available?"

She looked away from the phone. Jerry Boyd's voice, she decided, had the oily confidence of a television game show host; what terrible fall in life had reduced him to making cold calls at dinnertime? Probably a divorce. Now Viola was trying to trade for the truck. Unfortunately, she was offering Victor only a pinch of carpet lint in return. He wasn't interested. She shook it at him, repeatedly thrusting it into his face. Joyce took a breath.

"He's not here," she replied.

"I'm so sorry," he said, sounding genuinely regretful. "Please have him call me. Jerry Boyd, from Headhunters Transnational. We're very much aware at HT that his company is in post-9/11 transition. This may be the perfect moment for him to contemplate more lucrative challenges. As you know, he's extremely well regarded in the industry. We'd like him to meet with one of our clients, a Fortune 500 company."

Viola had just upped the ante to two pieces of rug lint. Victor wouldn't even look at them.

"I said he's not here."

"That's fine," Jerry Boyd said. "If you would give me a number where he can be reached—"

"He's gone. He left the country. He joined the fucking Taliban," she said, slamming down the phone. For a moment she stared at the phone and was rewarded with a vision of Marshall in a long white robe, bearded, sitting in an unswept cave and studying the Koran. It was totally plausible.

Viola concluded her negotiations with her brother. She grabbed the truck, pushing Victor aside, and then swatted him hard in the head.

"Viola!" Joyce cried. She took the truck away. It was a cheap plastic UN relief truck, some kind of Happy Meals prize. But Victor began to bawl and then wail a lament that seemed intended to express every sorrow inherent in human existence. His screams filled the apartment like a pervasive fluid and they could probably be heard down the hall and on the floor above. Joyce tried to hug him but right now he was unhuggable, his tiny frame tense and feverish and dedicated to making sound.

"He wasn't sharing!" Viola protested, and then she too started crying.

The door opened and Marshall entered the apartment, a carton of cigarettes under his arm. Victor bounded up from the floor past his mother and streaked across the living room.

Marshall laughed, and then Viola rushed at him too. He made a show of juggling them in his arms without dropping the cigarettes.

"Hey, kiddo-kiddos, what are these teary tears about? Whatsamatter U?"

Joyce glared as he brought the children into the living room. They had squalled for a moment, but now they giggled, oblivious to the reasons their faces were wet. Marshall ignored her.

"No smoking in the apartment," she said. "We've gone over that. It's in the interim agreement."

MARSHALL WAS STILL receiving his salary but his company, which had lost many of its key people on September 11, was hardly doing business these days. The firm had moved its surviving World Trade Center staff and other New York employees into a glass-sheathed skyscraper in midtown, deliberately choosing offices looking south with a view of Ground Zero. The CEO, his face flushed with emotion, freely allowing his tears to fall, had declared that they would never forget their colleagues' sacrifices. This had been at a multifaith memorial service in St. Patrick's Cathedral, with hymns sung by the Harlem Boys' Choir. In another ceremony in the new lobby a wall of the victims' photographs had been dedicated. The company had declared an unbreakable bond with their wives, husbands, and children. Grief counselors moved among the new offices with the suspicious alertness of fire inspectors.

Marshall had not been notably forthcoming during the individual and group counseling sessions: he was accused of repressing his grief. Even when he confessed that, yes, that was exactly what he was doing, that was exactly how terrible he felt, the counselors and his colleagues were dissatisfied. They had noticed that he had been the only one at the weekend retreat in the Berkshires to have brought his tennis racket. He was made aware again that he had never been very popular in the company. Indeed, this past summer he had suspected that some of his superiors were maneuvering to make his position at work untenable. Although 9/11 had suspended office politics—now, the company had become a family with stronger obligations to its individuals than were observed these days in most natural families—he sensed that his standing had resumed its decline.

In the meantime he spent his workdays strategizing against Joyce. The divorce proceedings had entered their final stage with the general terms of the eventual settlement fairly obvious, but Joyce was still fighting, taking advantage of his every mistake or scruple. Marshall worked against her in the same way, looking for vulnerabilities as he gathered intelligence. He developed a system of extracting information from the kids. He worked stealthily, drawing them into conversation without asking direct questions so that the questions never got back to Joyce. He made charts and lists; he kept a file of options and scenarios.

From Viola's passing comments—like, to Victor, "You're too *small* to be a ring-bearer!"—Marshall had established that Joyce's sister Flora was getting married, at last. He smiled. He had always felt warmth toward the girl, Joyce's fine-boned, luminescent, more frail, more tentative reflection. Flora was the younger sister who would not take the chance of moving to New York, the sister who had feared the mortal consequences of marriage—these past few months, he supposed, she must have seemed the more prudent, more fortunate sister. He liked her boyfriend, Neal, a bright, occasionally farcical computer scientist who had suffered for years under the unarticulated disapproval of the sisters' parents. Marshall recalled a protracted Thanksgiving weekend in Connecticut when Neal had made one offending mistake after another—unilaterally turning on the radio in the living room, wisecracking about

Monica Lewinsky like a stand-up comic...He had nearly knocked over a lamp too. Flora had been livid. On the Sunday morning, Marshall and Neal went for a walk together in the woods along the creek, and although they didn't speak about the weekend's catastrophes, Marshall's companionship put Neal at ease and somehow rescued the weekend. News now of the imminent nuptials was a small fact, but in Marshall's hands it carried the weight of opportunity.

He waited a week to call Neal, but still wasn't sure which way to turn the conversation. He reached him at his lab. Marshall identified himself and there was a surprised silence, as if Joyce's family had already pronounced him dead.

"Hi." Neal's voice was strained, wary.

"Hey, that's great, man! I heard about you and Flora getting engaged. Pardon me, did I catch you at a bad time?"

"Marshall?"

"It's wonderful news. I wish you both the best."

"Well, thank you, Marshall. I didn't..." Neal stopped for a moment, apparently wondering if he could say this. "I didn't expect to hear from you. You know, the way things are."

"Yeah, yeah, but forget that, I *had* to call. We haven't spoken in so long, Neal, how *are* you?"

They had never really been that close. Whatever bond they could claim arose from that one weekend, a few other family occasions, and an unspoken shared knowledge of two sisters similar in character and build. Now they began a halting, unfocused conversation, but Neal warmed when he started talking about his recent work—his lab had just won a contract modeling airport security systems—and he shyly mentioned that he and Flora were buying a house together. Then, almost gasping, he recalled that Marshall had worked in the twin towers. Marshall deflected his concern and condolences and said only that on the morning of the terrorist attacks he hadn't reached work yet. He congratulated him again on his wedding plans.

Neal said, "It must sound strange to hear someone looking forward to getting married..."

"No, no, no," Marshall assured him. "Not at all. I think marriage is great. Sometimes it doesn't work out, and that's sad, but getting married and having children, giving it a try, are the best things I've ever done."

As Marshall spoke these words he wondered if they were true. He had never actually considered whether he regretted marrying Joyce. Even now the marriage didn't seem like a mistake; the era of tragic mistakes came later. And having kids? Only a monster (like the monster Joyce insisted he was) would wish away his children, but he knew that he and Joyce had been much happier before they were parents—he couldn't even remember what they had argued about before they were parents. Of course he loved his children, but now he doubted that he would ever get his rightful enjoyment from them. Something else Joyce had ruined for him.

So, if it was not getting married and having kids, *what* was the best thing he ever did? Was it something at work? Or something altruistic? Would Lloyd's name somehow be included in the answer to that question?

He paused, momentarily distracted. Then he said, "And Flora's a wonderful girl. Beautiful, smart, accomplished, funny..."

"Yes, she is," Neal agreed.

Marshall gauged Neal's enthusiasm. He had thrown "accomplished" into the list as bait. Flora had enjoyed a brilliant university career, but since then she had drifted from one mediocre, unhappy job to another. He detected no hint of demurral. Maybe Neal liked having her work as a receptionist. Marshall pressed on.

"In fact, the entire family is great, really good people. I guess we all know that Joyce and I aren't going to make it, but I hope to always feel welcome in Canaan. You know, for visits and holidays." This was crazy, laughably crazy. His ability to say something this crazy made him feel immensely powerful and free. "I've always admired Joyce's parents. Deke's so well read and tough, Amanda's so elegant..."

Neal said, "Right."

Bingo. That was a false note. He had something there, and it was Amanda. Yes, of course, Amanda. She had always been uneasy about Neal's courtship of her daughter and everyone knew it. Joyce had hinted once that Neal was in Amanda's disfavor without ever specifying why, but Marshall guessed the root cause was a clash of tempers: Neal was an urban type; he could be overly familiar, too loose in the wrong situations, too quick with a joke. He made even Marshall cringe at times, and he could see how those traits would alienate Joyce's mother.

"I mean, Amanda is a beautiful woman—totally fastidious, everything has to be perfect right down to the very last strand of hair," Marshall said. "It's true, though, she can be reserved at times, there's ice beneath that glamour. She's also a bit high-strung, don't you think? But that's just the way she is."

"Yeah. I guess."

"You know, the girls have that glamour too. Do you remember how they looked at the wedding in Boston? Those matching high-cinched black velvet gowns, those bare necks, their hair in tresses down to their shoulders...I couldn't take my eyes off them." This was true: the two sisters had been lovely that day. "And, it's funny, they have that high-strungedness too, just like Amanda. I mean, Joyce certainly, it's a factor that's complicated her life, not only at home. It puts people off...Even sweet little Flora..."

"Um."

No, that wasn't it, Neal didn't concur at all. Marshall hadn't found the coordinates for the source of that dissatisfied *right;* he wished he could zero in on it, disrupting Neal and Flora's stately march to the altar. But Flora *was* high-strung, in several aspects at least, damn it. Why couldn't Neal see it? Why couldn't he see that the whole family was vicious, the very air they breathed soaked in malignancy, the whole damn house in Connecticut a den of vipers?

Marshall said, "Anyway, she *is* sweet. You'll be great together. I have so much to do, I should get back to work, but Neal, I just wanted to give you and Flora my very best wishes. Kiss her for me. And I'm not sure how it works, exactly, but I think I'll still be your kids' uncle."

"I think so..." Neal murmured, evidently contemplating the rules of avuncularity. "I'm so touched, Marshall. Really touched. Wow, thanks. Good luck yourself, I know you're in a difficult situation..."

"Well, take care..."

"Marshall, listen," Neal said, speaking quickly. "I'm having a little party in two weeks, going out with the guys. Not a bachelor party, really, just dinner at a restaurant in the city. My brother's flying in from California. I would have invited you... but why don't you come anyway? It'll be fun, low-key."

Anyone looking across the office at Marshall at his desk would have been startled, and even offended, by the huge grin that exploded across his face.

"I wouldn't miss it for all the oil in the world. Is Flora going to be okay with me being there?"

"Nah, she'll moider me," Neal joked, but Marshall heard a touch of nervousness in the reply. The invitation had been issued rashly. He was already reconsidering.

"You know," Marshall said, "we don't have to advertise this..."

"Right..." Neal was still wavering.

"Hey, it's not like I'm an enemy. Flora doesn't consider me

one, I hope. Even Joyce and I aren't *enemies*. We're still close in many ways, this is just one of those things that happen..."

Again, Marshall's declaration was laughably crazy—he knew the harsh words being said about him within the family—but Neal was allowing it to make sense. He was an emotional fellow: not only did he have romantic notions about marriage, he probably entertained a few in regard to divorce. He gave Marshall the time and place of the dinner, at an Italian restaurant in the West Village. Coordinates.

DR. NANCY, the child psychiatrist, neatly laid out the sheets of foolscap. At first Mr. Peter, the court-appointed guardian, couldn't make sense of the drawings. The human figures were recognizable, but what they were doing and where they were situated were not. The crayon work was sloppy and the red crayon had been used wildly, with tangles of scribble running across each sketch. The only other legible features were long rectangular blocks, set at skewed angles, some of them cross-hatched. Dr. Nancy placed a long, painted fingernail on each drawing as she explained: this is the mother and the father together, this is the father with the girl, the father alone with the boy, the mother with the boy, the boy alone, and look at this one, it's all four of them. Mr. Peter studied the drawing for a while. The figures were holding hands, partly shrouded in red crayon.

These are, he thought, pretty hot fingernails, varnished burnt orange. Dr. Nancy wore a mid-calf skirt, stockings, and a satiny blouse; most child psychologists tended toward the drab, projecting motherly and grandmotherly personas meant to reassure the children. He preferred this persona. Looking at the youngish woman, svelte and energetic, Mr. Peter wondered how the case would unfold and whether they would work together afterward. He tried to peer into the future and learn whether it contained a friendship, shared confidences and intimacies, romantic feints and parries and further complications—a conspiracy that would conclude either with love or without it. He was pleased that he was wearing his most lawyerly dark blue suit.

As he began to examine the drawings, Mr. Peter believed that the little girl, nominally his legal client, lagged in the development of her motor skills—this was common enough in children from troubled families and played well enough in court. But Dr. Nancy impatiently tapped her fingers on the drawings, urging him to look harder. He worked at separating and distinguishing the crayoned snarls. He became aware of the violent passion that had gone into these sketches; also, in the consistency of their subjects. The drawings came into focus. The psychologist had asked the girl to draw pictures of her family. In each one she had placed her family near or around the burning World Trade Center.

The World Trade Center was on fire; in one drawing the tail of a jet protruded from the left tower, about a third the size of the tower. The boy stood on the tail, on fire. In another picture the mother and father were poised on each of the towers' roofs, their mouths framed as solid O's of black crayon. Even though the figures were primitive, Mr. Peter received a strong impression. In the next few sketches the girl seemed to be leading the father away from the buildings, off the page; then the burning mother was carrying the burning father; then the girl's limbs, scribbled over by deadly red, seemed separated from her body. In the last drawing the four of them had leaped from the towers and were falling hand in hand.

MARSHALL PURCHASED an inexpensive telephone equipped with a simple earphone attachment. It rested on a hook next to the receiver. It allowed you to listen to a conversation that was taking place on another extension without lifting the receiver and giving yourself away. The packaging warned, "Federal law prohibits use without the knowledge of all parties." Marshall smiled, unable to contemplate an instance in which one would use the device *with* the knowledge of all parties.

He kept the phone hidden behind some books, though Joyce hadn't entered his bedroom in more than a year. He enjoyed the clandestine cleverness of the device and his reliance on technology of which Joyce would never conceive. She was resolutely low-tech. In this battle Joyce's advantages—single-mindedness, a keener hatred—would succumb to Marshall's superior tactics. He thrilled with an appreciation of his power the first time he listened in on a conversation, a call opening playdate negotiations from the mother of Victor's best friend. Marshall's greatest hope was to intercept communication between Joyce and her lawyer, but it seemed she was too cautious for that and presumably took counsel only through her phone at work. This meant he had to be patient, sifting through a thin data stream: updates to work-related appointments, haircutter appointments, further playdate negotiations that went on longer than the playdates themselves, a few guarded conversations with her parents. There was nothing like a breakthrough until Flora called one evening, furious.

Removing the telephone from its hiding place, Marshall missed her first words, but he recognized Flora's breathy, agitated voice at once.

"Christ, she's driving me nuts."

She could only be her mother, Amanda. He wished he had paid another hundred dollars for a recording device.

JOYCE: Over that thing?
FLORA: Yeah.
JOYCE: Mmm.
FLORA: I've given in to every demand. Neal's given in. But you know, he has a family too.

JOYCE: No rabbi?

FLORA: He doesn't care about that. It's been years since he set foot in a synagogue. His parents don't care.

JOYCE: So.

FLORA: Gottschall's going to read a Hebrew prayer. Mom's going to stroke but—

JOYCE: Yeah.

FLORA: But they want this thing. It's like, I don't know, nonnegotiable. They'll pay. But Mom has her country club friends. It's not my wedding. Everything has to be perfect, for her. She's going to impress the Pruitts, the Masons—

JOYCE: Whose son is gay. Does Mom know that? Look, call me at work. I can't talk. Osama's holed up in Tora Bora.

FLORA: Right. Kiss-kiss.

JOYCE: Kiss. Sweetie, we'll talk tomorrow.

Joyce called him Osama? He *loved* that—this was great, this was better than any intelligence, better than anything tangibly useful. He didn't want to get back at her now, he just wanted to prolong this feeling of mastery, this sense of being *able* to get back at her. So he would have to get back at her; he would have to press his advantage. By the time this divorce was finalized, she was going to think he was Hitler and Stalin too.

The friend of my enemy...Roger came into the Afghan restaurant with his eyes hooded, his demeanor solemn. He looked hot under his coat, which was much heavier than it needed to be on this summery November evening. He unzipped it violently. Joyce slid out from her table by the bar and presented herself to be kissed. He lightly brushed her cheek. She squeezed his arm as he looked away.

It was an Afghan restaurant, but this was Brooklyn Heights: Joyce noted the mojitos on the drinks menu. "C'mon," she said. "They're fun."

They were meeting only for drinks, so that Joyce could return a photo album she had borrowed from Linda years before. She couldn't return it herself: she and Linda were no longer speaking; they had ended, abruptly, a conversation they had begun in the third grade and had carried through the most fraught, significant, character-determining years of their lives. Each had now become the other's unperson, whose name you couldn't even think. Joyce had left the album in the apartment, however. Marshall and the kids were out of town for the weekend.

"Thank you for coming, Roger. I feel just terrible not seeing you guys. I miss Linda. I miss *you*."

His hand sketched a vague outline in the air in front of his face. "Yeah, well, you know."

"I know," she said warmly.

In fact she didn't know. Linda had been her best friend. Now Marshall had somehow seized the friendship and carried it off with him.

"So, how have you been holding up?" Roger asked, after they were served their drinks.

Joyce knew he would ask her this question, in precisely this way—eyes down at the table—but she took a while before replying.

"All right," she said heavily, and then shrugged. "But talk to me about something else. Something pleasant."

Roger was visibly relieved not to have to discuss Joyce and Marshall's breakup. Instead he told her what had happened to him on September 11. He pronounced the date in a grim whisper. He had been in Florida on business. He had been washing his hair in the shower in the hotel room, with the TV on, if only to keep him company. He couldn't hear what was being said, not with the water running, but through the bathroom's walls he had sensed a change in the broadcast's pitch or temperature, the voice of Tom Brokaw at the wrong hour of the day. He had rushed out without a towel and was instantly mesmerized by the television images. He had watched for hours while his hair dried and the lather caked. Later, after days of confusion, he was bumped from his return flight. He detailed his maneuvers to get a new flight—dozens of phone calls, being put on hold for hours, urgent appeals to the corporate headquarters in Atlanta—concluding bitterly, "Delta wouldn't tell me a thing."

"Hmm," Joyce said.

Roger was a burly man with bushy eyebrows and thick, cushiony lips; Linda's endearing nicknames had always been drawn from the ursine: Smokes, Yogarama, etc. Of the four friends, he was the most intellectual and level-headed yet, Joyce realized, he considered himself a significant actor—a victim—in the September 11 tragedy. And didn't she think she was a victim too? After all, she had *seen* the buildings fall, with her own helplessly naked eyes. She was supposed to have been on one of the planes. But so what. *Every* American felt that he had been personally attacked by the terrorists, and that was the patriotic thing of course, but patriotic metaphors aside, wasn't the belief a bit delusional? There was a difference between being killed and not being killed. Was everyone walking around America thinking they had been intimately, self-importantly, involved in the destruction of the World Trade Center?

She studied him carefully, alongside the image he had brought to the table: himself rushing from the shower. The comment didn't appear to be a come-on. He was much too somber and uncomfortable for that. Her phone call and simple request that he meet her for drinks had nearly seemed to break his heart. Their foursome had been inseparable once, each friendship within it tight and direct. She was touched, for she felt the same grief he did. Still, he had just placed his dripping, untoweled self in play.

The restaurant filled with customers and the kitchen started disgorging clove-scented fumes. Lifting her iced glass, Joyce took a long pull on her straw. Dented copper and bronze tea-pots were lined on a shelf on one side of the room, wall tapes-tries on the other. Diners leaned on embroidered pillows. Their murmurs rose just to the point of audibility. The bearded wait-ers wore loose white shirts, belted around their waists and left to fall untucked over their cotton trousers, and stiff sleeveless black waistcoats. She wondered if they carried knives beneath their waistcoats, and not only for cutting meat.

"Too bad about those Yanks," she said, trying to turn the conversation away from September 11, but that was impossible. In the seventh game of the delayed World Series earlier this month, the Yankees had lost to the expansion team from Ari-zona. The games, found in the back pages of newspapers dom-inated by terrorism and war, had been played in a spacious vacuum, despite the 9/11 ceremonies that preceded them. After the president, wearing an FDNY windbreaker, threw out the first ball—a perfect strike, the papers called it—the players were unable to fashion a story that either countered or honored the tragedy. The Yankees should have triumphed, demonstrat-ing the vigor and resilience of the world's greatest city—or the team should have been too demoralized to have made it into the Series at all. Not that many of the players ware actu-ally from New York. Roger scowled at the table. He had downed his drink as if it were medicine.

Joyce blurted, "Does Linda miss me?"

Damn, that wasn't what she wanted to say; she had hoped to avoid bringing Linda into the conversation. She felt blood rush to her face. Roger was taken aback. This meant talking about the breakup.

"Yes, of course," he said, frowning. Roger usually preferred precision and didn't wish to make an automatic response. He thought about his answer. "It's complex. Of course she misses you. She misses the friendship. She understands, though, that it can't be what it was."

Joyce wanted to ask, *Why not?* What did Marshall have to do with her and Linda? And how could Linda and Roger be so spineless? She wanted to smack him. They had always been weak. Now incidents from their lives came to mind. Linda had stayed with her loutish college boyfriend for years past college, unable to stand up to his abuse. Roger was perennially troubled by some complicated problems involving a rental property he owned with his sister and mother—problems whose solutions were obvious, requiring only some minimally tough determination. The way they shied from conflict could have been described as generosity and easygoingness—and it was these qualities that defined what looked like a relaxed, smoothly humming marriage—but Roger and Linda needed more than anything to be well liked. Roger hid his desperation behind an affability that pleasingly contrasted with his bulk and bearing. As for Linda, her defense was an affected ditziness that had gradually become an intrinsic part of her personality. She had been a dope to let Marshall come between them. But Joyce's anger had gone cold a long time ago, she reminded herself. She was here to do what she was forced to do; she had begged Roger to meet her for a drink not because she wanted to repair her friendship with Linda. *The friend of my enemy...*

"Do *you* miss me?" she said instead.

"Yes, sure, sure. Linda and I are heartbroken about this. We didn't want to take sides, our friendship meant a lot..."

Joyce reached across the table and seized his hand. This was something she would never have done before, back when they were still friends and she had no enemies. She would never have touched him like this, even though their rapport had always included some physical warmth. Before they had kids the four of them had moved around each other with a light, unembarrassed, meaningless physicality. Nothing was meaningless now: the waiters had witnessed her gesture, possibly; she thought she saw one of them flick a signal to the other, who had perhaps passed it on to the third. Everything was known. At the next table, a platter of sizzling kebabs had been brought to another couple, held high above the waiter's head like the spoils of war.

Roger was startled by her touch, but he didn't pull his hand away. She squeezed it. She became aware that a lute was playing on a tape or CD in the back of the restaurant, accompanied by quick, galloping, hand-beating percussion. A man sang: nasally, his voice strained, perhaps in solicitation, punctuated by frequent glottal stops. The singer paused, the lute called for him to continue, and it was joined by a stringed instrument, very tightly, sinuously wound. The rapid drumming was followed by forceful hand-clapping and the ringing of finger cymbals.

"No, I mean *you*, yourself, Roger. Do you miss me?"

He was blushing, smiling shyly. The proper hand squeeze could change the world.

"I miss you," she said. "Our friendship was, is, important to me. And, you know, I always thought we had something more than a friendship. I mean, I think we always saw each other as good friends, but there was always some boy-girl stuff involved, am I right?" She smiled with warmth, putting herself on the line. "There was some heat between us." Roger's smile didn't confirm this. It had become pained. This turn in the conversation made him anxious. "It was obvious, we're as transparent as two glasses of water. There were times when I thought...well, I don't know what I thought. You remember we were taking the cab together, back from that cocktail party...?" He remembered it with a jolt: she saw it in his eyes. That evening Marshall had been out of town and Linda had a dinner appointment.

Roger and Joyce had paired themselves at the party, even though they saw each other all the time. They shared a taxi to Brooklyn. Joyce went on softly, "I guess we were drinking a bit. It was cold, the cab had no shocks, we kept on bouncing against each other in the backseat, giggling. I thought you were going to kiss me. I think I wanted you to. I wasn't sure what I wanted. I think if I had only looked at you or said something or stopped giggling…" He pursed his lips, unable to contradict her. "It seemed like it wouldn't have taken much. But that's what's wrong with me, I don't take risks, and look where it's left me…"

She trailed off. She wasn't precisely clear in her own mind how her fear of taking risks had wrecked her marriage, but it seemed to make sense. For example, if she had taken the risk to confront Marshall earlier with their marital problems…No, that wouldn't have worked. She still held Roger's hand, cool and damp from his drink. She moved her hand slightly without squeezing. The motion was almost a caress.

"I'm sorry, I should go," he said, but he didn't remove his hand. He could have removed it at any time.

"I'm sorry," she said, pulling hers away. "I didn't mean to embarrass you."

"No, not at all. What happened happened, and what didn't happen…" He looked confused by his own tautology. In the taxi he had actually put his arms around her for a moment, ostensibly to keep her warm.

"Oh shit," she said.

"What?"

"I forgot the photo album!"

Roger shrugged. "It doesn't matter. Linda can get it some other time."

"I feel terrible."

"Mail it," he said, a ridiculous suggestion. The postal service had just reopened and no one was mailing anything. "UPS it."

"They're pictures from elementary school!"

Nothing could have compromised Roger more than the obviousness of her tactics. He would return with her to the apartment because he wanted to. Many deceptions were practiced in this way, in bazaars and counting halls, at the marriage broker and house of assembly, against those who needed to be deceived so that they could acquire in good conscience something they wanted.

It was difficult, though, to hold the moment in the two blocks home, after he paid the bill and they faced the sting of the quickly cooling, sobering evening. Joyce took care not to brush too heavily against him. She had to exercise caution. She had to keep the matter on his mind without being so flirtatious that it would register consciously. They walked quickly, hardly speaking. The lute continued to sound in her ears; she heard mourning now in the voice of the singer. The fiddle was nearly made visible by its whine: a hunter's bow scraping against a metal wire. She thought she might lose Roger again while she fumbled for the key to the building. He would remember all the times he had been here with Linda and Marshall. Now there was too long a wait for the elevator, a full minute, enough time for them to reconsider. As they ascended to her floor, she suppressed her misgivings and smiled, virtually batting her eyes. His smile was burdened with awkwardness and anxiety.

Then she was sure she lost him when she opened the door to the apartment. The sour odors of family life spilled from it, replacing the scents that had accompanied them from the restaurant, the cloves, the cardamom, the ginger, the saffron, the pepper, the turmeric, the fenugreek, the anise. She had straightened the apartment this morning, picking up toys and sweeping and dusting the living room. She had put Snuffles' food and water dishes away. She had removed her bed linen from the couch and stuffed it into a closet—but now she saw that she had neglected to remove the clock radio from its incongruous, telltale position on the side table. Some water damage around a window, dating from a storm last spring, had gone unfixed, conspicuously awaiting a settlement on the property. Marshall's bedroom door was closed, as always. She saw the apartment through Roger's eyes: it *looked* like a broken home.

"Okay," he said, stopped at the threshold.

"Come on in, I'll get the album."

He remained in the doorway.

"It's okay," she said, taking his hand. "They're not coming back till Monday, I swear. Take off your coat. How about a drink? Those mojitos were almost all Seven-Up and sugar. The Muslims can't make a decent cocktail. How about a Scotch?"

She poured it right away. She needed a Scotch now as badly as she needed oxygen. Her hands trembled. She had never before done anything on any field of battle this daring or this treacherous. She had never cheated on Marshall, to whom she was still technically, legally married. Roger stood at the entrance to her kitchen, sweltering in his coat, which he had only partially unzipped.

"Cheers," she said. She handed him his glass.

His eyes darted glances around the apartment, taking in the debris from their marriage: a CD rack with half its discs missing, a nonworking samovar Marshall had expelled from the master closet when he took control of the bedroom. Perhaps he was also looking for signs that Marshall was hiding behind the couch or alongside the TV. She had done a quick, panicked survey herself. Turning to her, Roger replied, *"Khodai de mal sha."*

"What's that?"

"A Pashtun saying. You know, from Afghanistan. 'May God be your companion.'"

"How'd you learn it?"

He said, "I don't know. Picked it up from the news, I guess."

His smile was mysterious, as if he knew exactly where he had picked it up.

"*Khodai de mal sha,*" she echoed. She loved saying it, the strange, steaming syllables gliding over her lips. For the moment her mouth was Pashtun, capable of Pashtun lies, Pashtun courage, Pashtun romance, and Pashtun desire. "*Khodai de mal sha,*" she repeated.

They fell on their drinks, each taking half a glass at once. She tracked the descent of the alcohol into her gut, waited a moment, and then felt the consequent familiar little explosion and the warmth rising to her ears. She gazed at him, hoping he was experiencing the same effects.

She wasn't going to wait for something to go wrong. She reached up to kiss him. His lips were warm, as soft as she thought they would be, yet they responded to her kiss with solemn insistence. He had wanted her to kiss him all this time.

Joyce removed his coat. His blue oxford shirt was soaked and his perspiration was not simply from the heat. He touched her breast gently, but without the least hesitation. *Roger touched my breast!* she told herself, amazed, and another voice responded: *The friend of my enemy is my enemy.* She kissed him harder. It was all happening very fast: he didn't want to lose the moment either. She slipped out of her shoes and then, trying to move closer, she nearly fell over them. He caught her. Their drinks swirled around in their tumblers but didn't spill. They each took another swallow.

He was trying to drift toward the couch, but she resisted. It wasn't the couch where they needed to be. She wrestled him over to the door to Marshall's bedroom. She dropped her left hand, allowing it to caress his side as she reached to turn the doorknob.

He stopped, frozen, as if suddenly aware of being within the sights of a rifle. He knew this was Marshall's room. Joyce herself sensed the trespass, but she pushed the door open wide, without turning to look in. Roger peered into the gloom over her shoulder, scared. He had probably never done anything like this either—and Marshall, until a moment ago, had been his best friend. She slid her hand along the front of his pants to determine that, no, the moment hadn't been lost. She pulled him into the bedroom.

When their glasses were empty their clothes came off. As she had known, he was extravagantly hairy: across his chest, his belly, his buttocks, his legs…The naked, sweaty bulk of him verged on the grotesque. She wasn't repelled: she had done this because she desired to enter into the grotesque. Joyce felt his hands and lips on her body, but she experienced the lovemaking, if that's what it was, as something happening to someone else. The Joyce who observed was still a successfully married mother of two small children. Yet she observed with grim approval. He was hunched over her, his lips on her right breast, coaxing blood into her nipple. If only Linda could see this, if only Marshall could…But that wasn't necessary, the violation was sufficient in itself, treachery was its own reward, independent of anyone's knowledge; and in any case, Joyce would know, and this knowledge was a poison, transferable by dart or whisper, a tincture added to the rosewater.

She perched at the edge of Marshall's bed. Her distance from these events closed as Roger put his hands on her shoulders, lowered her to the bed, and climbed onto her body, kissing the hollow of her neck. Then she saw him slide in. His *penis*! Linda's husband's *penis*! Inside her! She was stunned by how easily this had been accomplished. The seduction had been no work at all. It was as if…Now the lovemaking *was* happening to her, his hands and mouth on her breasts, his pelvis grinding hers against the bed, a great store of energy being summoned from within her. His hair, his bulk, his sweat, and his masculine odor gave him a fearsome, primitive aspect. She was suddenly overcome by a flood of sexual feeling: every nerve ending in her body seemed to be in contact with Roger's penis. *She* was Roger's penis. *The penis of the friend of my enemy...* Joyce had thought she was hardly attracted to Roger—there had *never* been any boy-girl stuff between them—but she suddenly wanted him. She moved with him, laid out across a textured beige bedspread Marshall had purchased on his own, and recalled now the easy delight she had once taken from the sex act.

When it was over, the waves of feeling continued to rock her and Roger rolled over, falling heavily onto the bedspread. He was soaked again with perspiration. "Well," he said, and she found herself beginning to turn into the dim, slow, luscious arc toward a nap. Then she remembered to arch her back, spilling semen. The new bedspread was eminently stainable. She wondered if she was pregnant. That would be a disaster and it would also be almost perfect.

She hadn't been in this bedroom since she had moved to the couch. From where she lay, flat on her back, her breasts bare and still heaving, the room didn't look as if it had been dusted or cleaned in all that time, though Marshall had outfitted it with a new television and a CD player–clock radio, much better than her setup. There was a picture of the kids on the dresser, taken when Vic was no more than a year, the happiness of the moment locked within the picture frame like a gemstone. She saw a new phone behind the books on Marshall's night table, relationship books and histories of the Middle East: *Winning Divorce Strategies; The Ottomans Break Up; New York State Family Law for Dummies; Partition and Exile; How to Keep the House, the Money, the Kids, and the Homeland; The Great Game; Screw Your Ex!* Marshall's streamlined, LED-equipped telephone seemed gratuitously high-tech, with some kind of weird attachment hooked into it. What was *that* for?

"We wanted it," she said, returning to Roger. "We both wanted it." Her voice was choked, a bit husky. She liked the sound. At that moment she found herself fantastically sexy.

"That cunt," he said, gasping. "She had it coming!"

Joyce wished she had a cigarette. It had been accomplished: this stain on Linda's marriage as sure as the one on Marshall's bedspread. She pushed her pelvis forward again, releasing another trickle. But wait a minute, what did he mean when he said, "She had it coming"? Who did, Linda? Why? How? So caught up in her divorce, she had hardly wondered about the state of Roger and Linda's marriage. What exactly were the circumstances that made him capable of doing this? She didn't know. She didn't know a goddamn thing. She hadn't spoken to Linda in a year and had no knowledge of what went on in her life—who was her new best friend? what had she done to Roger? how could Roger call her a "cunt"? yuck—and now Joyce felt the loss of friendship echo through her all over again.

"Could you give that to me?"

"What?"

He slid his fat fingers down her leg to her ankle bracelet. He pulled on it gently. She had forgotten she was even wearing it.

"What for?"

"Oh, you know, just to have. As a keepsake."

As a trophy. Linda would find it in the back of a dresser. She would know it was Joyce's; she would learn that Roger had found a new way to hurt and dishonor her. Joyce reached for the bracelet, flicked the clasp, and passed it to him. As she lay there, staring at the ceiling, she knew she had not seduced Roger at all. He had his own reasons for making love to her, something to do with Linda. She had seen him as a pawn in her struggle against Marshall, but each person had his own tragic secret history, his own rationalizations, his own formulas of conflict, his own imperfectly understood needs. Every human relationship was a conspiracy. Roger, too, was working in the shadows, for his own survival, against his own enemies and friends of enemies... Her body cooled, turning taut, and she wondered where Marshall kept his cigarettes.

DECEMBER

ANOTHER RESTAURANT, on Saturday night a week later: Marshall arrived early to reconnoiter. The restaurant was small and softly lit, with bare walls and creamy linen tablecloths, and packed with diners, mostly couples. He found only six places had been reserved for Neal's bachelor party—a miserable turnout for someone known for his friendliness and good humor, Marshall noted with pleasure. When Neal stepped through the door he waved at Marshall and, radiant in anticipation, was brought to the table by the hostess. The two men hugged, despite the sea of strangers around them. Again Marshall considered how little he knew the guy, and how pathetic it was that he might be considered his fifth best friend. Neal was accompanied by his brother, Joel, who managed to take the chair between them.

The other men arrived shortly and all at once, guys in their twenties. Marshall had met one of them before, Howie, who appeared to be Neal's closest friend, though Marshall uncharitably intuited that Neal was probably not Howie's. There was a Steve and somebody named either Alan or Albert; engaged in scheming, uncharitable thoughts, Marshall missed the name. Alan-Albert apparently worked with Neal. They were all big-boned men in chinos and blazers, much too large for the restaurant, and they squeezed against the tables as they filed in. Neal, Joel, and Marshall rose to shake hands and then the men wondered, at length, about who should occupy which seat. One of the waiters hurried over to get them settled.

Steve turned in his seat and craned his neck, looking over the room. He said, "Where are the hookers? What kind of bachelor party is this without hookers?"

The men tittered and this appeared to break the ice. There were a few jokes about where they could go for hookers or lap dancing, or simply a bar where they could meet girls. A few murmurs of appreciation were elicited as the curvy hostess in a red sweater and tight slacks passed, gliding by on high heels. "Sweet," Howie said. Marshall detected an undercurrent of uneasiness, the good humor forced by the occasion. These men weren't accustomed to making suggestive remarks about women. "Red means go," Steve said. "It's your last chance, Neal." This was passed over in silence, as if he had just revealed too much about his sexual preferences. As it happened, Marshall had originally hoped to hire an "escort" for the party and had begun doing the initial research in the yellow pages. He had made phone calls and discovered that bachelor parties and "deflowerings" were a popular specialty, but once he began discussing what he wanted the woman to do, he realized he would be paying several hundred dollars or more. Real sex would cost a fortune and a rebuffed seduction would be just as expensive as one that was carried through. He had thought better of it.

Joel made a big deal about ordering the wine for the table, and when it came he rolled it around in his glass and sniffed it hard. He swallowed a mouthful and looked vacantly across the restaurant. Finally, he nodded at the waiter. When the waiter left, Howie rolled his eyes and said, "A Jewish wine snob. God help us."

"Jews make good wine snobs," Joel shot back. "It's all in *le nez*."

They all laughed except Marshall, who knew that he did not have leave to laugh at Jewish noses. He wasn't inclined to anyway, since Jews hardly held a monopoly on large noses—the curvy Italian hostess, for example, owned a wonderfully carnal prowlike schnozz he would have loved to kiss and caress—and he never understood the humor of self-deprecation. Jews thought it was funny simply to be Jewish; this mystified him. He couldn't understand why being Jewish was any more humorous than being, say, Norwegian; but if you expressed this perplexity to a Jew, he'd be offended. These guys were all Jews. He studied Neal's brother, Joel, who in fact did have a sizable nose, as well as a cropped black beard that might qualify as rabbinical, now that Marshall was thinking about it. His eyes were a deep nutlike brown and his expression, even when he made a weak joke, seemed aggressively intelligent. He hardly resembled his much fairer, easygoing brother.

Marshall pretended to be shy as the conversation circled the table, touching on their jobs and the war in Afghanistan. Relieved that the obligatory sex conversation had concluded, they debated the merits of a land invasion and the whereabouts of Osama bin Laden. Neal told a very funny joke, perfectly delivered: bin Laden and Saddam Hussein walk into a bar...Marshall hardly laughed and didn't speak. He studied the menu, listening for an opening. At some point he became aware that his reticence disturbed the other men, an unexpected but interesting effect. He prolonged it and moodily darted his eyes down at the table. Aspiring to be the live wire, Steve broke in on his reverie to ask how he knew Neal.

"My wife is Flora's sister."

Marshall said it lightly, but a shadow crossed Neal's face. He had evidently told himself that his friendship with Marshall had nothing to do with the two sisters. Marshall's reply had re-minded him of the serious recriminations he risked in extend-ing an invitation to the dinner.

Steve pushed on unawares. "How long have you been mar-ried?"

"Seven years."

"That's great!"

"Actually, we're getting divorced now. We're litigating, we're counterlitigating..."

Marshall smiled. Steve smiled too, as if Marshall had just told him something optimistic. None of these men were mar-ried, so they knew nothing about women. Probably few of them understood divorce; perhaps they simply equated it with being single again, which was like equating death with being unborn. But the word "divorced" had electrified Neal. He was already imagining his own divorce, wondering if it would be as awful as Marshall and Joyce's. Marshall guessed their divorce cast a pall on the wedding preparations in Canaan. Good.

The moment passed and the men dug into their dinners, their bonhomie returning. Two more bottles of wine were ordered. Marshall wondered how he could return to his divorce, but the conversation had drifted away. Now Joel, a microbiologist at Stanford, was holding their attention with an amusing story about how he had nearly missed the events of September 11. He had slept late that morning and had driven off to the university listening to a CD. On the highway he had noticed that nearly every driver was talking into his cell phone. Students were standing in clusters on the campus, also with cell phones. No one seemed to be in their classes. As a scientist, he drew from the empirical evidence the only pos-sible conclusion: cell phones had become ubiquitous. He was in his lab for more than an hour before a postdoc from New York stopped by, nearly in tears. Joel told the table, "I was the last person in America to find out about the attacks." He paused for a beat, his eyes sparkling. "I mean, not counting the FBI."

The men snickered, all except Marshall.

Neal noticed that he held back. He explained, "Marshall worked at the World Trade Center."

They looked appalled. Joel said quickly, "Sorry."

Marshall laughed and waved away the apology. "No, no, don't worry, I'm not traumatized or anything like that."

"He hadn't reached work yet," Neal said, recalling their telephone conversation. "You were delayed, right?"

Marshall winced and made an embarrassed little smile. "Actually, I *was* in the building when the second plane hit, in an elevator on the way to my office—which had just been obliterated. Never heard the first plane. The elevator stopped for a while and then left us off in the lobby on the forty-fourth floor. We had to walk down the stairwell. It was chaos, let me tell you: smoke and dust, people bloodied, people crying. I saw the firemen going in. I saw dead bodies in the plaza, people falling... Yeah, it was awful," he concluded.

These words, spoken matter-of-factly, had been enough to stop the other men from eating, some of them with their forks in midair. "Wow," Alan-Albert said at last. "Jeez," said Howie. Neal beamed, aware that his bachelor party had suddenly been swept within the circumference of contemporary world events.

Joel said, "My God, what were you thinking?"

Marshall chuckled. "Mostly about how to get out of the building."

"Did you know what it was?"

"A plane? No," Marshall said. What *had* he been thinking? His recollection of that morning was like the underground lobby in which he had seemed trapped: murky, smoky, dangerous. He remembered making a friend in the plaza and then losing him. It had also been the morning he realized that Miss Naomi was a babe. "I guess we thought it was some kind of bomb. I wasn't working there in 1993, when they blew up the parking garage. Six people were killed then. But everyone thought of that. It was part of the building's memory."

"So you didn't think it was an accident. You knew it was terrorists," Joel confirmed.

"Right, sure," Marshall said. He observed Joel's satisfaction. Neal's brother was driving at something. "Of course it was terrorists. No one thought it could be anything else," he added. The other men grimly shook their heads, as if he were speaking of a greater truth. He ventured, "Look at the world today. I knew it was Middle East terrorism come home."

Joel murmured, "That's what it was, all right."

Marshall allowed himself to be egged on. "I felt like *I* was in the Middle East. I was looking for an exit, looking for daylight, and I was trying not to get hit by falling debris, and all these thoughts were going through my head. Why am *I* in this fucking war?—that's what I asked myself." Marshall looked around the table: five Jews. They were letting their pasta get cold. They shared his anger and grief, as if they had been in the World Trade Center with him, as if they had lost a friend in the plaza too. "Why was this happening?"

"Yeah, why?" Joel said bitterly. "What's wrong with these people? Why—"

"I was just furious," Marshall continued, "thinking of everything that had put us at war with the Arab world: irrational Islamic fundamentalism, oil lust, fanatics from Brooklyn, Third World poverty—the list of reasons goes on, and meanwhile bodies were dropping into the plaza. That's what I was thinking."

Howie sighed and began cutting his steak. Steve and Neal looked sorrowful. At the next table a middle-aged couple had heard at least part of the exchange and had paused in their own conversation.

Joel smiled, as if in mild incomprehension. But Marshall

guessed he did comprehend. Joel said, "Brooklyn? What do you mean?"

Marshall nodded, conceding, "Well, perhaps they're not all from Brooklyn, but many of those Jewish settlers on the West Bank are American. And they go to Israel specifically intending to build settlements—knowing they're illegal under international law, knowing they're an impediment to peace, knowing they hugely complicate our relations with other countries in the Middle East."

"I think if you met them," Joel said gently, "you would discover that they're not fanatics. Most are well educated, and many are professionals who commute to work in Jerusalem. Many are not even religious. They simply want better lives for themselves and their families, living as Jews in peace with the world."

"On Arab land," Marshall declared, and he saw a flash of anger in Joel's eyes, quickly suppressed. The other men looked uncomfortable. Marshall brought a little heat into his voice. "They bring small children to these ugly outposts in a place where the people want to kill them. They take the land by force, they take the water, and then they claim the Bible as their authority. I call that fanaticism. And somehow the U.S. has made its entire foreign policy hostage to these few thousand dickheads."

Joel grinned in a friendly way. He pushed out a little chuckle. "Perhaps you could be better informed, but this reflects the bias of the American news media. First of all, if you look at bin Laden's statements before September 11, there's no evidence that he ever cared about the Palestinians; his complaint is with the American military presence in Saudi Arabia."

"Yeah, right." Marshall let his sarcasm congeal for a few moments in the garlic-laced steam over their table. "The settlers have nothing to do with Arab anger at the U.S.—"

"Second," Joel said more firmly, locking his eyes on Marshall's, "the concept of this so-called Arab land. What does this mean? Jews have settled in what you call the West Bank for millennia. This was the center of Jewish civilization, this is where our patriarchs are buried. This was always part of Palestine, under the Ottomans and under the British Mandate, always Jewish territory, Judea and Samaria. Now the settlers are developing the land, irrigating it and farming it and making jobs for everybody. The Arabs want to ethnically cleanse the land— while a million of their people maintain full citizenship in Israel, freer than they would be in any other country of the Mideast, and better educated and better paid!"

Neal broke in, his smile good-natured. "Hey, guys, ease up. What is this, *Crossfire*? I invite you to my bachelor party and I get *Crossfire*?" The other men chuckled.

"C'mon," Marshall replied. Sneering, he raised his voice to reach the other tables. "Something like three million Palestinians live on the West Bank and in Gaza. Do you really think you can keep them down forever? And when the Arabs see Israeli soldiers killing Palestinian civilians—Palestinian *children*— to protect the settlers, they blame America! That's why the World Trade Center was attacked!"

Joel rapped his knuckles on the table. "This is scapegoating. The Arabs are mad at Israel and America because they're the only things their corrupt, repressive governments allow them to be mad at. Their anger is unjustified. To appease it would be craven."

Marshall shrugged, as if the argument weren't important to him, and as if Joel had been the first to get angry. "Perhaps, but this is what most of the world thinks. This is what most of America thinks. The Israelis have their country, why can't they leave the Palestinians alone in theirs?"

"What Palestinians? Did you ever wonder why there wasn't a clamor for a Palestinian state all over the world in the nineteen years when the West Bank was held by Jordan and Gaza was held by Egypt? I'll tell you: no one ever thought of the Palestinians as a distinct nationality until after the territory was captured in the Six-Day War—a war that Israel fought defensively, for its own survival. These so-called Palestinians are only a tool that the Arabs are using in the pursuit of their ultimate goal: the total destruction of Israel. That's obvious to anyone who knows the first thing about the history of Israel."

Marshall screwed his face into a mask of disgust.

"How informed do I have to be about Israeli history? I'm an American. When we went to war in Somalia and Kosovo, how much history did I have to know? How much does anyone know about other places' just-as-complicated histories? I don't need a course in Zionism, the Balfour Declaration, the Holocaust, UN Resolution Five Million and Three...Fuck it. The only thing that's important to me as an American is America's national interests. And Americans are starting to ask themselves, what's so necessary about this crappy little country that our people have to die for it? Why do we have to make all these foreign policy accommodations for a single ethnic group?"

The men at the table had put their forks down. Until Marshall had spoken the words *crappy little country*, this had been an argument between only him and Joel. He had seen a few flickers of demurral in their faces when Joel had defended the settlers. Steve had seemed to want to jump into the conversation, to mediate it. Now he was paralyzed. Neal's face had darkened.

Joel's smile was rock hard. "Spoken like a true anti-Semite."

"What do you think makes people anti-Semites?" Marshall blurted, or, rather, pretended to blurt. He answered himself in a low, even voice, his mouth tight. "It's the way every dissent from Israeli policy provokes an accusation of anti-Semitism. It's the fact that we're not permitted to talk about Israel in this country, even though it's our number one foreign problem. It's the way that every remark by every non-Jew has to be tested for the stain of anti-Semitism. And I ask myself, in this day and age, why is anti-Semitism the greatest evil the world must contend with? Why is it worse than being anti-Arab?"

Joel shook his head and turned to Neal. "See? Scratch a Gentile. You thought I was making this up. They'll never accept us, never. Look at their white-bread private schools and the no-Jews country club. That's why they fought so hard against you and don't want the least Jewish content in your wedding: no rabbi, a single lousy Jewish prayer, a huge argument just to get the chuppah. I'm not blaming them individually, but their environment is totally inimical to everything you are."

He turned to Marshall. Marshall recalled that at one time he would have been intimidated by his passion and certainty. Now he didn't care, he had won complete freedom of expression, even if he was still imprisoned within his marriage. He was crazy! Joel said, "You should educate yourself. Israel's not going away and neither are the Jews."

The men were silent and the other diners stared. They expected Marshall to storm from the restaurant. But he smirked, lifted his knife and fork, and returned to his plate. He kept his head down, taking an animal-like pleasure in the meat. After a while the other men resumed eating. The conversation was dead, except for a few murmurs about how good the food was. In fact it was cold. The table was cleared and Joel signaled for the check, but Marshall demanded the dessert menu. He ordered a tiramisù. The other men reluctantly ordered desserts as well. Then there was coffee. He ordered a refill. Even after the check had been paid, Marshall lingered sullenly with Neal, his brother, and his friends on the sidewalk in front of the restaurant, so that they couldn't go off for a nightcap without him. When they each had finally been deposited in their respective cabs, Marshall walked by himself to the subway. He felt like singing. Flora's *thing*. That was it.

JOYCE'S FIRST IMPULSE was to tell Flora about her affair with Roger, even if it wasn't really an "affair"—he hadn't called her since that evening and she hadn't wanted him to; nor had he called her back after she left her number at his office, several times. But while Flora would have been impressed and deliciously scandalized, the fling with Roger could also have confirmed suspicions, if Flora possessed them, that Joyce was responsible for the failure of her marriage through other self-indulgences and betrayals. The divorce had already lowered her standing in the family. Joyce knew her parents blamed her; they probably recalled from her youth precursor catastrophes. Flora would have heard comments.

As soon as Joyce arrived in Connecticut, she saw that her concerns about Flora's response were moot: Flora had no time for her confessions. She rushed at her in the driveway, her face flushed, her hair unclipped, desperate to unburden herself, and she hardly said hello to Victor and Viola. The kids had squabbled all the way from the railway station; their grandfather Deke had pretended not to hear, or perhaps truly had not heard. His radio had been tuned to a loud, biliously contentious call-in show. Once the kids were settled the sisters sequestered themselves in Joyce's childhood bedroom, which had been renovated into a charmless but convenience-rich hotel-like guest chamber, furnished with a television, a writing desk, a dressing room, and, in the adjacent bathroom, little packets of soap and shampoo. Her voice tight, Flora said that certain details involving the caterer and the florist had not yet been finalized—Amanda was still tinkering. Also, she had added to the musical selections some awful seventies pop numbers. Meanwhile, Deke was absent most of the time, apparently indifferent to the wedding.

Joyce asked, "How's Neal?"

Flora frowned at the non sequitur.

"All right. He's occupied with his own family. His brother came in last week, they had like a bachelor dinner with some friends, and now they're picking up their folks at JFK. They're coming for dinner tonight. Meanwhile I had another argument with Mom. You know, we agreed to that thing. Now it turns out there's something else, a glass. I didn't even know about it, but all of a sudden it's important to Neal. He told me on Sunday. He was adamant about it."

At that moment they heard their names lofted upward, sung as they had been sung since their infancies: liltingly, with an extra syllable in each name—*Jo-oyce! Flo-ora!*—the extra syllable buoyed by a measure of hope. The hope was that her daughters would not disappoint her. Without another word they went down to the living room, where Amanda had put out on the carpet a flowerless centerpiece basket for Flora's approval. She was wearing slacks and a cashmere sweater. Joyce was struck by how youthful she looked. She must have been dieting rigorously in the months approaching the wedding.

"Hello, sweetie," Amanda said, kissing her. "Your munchkins are adorable. The flower girl says the wedding will be on fire." She smiled. "What can she mean by that?"

"She means it's going to be exciting," Joyce said. "She can't stop talking about it. Vic still isn't sure what the fuss is about."

"It's not a fuss!" Amanda objected, and Joyce saw that she had stumbled into one of the side alleys of the dispute. Flora had probably told Amanda that she was making an unnecessary fuss over the wedding. Joyce regretted her remark, the manifestation of a reflex never to speak of one child without mentioning the other. Oblivious to the wedding preparations, Victor hadn't observed the fuss at all. Amanda said, "It's only a great deal of busyness, a few complications. I'm just trying to get this wedding right."

Joyce wondered if her mother meant to bring to mind her wedding seven years ago, which had been accompanied by several embarrassments: an unwanted guest, Marshall's cousin, whom they were obliged to invite; a scarily nearly inadequate supply of champagne; Marshall's ill-considered last-minute mustache; Deke's rebellion against the affair's add-on costs; Marshall's slacker best man, who performed his duties half stoned. Joyce had specifically asked Gottschall to delete the word "obey" from her vows. They had practiced it without "obey" every time. On the day of the ceremony he had employed it anyway. Joyce had replied, "I do," and had immediately hated herself for it, and hated Marshall too. Did Amanda believe that if they had gotten *that* wedding right, Joyce and Marshall wouldn't be getting divorced now? It was an offensive thought, but not entirely without reason. Their marital arguments had been prefigured by the premarital, unlike their sex. Joyce sucked in her breath, signaling her displeasure with her mother's comment.

"Flora says I never consult with her," Amanda went on, perhaps pretending not to notice Joyce's vexation. "Well, the florist has kindly allowed me to take home the centerpiece basket, so that Flora can give us her judgment. What do you think, dear?"

"Mom," Flora said wearily, "I can't judge the centerpiece without the flowers."

"You've seen the flowers!" Amanda exclaimed, her voice wavering with emotion. It was hard to determine to what extent this drama was being performed for Joyce's benefit. "But you didn't like the baskets. You thought they were too formal. This is less formal. Please, use your imagination. If you don't care for it, I'll try to locate another."

"Fine. It's great."

"You don't think it's great."

"I do."

"You think it's something else I'm imposing on you."

"I don't," Flora said. "Call the florist. This is the center-piece I want and demand. Please, Mom, can't we just move on to something else?"

"No more arguments!" Amanda agreed, holding up her hands in surrender. "I have to get into the kitchen and see about dinner. They'll be here at six." She confided to Joyce, "It's veal. I was going to make a pork dish, then I remembered."

Flora protested, "I've told you a hundred times, Mom, Neal loves pork. They're not religious and they don't observe kosher regulations. And if they did, nonkosher veal would be just as inadmissible as pork." She paused. "I think."

"You think," Amanda said. "But you don't know. How could you? They themselves don't know all the rules and regulations, which as far as I can see are completely arbitrary. Certain butchers are kosher, some are not—but isn't the meat the same? They have kosher *salt*, for God's sake. How can a grain of salt be more Jewish than another grain of salt? I'm glad to oblige them, of course, as best I can, and it's all very colorful and exotic—I've always been pro-Israel—but really. They say they're not religious, and then they come up with one religious demand after another. Now there's this to-do about a glass."

Joyce nodded. "Flora started telling me."

"Oh, the glass! The glass! First, we offered to have Gott-schall read a Jewish prayer. Then they came back and said they wanted this thing carried into the church, some kind of canopy thing they wanted to stand under when he read the prayer. Who's going to know what *that* is? It will look very silly up there in Canaan Christ Church. There was never any question of this being a Jewish wedding. They knew Flora was Christian and we were Christians, and in fact, some of us take our faith very seriously—never mind that. But they insisted on a Satur-day evening wedding after the Sabbath they don't observe and we agreed to it and they insisted on the canopy and we agreed to it. Now they've just came back and said they need to break a glass."

"That's right, Mom," Joyce recalled now. "I've seen it done at Jewish weddings, even mixed ones. Like at Annette's. They drink wine from a glass, put it under a blanket, and step on it. The glass-breaking symbolizes that even in moments of great joy they have to keep in mind the sorrows of the world, especially the Jewish exile from Jerusalem. And the canopy's a symbolic new home for the couple: it's called a chuppah. The ceremony's very sweet, actually, very moving and not religious at all."

"Okay. Great. It's not my wedding. You want to break a glass, Flora, go ahead," Amanda said, heading toward the kitchen and pretending not to be mollified. In fact, Joyce had said precisely the right thing, probably by mentioning Annette, whose family represented serious old money up in Boston. Joyce felt she had just scored points as a peacemaker.

Flora sighed. "It's been like that all week, one argument after another. And Neal! He admits he just thought of the glass, but he says it's vitally important. You know, it wouldn't be so annoying if he'd been more involved from the start, but everything with him is an occasion for another one-liner..."

Joyce went to her room to shower and change for dinner. The kids were playing on the front lawn by themselves, taking advantage of the liberties granted by the suburban civil order. They had been generating an enormous amount of noise, but her bedroom was in the back, putting her out of range. She was pleased by her intervention in her mother's dispute with Flora. It had been timely, shrewd, and genuinely fair-minded. She felt like Jimmy Carter.

After her bath she wrapped herself in a towel and lay on the double bed that had replaced the one from her childhood. She marveled at how impersonal the guest room was and how much she welcomed its impersonality. Close your eyes and you couldn't recall the subject of the print hanging over the desk, nor the color of the walls or the bedspread. Here lingered no trace of family or self. You could forget history. Everything that had ever happened to her seemed to have taken place on another continent, in a distant century.

MARSHALL WAS CRAZY, no doubt about it. He drove crazy down the Merritt Parkway, speeding, chortling, cackling, pounding the top of the roof of his car with his windows open as his radio blasted away. It was forty degrees outside. He was crazy and crazy made him strong. He could do whatever he wanted now, absolutely anything, he was a crazy fucking divorcing superpower.

He had no idea how this was going to turn out. He was operating on blind scamming instinct: say this, do that, yes sir, I'm calling on behalf of Neal Weiss. From the moment he first wished Neal good luck, Marshall had bulled his way through enemy territory without any idea of where his next opportunity would present itself. His trusting to chance was the true mark of a madman.

It was like going back into the building and finding Lloyd. He didn't know what would happen next and he didn't care. Fuck Joyce and fuck her whole fucking family.

NEAL'S FAMILY ARRIVED at six, precisely on time as if, Joyce speculated, they were conforming to what they thought were the rigors of WASP punctuality. This speculation wouldn't have occurred to Joyce if it hadn't been for the discussion about the glass-breaking ceremony. She didn't think she usually entertained generalized expectations about Jews, among whom she had lived and worked her entire adult life, or about what Jews thought of non-Jews. She had hardly ever considered her putative brother-in-law's faith. But just as she had begun to expect his family to be something more old-country than he was, or at least something more Long Island, Harold and Elise Weiss arrived at the front door tall, tanned, and fit like Neal, perfectly Californian. The couples exchanged handshakes within the conventional American boundaries of social warmth. No one kissed. Flora and Neal eyed each other, trying to determine from each other's expression before Neal's parents and brother even took off their coats how the other thought the dinner was working out. Amanda waved her guests into the living room. Deke poured some Scotch for Harold and the two men hastened to discuss Sunday's football matchups, ignoring the Saturday event.

Only Joel approached what she would have expected as Jewish. His coloring was darker than Neal's and he maintained a diffident, attractively serious air after being introduced to Joyce's family. He shook their hands hard and retreated. It transpired that Elise and Amanda had once attended the same cooking school in Toulouse and Neal and Flora were hashing out some ever-expanding complications involving the wedding, so that left Joel with Joyce, but he didn't show an interest in chitchat. He was walking around the living room, inspecting their furnishings—the pictures on the wall, the secretary—like an anthropologist.

In any case, the kids had to be roped in before dinner. Joyce had deliberately left them outside, since they were playing unusually well together. The game they had devised that afternoon, its rules ramified and mysterious, mandated hours of running and shouting, as well as repeated leaps off the side of the porch onto a small slope that declined toward the woods. They always jumped holding hands and rolled down the lawn screaming and whooping. When she found them they were a mess of tangled hair and grass stains, but she reveled in their freedom. She wondered, as she had even before New York became a terrorist target, whether they would be better off living outside the city. She quickly dismissed the thought. Any proposal to change domiciles would have been impossible, reopening all the previous, provisionally settled negotiations. Marshall would have used the proposal against her.

Dinner was ready by the time the children were changed, washed, and made presentable. The Weisses were charmed as Viola and Vic went around the table introducing themselves. The kids were comfortable with Neal and let him grab them by their heads and administer noogies. Amanda was taken aback for a moment, never having, probably, experienced a noogie herself. Then she smiled coolly. Joel's smile was cool too, Joyce discerned.

As Joyce and her truncated family took their seats, the table, as a committee of the whole, returned to the business before it: finalizing the logistics for the next two days. The arrangements were too urgent to wait for after dinner. Beyond the florist and the caterer lay encounters with dry cleaners, hairdressers, and the Beverage Barn, every one of them at different points on the compass. Even with three cars at their disposal, the scheduling was complicated. Joyce feared to mention that she needed to have her nails done. Tomorrow before the rehearsal dinner Neal had an appointment for the final fitting and pickup of his tuxedo. Flora insisted on being there to give it her approval.

"I want you at your cutest," she said, reaching over and squeezing his cheek. Neal giggled.

Joyce couldn't recall whether she had ever done anything in public like that to Marshall.

"Fine," Joel agreed, "but then we have to go to Hartford."

These words were delivered like a judgment from the bench. His family nodded.

"Hartford?" Amanda said. "That's more than an hour away."

"It's the location of the closest Jewish religious supply store,"

Joel replied, almost reprovingly. "It's the only store in the region that has a chuppah rental. We made a reservation."

The chuppah. He had been quiet during most of the logistics discussion, waiting for this moment.

"No problem," Flora said. "You can leave me off here. It's on the way back from the tuxedo store."

"And we have to get a wineglass," Neal reminded her. The mark left by Flora's pinch hadn't entirely faded. It occurred to Joyce that the cheek pinch was a characteristically Jewish gesture. Flora was becoming more Jewish every day.

"We have glasses. Right, Mom?"

"Of course we do." Amanda asked quietly, "Is there a special kind of glass that you require, Neal?"

"No, I don't think so," he said, and grinned. "It shouldn't be expensive, since, you know, we're going to be smashing it."

"As long as it's Waterford," Harold broke in. He was a big man with a large bald forehead and a rakishly droopy mustache. He gazed unsmilingly with cold, dark brown eyes into Amanda's. When she didn't respond at once, he rushed to say, "I'm joking. I have no idea what kind of glass. A Flintstones glass would be fine, I'm sure." He paused thoughtfully. "If the jelly was kosher."

Joyce saw Amanda flash something at Flora. The expression was obliquely observed and so short-lived that Joyce couldn't read its meaning, but she guessed it contained several quanta of exasperation.

Joel told them, "Getting the chuppah, though—for that we need the religious supply store."

Flora repeated, "No problem. You'll drop me off with the tux, I'll hang it, and you can go on your way."

"The chuppah's important," Neal said to Flora's family in apology. He grinned, eyes wide, and suddenly threw up his hands. "It's just one of those wacky desert-nomad chosen-people things."

"Okay, okay," Flora said. "Get two."

JOYCE WAS LEFT with the kids the following morning as the machinery of the wedding was put into motion, each car dispatched with a list and a fully charged cell phone. Joyce was relieved not to rush off anywhere and not to be at the center of the drama, with time to linger over her coffee at the breakfast table. It wasn't her wedding, hurrah. She considered the personal baggage Neal and Flora had assembled for their honeymoon and beyond. It wasn't her marriage, hurrah. She resolved to do her nails herself and not even mention it. She was pleased not to be in the way—not, for a change, to be the problem. Indeed, there were times, like yesterday afternoon, when she thought she could demonstrate to her mother and sister her clearheadedness and good judgment. At some point, perhaps, she would make obvious to her family and to *herself* just how well she was handling the turmoil in her life.

As the morning warmed the kids agitated to go out and she walked them through the country neighborhood, pointing out where her best friends had lived, where she had gone to school, and in which homes she had babysat. The walk proved slightly deflating: Victor and Viola were more interested in kicking stones, especially a particular blue-black rock they had found in the gutter. Viola declared that it was a piece of an airplane. Within a few blocks Joyce had changed her mind about the excursion. Almost every one of these houses provoked memories of her childhood; it had been a happy enough childhood, but the markers of her past innocence and promise now reminded her only of her present misery. At the same time familiar neighbors still inhabited most of these homes. A single glance from a window would resurrect *their* recollections. They knew of her pending divorce. They would sigh when they saw her. Some were sighing behind the curtains right now. It was a Friday

morning and she was walking aimlessly through streets in which
no one commonly walked at all.

After lunch the kids went to the porch to resume the game
from the night before. Joyce watched them for a minute,
amused, and returned inside the house to read the newspaper,
which detailed the stepped-up war in Afghanistan, where continuing betrayals were followed by further chicanery and rival
factions duped the U.S. into targeting more innocent civilians.
But the war proved to be considerably less interesting when
read about in Connecticut, rather than in New York City, where
the towers' absence was still palpable. Here New York and
Kabul seemed equally distant and foreign. New York remained
part of the world's current history, its streets teeming with im-
migrants and refugees, its ethnic, corrupt politics kin to the
strife that redrew maps and toppled regimes elsewhere. Connecticut was almost shut off from the times—but then she
recalled that her sister had recently mentioned that an Ethiopian restaurant had opened in the adjacent town. And Joyce
had heard something Slavic being spoken in the Rexall.

Flora, Neal, and Joel returned late with the tuxedo, nearly
at two. As Flora brought the suit bag to her bedroom, Neal followed her on a run into the house, to use the bathroom. Joyce
saw that the three of them were hardly speaking to each other
and were even grim. Things must have gone poorly at the tuxedo rental. Joel remained in the car with the motor running,
strumming his fingers on the roof. She thought it would be a
kind gesture to keep him company for a minute. Observing his
nervous impatience as she approached the car, she regretted
the courtesy, but it was too late to turn back.

"That took a while," she ventured, smiling.

"Yes." He glanced at her. A map of the state lay in his lap.
"Your sister wasn't happy with the fit."

"You'll have plenty of time to get to Hartford," she assured
him, though she was probably only making matters worse. She

should have remained in the house. The day had turned cool and she wasn't even wearing a coat.

"The sun sets at four twenty-seven tonight," he said evenly. "It's the Sabbath. The store closes at four."

"He'll be out in a minute and it's a quick shot down. I promise."

Just as she said this, regretting that she was making promises to Neal's brother, a shriek ricocheted off the trees in the woods alongside the house and pierced them both. Whatever her deficiencies as a mother—her self-centeredness, her inattentiveness, her temper, her poor judgment, her foolish fantasies of total freedom, all of which had been reconfirmed in recent months—she knew at once that the shriek belonged to Viola.

She sprinted around the side of the house, where Viola lay sprawled halfway down the side of the hill. Victor stood at the edge of the porch, looking over it, his hands covering his face.

"Ow-ow-ow-ow-ow-ow!" Viola cried.

Joyce rushed at her, searching for blood. There wasn't any, but the girl was in great pain. She was holding her forearm while simultaneously trying to writhe away from it, howling. Joyce knelt. "Sweetie," she murmured. But the girl couldn't see. Her face had gone puffy, melted into a stew of tears. Without thinking, Joyce wished Marshall were there.

"It not my fault!" Victor protested.

Joel had left the car and had come around the corner of the house, climbing the lawn in laborious strides. As he approached the tableau of mother and stricken child, he crossed his arms and frowned in contemplation.

She tried to speak to her daughter. "Sweetie, sweetie, where does it hurt?"

"Ow-ow-ow-ow-ow-ow!"

Her screams were broadcast up and down the street. The neighbors who had spied her through their curtains this morning were sighing again.

"Can you stand, sweetie?"

The girl was encased in the soundproof shell of her own cries. Vic was bawling too. His tears rained down on them.

Joyce lifted her to a standing position and coaxed her to show the arm. It was swelling already. As Joyce touched it, the girl yelped. Joyce snapped back her hand.

She said, "Oh my God." Viola had turned pale, her lips completely bloodless. "She must have broken it."

Neal and Flora appeared, emerging from the back door with quizzical half smiles, apparently unable to identify the source of the wailing or even to identify the wailing as an expression of pain. Was Joyce the only one who had never heard anything worse than this? Or was it simply impossible for another individual, even an aunt, to hear a child's cries as her mother did? There was no blood, this was going to be okay, and still Joyce thought of the children trapped in the world's wars. You couldn't bear to hear their cries either, not while you were pursuing the serious, challenging business of your own life. Viola was still screaming, and Victor was weeping, his arms raised in the hope that someone would pick him up. Joyce's mind seemed marooned in the Congo, Gaza, and Afghanistan, yet she was sufficiently composed to note that Flora's cheeks were flushed and that the cups of her brassiere rode loose beneath her sweater. She and Neal had been making love, a desperate quickie while Joel was waiting in the car.

"It's not broken," Joel declared.

She wondered. He was a microbiologist, but that didn't mean he was medically trained.

"You don't know that."

"The ground's soft." There had been rain that night. To demonstrate, he rocked on the lawn with one foot. "She couldn't have broken it."

"She could have fallen in a hundred different ways." Joyce didn't understand what capital Joel had invested in the wholeness of Viola's wristbone. "We have to take her to the emergency room."

"You could put ice on it."

"Joel!" Neal intervened. "Stop being a schmuck."

Flora led Victor, who was still sobbing, inside the house while Joyce huddled with Viola in the back of the car. She gave the brothers directions to the hospital, located on the other side of a construction zone. Viola moaned. Joel drove quickly, nearly running a light. Joyce realized that he was worried about making it to the religious supply store in time—and she shared his concern. She didn't want Viola to make them late. "You can just drop us off at the ER," she offered.

Viola was blubbering about her brother.

"Now come on, honey, let's be fair," Joyce said. "I think you did this on your own."

"No! He did it!"

"Are we going to blame Victor for everything? Joel, make the next left—here. You were jumping off the porch all day and yesterday too. I watched you. If it was anyone's fault, it was mine, for letting you do it."

Of course the accident was Joyce's fault, she realized. *Idiot!* Marshall's lawyer was going to love this, especially if the wrist was broken. He had been building an increasingly persuasive case against her all autumn. She had *watched* them jumping from the porch?

"It's because of Victor!"

"No, honey—"

"He let go! That was the game we were playing."

"That was—"

"The World Trade Center was on fire and we had to jump off together! But he let go of my hand!"

Joyce kissed her forehead, which had gone clammy. "Well, that was the game, honey, but I don't see how him letting go made you fall on your wrist."

"He made me lose my balance!" she howled. "He broke the rules!"

Joel half turned in the driver's seat, wincing. "The porch was the World Trade Center? That was your game?"

Joyce held the girl more closely to her. The kids had been jumping for hours today and the day before, hundreds of leaps from the side of the porch. And every time it had been like new, with the towers still standing, spewing flame and black smoke. Viola whimpered, "We were playing 9/11."

"Drive, Joel," Joyce said. "Two lights. We're almost there."

THE EMERGENCY ROOM PERSONNEL were pleased by Viola's arrival, as if they hadn't seen an emergency in years and needed one to stay in business. Joel and Neal drove off. Three nurses became involved at once, cooing over the girl, while another brought Joyce a cup of coffee. The doctor tenderly examined Viola's wrist. She was put in a wheelchair and sent to Imaging. By now she had stopped crying, amazed by the wheelchair and the enormous attention she was receiving.

It turned out that the arm wasn't broken, only badly sprained. Viola required a cast anyway. Joyce was left alone in the waiting room, glad to leave her daughter in the care of trained professionals for a few minutes. The light in the windowless room was muted and classical music was piped in as soft as mist: there was nothing *urgent* in this emergency room. She leaned back and extended her legs, pleased to be in Connecticut, distant from her divorce. She slipped off her shoes and wiggled her toes in the beige plush carpet as if it were sand. A sprained wrist, no big deal after all. She imagined herself blessed with perspective, capable of seeing these petty crises for what they were. Her epic struggle with Marshall: what did it matter? They'd get divorced, one of them making out slightly less well than the other, and other worlds would continue to move in their orbits around the anonymous stars within galaxies unseen by the biggest telescopes, and they'd all be dead soon enough. She told herself this while dreading that at the very moment she took the long view, Marshall would gain some trivial and incremental advantage.

Flora arrived with Victor, who entered the waiting room tightly grasping her hand, terrified. He burst into tears when he didn't see Viola. Joyce took him in her arms.

"It's my fault!" he bawled.

"It's not your fault."

"We made a suicide pack!"

"Pact. It's okay, baby. She's going to be fine."

Joyce explained that the wrist wasn't broken, but Victor continued to cry and Flora seemed distracted: one of her bridesmaids, she said, had come down with walking pneumonia. "I asked her if walking meant she could attend the wedding and she was offended. Is it all right if I leave Victor here? I want to pick up some chicken soup and bring it over. Is that appropriate?"

Her cell phone responded first, performing several bars of some Middle Eastern–sounding music.

Flora put it to the side of her face and grimaced. "What? I can't hear you. What?" She put her finger in the other ear. She still couldn't hear. "Wait, wait, Neal. Let me go outside."

Joyce looked at her watch: twenty-five past four. *Shit.* The overcast sky's afternoon grays would be sliding now into the deeper registers of sacred twilight. Heads were being covered, candles were being lit in muffled, God-infused homes up and down the East Coast. That was the long view. She bounced the boy on her knee, a nervous fidget on her part, but it quieted him. After a few minutes Flora came back, shaking her head.

"Is everything okay?"

"He's driving me nuts," Flora said. "They made it to the store in time, but the chuppah wasn't there, even though they had it reserved. They were told it was already picked up and paid for. Some kind of screwup."

Joyce pressed to confirm: "But they made it to the store before it closed."

"Just as they were pulling the gates. Joel virtually forced his way into the store, but there was no chuppah. He went nuclear. And Neal acted as if it was *my* fault! He said, 'Your family didn't want the chuppah anyway.' He's lost his mind, he doesn't even *care* about religion."

The two women settled back in the chairs and Flora closed her eyes. She too was trying to lift herself beyond the difficulties of the present moment. Victor had curled up against his mother's body. Joyce felt ashamed to be so relieved, and she was still confused.

"Didn't they have it reserved?"

"*Yes,*" she said irritably, as if Joyce were being dense. "There was a mistake. Who knows, all these Jewish names sound alike."

"They can't go elsewhere?"

"There's only a few Jewish religious supply stores in the state and they're all closed for the Sabbath. The guy had to leave the shop before sundown. He was nearly in tears himself but wouldn't look up who signed for it. And it's supposed to be my fault!"

At that moment Viola was brought in, a cast at the end of her left arm. Victor stared in terror at the wheelchair and plaster-encased forearm. Joyce's own body tensed. Viola's hair had come undone and fell across her face in strands. She was weary, fully cried-out. Beyond the doors of the ER, the line of her jaw had firmed and the wary expression around her eyes had deepened. Joyce was vouchsafed a view of the face her daughter would take into adulthood, a perfect mixture of her features and Marshall's, into a world whose real conflicts and dangers couldn't yet be fathomed.

OTHER PROBLEMS HAD DEVELOPED that afternoon, some
of them more serious than Viola's wrist sprain, the ill brides-
maid, and the lost chuppah. Flora's wedding shoes, perfect on
Wednesday, no longer fit. The caterer had worked off a long-
ago-revised seating chart when she made the place cards. Intending to confirm the musicians' presence at the reception one
more time, Flora couldn't reach them, despite repeated calls.
The out-of-town guests were arriving at the local hotels, some
having neglected to book rooms in advance. At the rehearsal
that evening some confusion about the conduct of the ceremony was revealed and had to be resolved, as if no one had
ever been married before. Then when the Reverend Gottschall
reached the Hebrew prayer he was supposed to read, he asked
about the chuppah. Joyce felt blood rush to her face in mysterious, conspicuous embarrassment. Flora rushed to say that there
wouldn't be one. Speaking in the same chilly monotone he had
employed since returning from Hartford, Neal insisted that
they pretend it was there. Joyce reminded herself that if she did
nothing but keep the kids (now both subdued) out of the way,
her family would be grateful.

The Weisses had chosen an Ethiopian restaurant as the
place to host the rehearsal dinner. It was located in an
eighteenth-century stone farmhouse, with exposed stone
walls and hand-hewn cherrywood rafters supporting the high
roof, but its interior was entirely African: tribal masks, woven
baskets. The party was led to a perimeter of embroidered pillows around a low table, and an army of servers placed the
food on a layered bed of doughy crepes that served as both
platter and tablecloth. Their Ethiopian waitress, a tall young
woman with model-class cheekbones and a minute voice
whose unpredictably stressed syllables eroticized the most
commonplace English words, instructed that there would be

no napkins; Amanda stared at her bug-eyed. They would have to tear off pieces of crepe to soak up the sauces and spices, as well as to wipe their hands and faces. The waitress watched them tentatively engage the meal. She towered above them, her otherworldly features serene and all-knowing. It was easy for Joyce to imagine that they were no longer in Connecticut. Yet every night this waitress, another token of a war-ravaged world, left the restaurant and drove down Connecticut roads to her Connecticut home to live among Connecticut people.

The Weisses had hoped, evidently, that a restaurant with such fantastic and informal eating arrangements, as well as a bar, would break down inhibitions among those who had just met. But Joyce sensed that she was dining at a banquet with two clans forced by hard circumstance to accommodate each other's interests, in peril of being massacred after the first martini. Neal, Flora, and Joel took the smallest pieces of crepe, and Deke and Amanda took none, consuming small morsels of the food directly in front of them, with forks.

Only Harold Weiss found the chuppah affair amusing.

"One chuppah in the state, and somebody else got it!"

He seemed unaware of his sons' anger or Joyce's family's discomfort. He was alone in having a great time with the food, tearing off chunks of crepe, standing to scoop up sauces and meats halfway across the table and shoving them into his mouth. A great red-brown stain blossomed on the upper part of his white shirt. He laughed at it. Joyce envied the waitress when he turned his voracious attention to her, demanding to know the Ethiopian name for every dish and condiment. The waitress smiled shyly and, her lips moving with delicate precision, pronounced each word in a breathy whisper: *berbere, zizil tibs, yedura alicha*. Each sounded like a promise. Joyce wanted to be like Harold Weiss and let herself go. She wanted to smear her lips with the same sauces, soaking herself in them. But she resisted showing her appetite for the foreign world, this time, lest she betray her sister, mother, and father.

After they returned home she put her exhausted children to sleep. She had providentially wrapped Viola's cast in plastic, but it was filthy anyway. And despite her restraint at the table, a droplet of sauce had ended its journey halfway across the world on the sleeve of Joyce's blouse, inexpungible. She didn't care; she was exhilarated by the foods she had consumed.

She prepared for bed. She scoured her face and applied a cleansing mask—Mousse Masque, it was called, and it was the color of chocolate. She spread the paste with a Kleenex to every part of her face, superfluously including her eyelids and the arches beneath her eyebrows. This didn't make her as black as the waitress or as beautiful, but for the moment at least, as she watched her reflection, she imagined herself the cast-off child of another country, an impossibly exotic one with an ancient unread history: an Abyssinian, or at least someone with Abyssinian cheekbones. And Abyssinian *legs*. She resisted brushing her teeth right away, to retain on her lips and tongue the warmth of the East African sun. She gazed at her white-rimmed eyes, and as the door to her bedroom was flung open, a savanna wind gusted through the bathroom.

"I can't stand it! I can't!"

"What now?" Joyce said, trying to suppress her impatience.

"Neal's ruining everything!" Flora cried.

"What? How?"

Flora did not remark on her sister's negritude. She herself had been transformed. Her face was now puffy and blotched—tears had freshly run—and her hair was tangled. At the restaurant she had barely concealed her anxiety. "Guess."

"I don't know—"

"He's going to Brooklyn! Tomorrow, before the wedding, with his brother!"

"For what?"

"A chuppah."

"Tomorrow's Saturday, still the Sabbath," Joyce said. "How's he going to get a chuppah in Brooklyn on a Saturday?"

"Steve has a friend who has a friend whose family owns a chuppah, one they use for family weddings. They called him. He's going to let them borrow it. They're going to leave very early in the morning, pick it up, and drive back."

Joyce's already-hardening facial mask cracked as she dropped her jaw.

"That's crazy. It'll take them three hours to get down and three hours to get back! It's a five o'clock ceremony. What if they have problems? What if there's traffic?"

"I know, I know!" Flora sobbed. She fell heavily onto the bed and buried her wet face in her hands. "I told Neal that. I told him he was wrecking the wedding. Oh my God, I told him he didn't really want to get married." She gasped and shuddered. "It's true. He *doesn't* want to get married. He doesn't! Because I'm not Jewish."

Joyce sat alongside her and stroked her hair, its texture and color so much like her own. Flora's quivering body was almost feverish. Joyce too had abandoned herself to tears recently, just this week two or three times. She worked now on Flora's hair, running her fingers along the snarls, picking some of them apart.

"He does want to, he does. He loves you," Joyce said, searching for the soothing tone that often eluded her when the children most needed it. She had a new thought, and the effect on her face ripped another fissure in the mask. She could feel a line of exposed skin. "Wait a minute, it's Joel who's so insistent about the chuppah. Why couldn't he go to Brooklyn himself and leave Neal?"

"Good question!" Flora cried, furious. "I'll tell you why. They're afraid we'll go on with the ceremony anyway, without him, without the chuppah. Neal's a *hostage!*"

———

BY THE FOLLOWING MORNING they were all moving in a grief-stricken stupor, as if preparing for a funeral. Even Deke was upset by his younger daughter's predicament. He asked her to clearly, soberly, repeat everything Neal had said the night before. He called Harold Weiss, who was no less dismayed by his sons' flight to Brooklyn. "I don't know what's in that boy's mind," he muttered. The mind he referred to belonged to Joel. Around ten o'clock Neal called Flora to say they had made it to Brooklyn in record time. Unfortunately, the chuppah was located at the guy's parents' house in Queens, but close by. Flora said, "Just come back, forget it."

Hardly speaking to each other, Amanda, Flora, and Joyce went to have their hair done. Even with makeup Amanda's face had gone gray and hard. She was probably wondering how she had raised these two daughters, one who was disastrously ending her marriage and another apparently incapable of beginning one.

Neal didn't call again until two, as the wedding party was being assembled. Now Flora just grunted and hung up. She dropped the phone at her side, her eyes misted with frustration.

"He said they just crossed the Triborough Bridge."

"They'll get here at four-thirty, at the earliest," Joyce guessed.

"And he sounded so chipper. He was *congratulating* himself for having found a chuppah! Like he hadn't done anything wrong. Like he had just gone down the street for a bagel."

She must have thought her mother was out of the room, but Amanda had hurried in when the phone rang. She was wearing a brocaded jacket with a matching skirt in pale sage. She barked, "This is no time for jokes."

If the wedding began late it wouldn't be the end of the world, especially with the end of the world elsewhere so palpable—but there was no way Joyce could tell her mother and sister so without seeming to make light of the situation.

The afternoon's remaining hours swiftly passed as the family and the other members of the wedding moved in their prescribed courses, as if there were a groom present. No one asked where Neal was, not even Gottschall. Viola raged when Joyce said she'd have to wait before she was allowed to hold the flowers. At the chapel the guests soon arrived. Amanda greeted them each with a cold, bony handshake, her smile as fragile as the wedding glass that had been procured from her cupboard. She mumbled to a few people that there would be a delay, but she couldn't bear to say it more than twice. Five p.m. came without Neal. Joyce presumed all the guests knew about his absence by now. The organist worked her way down her repertoire. Amanda and Joyce took shelter in the alcove next to the dressing room, where Flora was in tears.

Amanda said, her voice tremulous, "I have never been so humiliated."

Joyce was startled by her mother's confession; it made her feel closer to her than she had been in years, since before she was married. Amanda appeared vulnerable now, almost undernourished in her mother-of-the-bride suit, naked against other people's speculation and gossip. Joyce, who had been suspended in her own state of maximum humiliation for more than a year, wondered if she was witnessing the harbinger of maternal sympathy, or at least an opportunity to provoke that sympathy. Joyce wished she could think of something to say, not only to console her mother, but also to reveal the correspondences in their situations. In the meanwhile she reached out and squeezed Amanda's shoulder.

Several notes of Middle Eastern music sounded off within Amanda's tiny handbag. It was Flora's phone, given to Amanda for safekeeping. After the second bar Joyce recognized the song.

It was Afghan. Amanda withdrew the phone, frowned, and said crisply, "Yes."

But it wasn't Neal. Amanda had to move the device away from her ear because the caller was shouting with great excitement. The shouting was accompanied by both parties' confusion over who was calling and who was receiving the call. "No, this is not Mrs. Weiss," Amanda said firmly. It transpired that the man had failed to reach Neal on his cell phone and was now trying the alternate number. He was from the religious supply store in Hartford. A mask of steel descended upon Amanda's face. She declared, "You let us down."

"The chuppah was signed for!" the man protested, every word carrying to Joyce. "We're closed, but it's after sunset, so I came in to look in the book. Thirty years I'm in business and nothing like this has ever happened. The chuppah was picked up by a member of your wedding. They signed for it!"

"That's impossible."

"They signed for it!" he repeated.

"Well, what does it say?" her mother demanded.

"It says...scribble scribble." He sighed heavily. "No, H something...Harriman?"

Joyce was rocked back on her heels and something seemed to fall away in her gut, as if she herself were falling. The sensation was so intense that she was virtually blinded, unable to see anything but Amanda, who could see nothing but her. Her mother's eyes had locked on.

"I—I—didn't! No! Can't be!" Joyce stammered her denial, just beginning to put into sluggish gear the mental processes that would allow her to imagine how her name could have found itself in a notebook kept by the owner of a Jewish religious supply store in Hartford, Connecticut.

"Are you sure?" Amanda asked the man.

"It's written right here. Harriman. Morris…Moishe…Marshall! There's no one there named Marshall Harriman?"

"No," Amanda said.

She closed the phone in a very controlled motion, but with as much force as the instrument was built to withstand. She gazed at Joyce, registering her daughter's character in its entirety: her fecklessness, her unluckiness, her contagious shame. Then they both heard an abrupt, many-throated murmur in the chapel. The murmur was followed by a roar and then, after a moment's pause, amused chuckles. Joyce turned away and took a step toward the chapel, trying to escape Amanda's glare.

Neal and Joel had arrived, together carrying a folded blue awning attached to four poles: the chuppah from Queens, an hour late. Without a glance left or right the two men strode up the aisle. Joel removed some hardware from a plastic bag and the brothers, their backs to the wedding guests, quickly assembled the canopy next to Gottschall's still-unoccupied lectern. The chuppah was a fairly simple affair, open on all sides, a Star of David embroidered on the underside of its roof. Joel and Neal exchanged terse, whispered instructions. Something needed to be forced into a socket. Neal grunted from the effort. His tuxedo seemed wrinkled. Bolts of white linen were released to cover the poles. Not knowing which music was appropriate to the raising of a chuppah, the organist had stopped halfway through "Jesus, My Only Hope."

Once the chuppah was erected Neal pulled on one of the poles to make sure that it was steady. Joel went to the seat in the first row, next to his parents. His father scowled. Neal finally turned to face the wedding guests. He grinned warmly, showing embarrassment, but the embarrassment was transparently feigned to solicit sympathy. Now that he was standing in front of the congregation, fresh-faced and handsome, he was perfectly at ease.

"Sorry for the delay, folks," he announced, and the crowd laughed as if he had said something charmingly funny. He straightened, flexed his elbows, and smoothed his tuxedo. Even Joyce was charmed by the breezy, open-stanced way he occupied the front of the church. She stole a glance at Amanda: she was not charmed at all. She watched her imminent son-in-law, an hour late for his own wedding, with a fury that would resonate down through the decades. Neal allowed his gaze to roam leisurely among the guests, making eye contact. Many smiled in return. He extended his arms in front of his body, showing them the palms of his hands. "Traffic was *moider!*"

MAY

1. Victor's red-green-blue hard rubber ball shivered for several moments and then came to a complete stop. 2. The books leaned like a frozen wave as they approached the end of the shelf. 3. The brightest part of a lightbulb was invisible, lost in its own radiance. 4. Victor thought Barney was a real dinosaur; at the same time he knew there was someone beneath the costume. He couldn't put those two facts together. 5. They flew into the World Trade Center on purpose. 6. Her mother always rushed into the kitchen when her father came home. 7. Rachel and Maria were adopted. 8. Halloween was the best holiday. You were given candy for free and didn't have to pay. 9. When the television was shut off by the remote control, a high-pitched bug-buzzing from inside the white star was followed by a gasp and then a silence deeper than ordinary quiet. Try it again. 10. You could see Miss Naomi's nips when she wore her pink leotard. 10a. Her father saw them; he looked. 11. They should have figured out they were going to fly into the World Trade Center. 12. Her mother couldn't touch Snuffles. 13. You could make your poop come out in chunks if you wanted to. 14. *The Powerpuff Girls* was her favorite show. 15. At the new school lunch would be served in a cafeteria, without

Victor. **16.** What's the matter, you? **17.** Once in a while her mother straightened the books, but they fell over again. Her father took some into the bedroom. **18.** At Monty's, if there was too much sauce on your pizza, you could send it back, but Victor didn't have a reason. He did it to prove that he could. **19.** When you first bit into chewing gum the juice came out so powerfully it hurt the inside of your jaw. **20.** Yellow tugboats cruised the river searching for customers. **21.** Oops, I did it again. **22.** A bad smell that wasn't poop meant that someone was dying somewhere in the world.

Viola said, "How do we know?"

This was the Key Food. She called it the wanting place, secretly to herself, because she recognized the desire that was manufactured and then shuddered through her whenever her mother announced, Put on your shoes, that's where we're going. She knew she desperately wanted a magic ring from the coin machine—she had to have one and only Victor's misbehavior would prevent her mother from buying it for her—at the same time that she was aware she hadn't wanted one before. Now every time they turned a lane at the front of the store, the magic rings were there, sparkling in their magic glass chambers. Her mother didn't see them; she was staring at her list. She passed the dog food without stopping, blindly pushing Victor in the baby seat. She didn't see what he was doing.

"Know what, honey?"

"Know."

"What?"

They were at the dairy section. Her mother stopped to remember what she needed. It was not on the list. She took her blue milk and their white milk, not her father's red milk. She lightly touched her hand on the orange juice and closed her eyes, listening, but not to the music that came from upstairs. She was still. The orange juice was speaking to her, begging. She opened her eyes and placed the orange juice in the cart. Just in time. Victor looked as sweet as an angel in heaven.

"Know things."

"What kinds of things?"

"*All* things."

Her mother examined the butters now, deciding whether she wanted square or round. She had a slightly stooped posture, with her bare goose-bumped arms wrapped around her chest. She said, still undecided, "How do we know them? By going to school, sweetie."

"No!"

"Yes. School is where we learn. Doesn't Miss Naomi teach you—"

"I don't mean school. I don't mean learning... I mean how do we *know*?"

They had reached the end of the dairy section. The ring machines lay beyond the registers. They only had to get there. Her mother stepped away from the cart. She was looking at her list and then at the entire width of the store, trying to remember. What else. But she had parked the cart by the Tylenols, almost right against the boxes. She could see Victor but she wasn't watching what he was doing. She frowned hard, squeezing out a thought like poop. You think I'm in love. She mumbled, "About what?"

"About *things*. Everything. The world."

"The world," she repeated. She jerked the cart—Victor's head bobbled; he giggled; she didn't notice how wickedly—and wheeled it toward the registers. All the lanes were empty, but she wanted to figure out which was the best. The teenagers pretended not to care whose she chose, each staring at the back of the store. She picked the lane closest to the ring machines and started placing the groceries on the flat escalator. "Well, we see things."

"But we see so much."

"Right…" This register's teenager was listening to music, but not to the music in the store. It was music somewhere else: teenager music, not what adults and small children could listen to. Pimples spilled across his chin, neck, and forehead, little red and white spots in secret designs that told the story of what he was thinking if only you knew how to read them. He made no sign of seeing her mother, but the escalator moved and he put the groceries through the EZ Pass. As she continued to lift items from the shopping cart, she said, "You learn to filter—"

"Can we get magic rings?"

"Yes."

"And how do we know what to filter?"

"You learn. Please, not now, I'm trying to concentrate."

Unloading the cart, her mother was very quiet and still again. Her list dropped to the floor. She clamped hard against her lips, as if she were trying to solve a puzzle, even though unloading the cart was a simple task that Viola could have performed herself if she were tall enough. The upstairs music had become enormous. I'm not so innocent. Victor squirmed and began kicking the cart. He suddenly wanted to get out.

"How?"

"From experience. Stop, Victor! Look, can we talk about this later?"

"And how do we know what we see is true?"

"We see it."

Her mother froze, her hands above the escalator with a jar in her hands. She stared at the jar. The teenager continued beeping the groceries. Another teenager packed them. He too was listening elsewhere.

"But what if there are things we can't see? Not *things*, but what they *mean*? You can't see what they mean, you have to *know* them—and that means knowing other things. And how do you know how important each thing is, compared to the others? Especially when you know two things that may be opposite. And you're thinking about a third thing. And when we do know what something means, can we really say it all the way? Can we even say it to ourselves? That's what I don't understand."

"Pimentos?" her mother cried. "I didn't get—" She pulled a can from the cart. "Anchovies. Wait, what is this? Stop." She ran her hands along other jars and small boxes. The teenager boy was still moving them through the EZ Pass. He held a carton of Tylenol. Its lettering was entirely different from what was printed on the Tylenol boxes they usually bought, Viola thought; she couldn't read yet. "Stop! Please, wait, stop!"

He didn't hear her. He didn't know she was speaking, though he probably knew many other things.

"Stop! I don't want these. Don't ring them up! Stop packing!"

The teenager finally ground to a halt, like the Tin Man in the rain. His face remained slack. He didn't look at her mother, who was searching the groceries on the other side of the EZ Pass, but kept his face forward. His eyes were like two gray coins. Viola couldn't imagine what he was thinking, what he remembered, or what he wanted. He raised his head to the ceiling and called out:

"Void!"

They waited until the man arrived and did something to the register. Everyone watched. The teenagers unpacked the bags and her mother went through the groceries, pushing aside what she didn't want. She tried not to look at anyone. Her face had gone red and she made little noises to herself. She whispered, "I should have known. I should have known." And then her body shook and she began crying, sobbing hard. She dropped her face into her hands. Victor reached over the escalator, picked up a can, and threw it back into the cart. Her mother turned away and buried her head against the display of candy and chewing gum, several packages of which Victor had already grabbed. Her shoulder blades quivered, like an angel's wings. When it seemed as if she was finished, she started again. You could hear it over the music. Void and the teenagers stood by helplessly, horrified. They didn't know what to do. They had never seen her at home; they had never seen her cry.

On the way out, Viola reminded her about the magic rings but she was almost running, shoving Victor's stroller ahead of them—he was kicking at the footrest now—moving so fast Viola could hardly keep up.

THIS WAS HOW it was now: too much happening too fast, and no one would explain. Viola had to pay attention, but that wasn't enough. She had to make connections and draw inferences.

She knew her understanding was limited. You could identify what lay in front of you, but what it meant was invisible. You could never be sure that you had sufficient data. A person went around in her own shell, defined by what she didn't know. Victor's shell was a small, babyish toddler one, defined by his most elemental babyish toddler needs; Viola could see it from the outside, because hers was more capacious, and her parents' much more so—but limited still. Language failed: you could never know enough words to express everything you knew, and even what you knew was a microscopic fraction of what there was, and even this doesn't completely express the idea.

Something was going on. Comprehending it required more thought and a full review of what she knew. 1. The lady doctor with the fingernails. 2. Her boyfriend, the lawyer. 3. Her mother watching TV on the couch after she and Victor went to bed. 4. Her father hiding in the bedroom. 5. Why her mother couldn't touch Snuffles. 6. A fight about the tent at Aunt Flora's wedding. 7. Her mother was made very angry when they were out somewhere—a restaurant, say—and Victor kicked off his shoes. **8.** Her mother eating alone. If only Viola could stand away from these facts for a moment and quiet the commotion that swirled around her, she would be able to view the situation in its entirety. She would view her own shell.

Doing so would be like watching television, which also comprised a universe of information; the *television* was a shell, so big you could watch only a single channel at a time, or perhaps two or three. Her favorite shows were *The Powerpuff Girls* and *Dexter* and her hatred of the purple dinosaur was calibrated to the precise degree that Victor loved him. Every night after *Dexter* her mother turned on the News while she made dinner. Viola believed that teachers at her new school next year would look like the News. She paid attention. She didn't understand everything the News said. No one did. The News spoke about their lives in secret, like the teenager's pimples. The News could leak: her father's pants had ripped at the World Trade Center and the hospital had put stitches in his forehead. The News leaked all over the world.

One evening while her father was out, after the News, her mother argued over the phone about the purplish, long-fluted vase she kept empty in the Dark Corner of the apartment. She said that it was an ugly antique. Somebody was trying to take it away. She wasn't going to let him; she wasn't going to let him take anything. The person on the phone contradicted her, evidently. But if she said the vase was ugly, why wouldn't she let someone take it away? Viola loved the vase. It was a vase a princess would place in her private chambers and fill with eternally blooming magic flowers. Then her mother said she would call back tomorrow from the office and she sat by the phone a long while, staring through the living room window but not seeing the city at all—closed up blind within her shell. Viola watched from the couch, pretending to draw. When her mother finally rose she saw that Victor had knocked over the kitchen garbage pail and kicked through the mess, scattering it.

Her wordless cry was like ice and, also, a bolt of electricity. Her hand sprang from her side and struck Victor hard on the upper part of his arm. He fell right to the floor into the trash.

This was good for Viola, good beyond words. She desperately wished that her mother would do it again, immediately. Victor was on the floor, his legs splayed, his head down among rinds and coffee grounds. His mouth was open. His eyes were wide. And then he began howling, his sobs without any sort of arc toward cessation, as if the force and surprise of the blow were still current. Her mother must have hurt him. Now Viola recalled her friends at preschool, Rachel and Maria and the mystery of their being adopted, their pasts of evil stepmothers and punishing orphanages. They must have been hit like this all the time.

Her father came home. He opened the door fast as if someone had been pushing against it and stomped in. His face was hard and dark and somehow cloaked by itself: you couldn't see his face even though you were looking right at it. His face had turned into a secret about itself. Victor was still wailing. As if in a trance, as if controlled by aliens or monster robots or Dexter, her father went to his room without speaking.

Now that it had been established how easy it was for Victor to be hit, Viola watched him more closely. From once being no more than an annoyance, his misbehavior had grown in ambition until it was a danger to them all. He threw to the floor every glass, jar, and dish he could get his hands on. He spilled cleaning fluids from containers under the kitchen sink. He wasted expensive paper, scribbling. But she knew she couldn't simply report each mischief: her parents would stop listening. She had to be patient.

She studied them as well. They had secrets, they had plans. Quite suddenly it occurred to Viola to ask herself why it was that if she and Victor spent one weekend with her mother they would see only their father the next. She had taken this arrangement for granted, as a detail in the way the universe was constructed, but she forced herself now to take another view, to overcome the constraints on her imagination. She thought hard: parents of other friends saw their children every weekend. This observation was, in itself, a revelation, and it spawned another: Victor was simply too difficult to be with two weekends in a row. But Viola had to be with him every weekend and every day, and nearly the whole day. The only solution—and this, she thought, must be the subject of her parents' secrets, their frustrations, and their bad moods—was to remove Victor from the household. He would have to be adopted.

The next day Victor took the rubber band in which the mail had come bound. He pulled at it and giggled as it pulled back. For hours he sat on the floor, almost *drooling* as he studied its elasticity, as if the rubber band were the greatest invention since...since snot, his other fascination. He smelled the rubber band and put it in his mouth. He brought it close to his face. He learned how to pluck it and demanded that she listen. He repeatedly flicked at it with his thumb but, pathetically, didn't know how to shoot it off. When she was three she had certainly known. It wasn't something you had to be taught.

DR. NANCY CONTINUED to ask questions. She was searching for something, also trying to figure what was up. But she asked the wrong questions—how do you feel? what is it like to be with your father? what is it like to be with your mom? *never* what is it like to be with Victor, *never* if you could choose to have any superpower, which would it be?—so their answers made little sense. She took notes in a green spiral book, frowning. Observing her frustration this week, Viola told her that her mother hit Victor. The effect was very good, at first: the doctor was jolted, she sat upright and looked at her as if for the first time. Then she wanted to see Victor's arm and, gently cooing, began inspecting other places all over his body, even his bottom. Victor giggled for a while, until he started crying, and Viola felt weird, as if she had asked her to look there.

When their mother picked them up, Dr. Nancy said nothing about it and her mother didn't notice how red-faced Victor was. He behaved on the walk to the subway, holding hands, keeping pace and ducking properly under the turnstile, and not flinging himself onto the tracks, but once the train arrived and they had rushed to their seats, she saw him working the tip of one sneaker against the heel of the other. Just as she was about to warn her, her mother flinched. She cried to the stranger sitting alongside her:

"Agent Robbins!"

The man didn't respond right away. He was slumped in his seat and slumped, too, within his suit. His face was bristly and gray and he stared at the floor of the train with sad droopy eyes. Viola was unnerved that her mother had spoken to a stranger.

He turned slowly, taking another moment before he looked at her. She blushed. Pressed against her arm, Viola could almost feel her body temperature rise. As quick as an EZ Pass, the man's eyes scanned the children's faces. He didn't smile.

"It's me, Joyce Harriman!"

Now Viola's ears burned. Other passengers watched them. They heard her mother pronounce her name: the passengers knew it now; her name belonged to them, another fact. What would it mean? The man looked at her mother intensely, baring his teeth in pain. He must have been thinking hard, but not about them.

Her mother said, "From the anthrax scare?"

He opened his mouth but some time passed before a word was dropped from it. "Right," he said without conviction.

"You took a nose swab. I called you..." She stopped, unsure

what to say. Her face was still dark. "I guess you never found who sent the real anthrax."

The man's sigh was nearly a groan and he turned to watch his reflection in the window opposite their seats. The tunnel's walls and pillars sped behind the ghostly image. In the window he was nearly handsome. "No, I guess not."

"That was silly, I'm sorry. I didn't mean to blame you—"

"It's all right. We should have got him." He dropped the back of his head against the glass behind him and showed his Adam's apple. "Five people dead. We collected plenty of intelligence, with every agent in every office working hard. Our best guys are still on the case, studying the material and the facts and the clues, employing the most advanced forensics. We *have* all the evidence we need, I'm sure of that—in a certain file, in a certain test tube, in a certain evidence bag, on a phone log, and in an e-mail. We have supercomputers crunching data right now, trying to get these pieces of evidence into alignment. But we're missing something, something big and obvious..."

"I know, I know," her mother said, as if he were one of her children. Her eyes had become soft and warm. She offered him a tiny smile. He didn't see it.

"This case is all I can think about, and thinking about it puts it even further out of reach. Ach," he said wearily, straightening up and waving his hand as if to swat a fly, "it's been a bad week for the agency. You've seen the News, it turns out we had good intelligence about al-Qaeda before 9/11...The Phoenix office reported that Arabs connected to bin Laden were taking flying lessons there; in Minnesota they arrested Moussaoui, but didn't search his computer, which had Atta's phone number on the hard drive. Two other guys on the foreign terrorist watch list were let into the country. The French sent us warnings. But we couldn't collect that intelligence in a single place. We couldn't communicate it from one office to the next, or between agencies, or to the local police. And every new corrective system we establish, every overseer or liaison or central collection office, adds to the data dump. We monitor al-Qaeda, the other crackpots...But there's too much chatter in the system, so we report only on the *volume* of the chatter, rather than its content. Then the volume becomes another piece of data...On my desk I have tons of intelligence—about another terrorist plot, the importation of illegal drugs, some ex-army gun nut in Washington State who may go on a rampage someday, the presence of extraterrestrial visitors at a mall in Piscataway and the Second Coming of Jesus Christ. But I can't know which of this is worth acting on. I send it upstream and it clutters the desk of someone trying to decide what to do with *his* intelligence. And no one in the government has the ability to look at this mess in its entirety and make sense of it. Do you know what I mean?"

Her mother nodded and she too gazed into the opposite window. From where Viola sat, the attenuated reflection didn't include either her or her brother. The two adults rested, not looking directly at each other, yet aware, she thought, of being framed in the window together. Two worn-out people. It was as if the man had suddenly become their father. The thought cut her open like an ice pick. Her mother murmured, "Yes. My life's like that too."

The roar of the train abruptly dropped in pitch as they entered a station. The train shuddered and slowed. "Oh," her mother cried. "This is our change! I'm sorry, Agent Robbins—"

"Please, call me Nathan."

"Shit!"

Victor had kicked off both his sneakers and they had slid beneath the legs of a sleeping man who held a brown paper bag to his chest. Her mother had already collected their things and had taken Viola's hand. She crouched to pick up the sneakers just as the train slammed to a stop, making her fall against the man's knees and then to the floor. "Shit," she said again.

The man woke to examine her through traffic-light yellow eyes, but he didn't move his legs. The door to the train opened and new passengers rushed in around them, taking their seats while she jammed the shoes onto Victor's feet. A scuff mark showed up near the hem of her dress. Agent Robbins rose, unsure how to help. Someone took his seat. Without looking back, a child in each hand as the doors started to close, her mother propelled them from the train.

THERE WAS a flat slapping sound, a little hum, the whirring, whistling, trilling insectlike beating of nearly microscopic surfaces against the rushing air, and then she was stung on the back of her neck. The rubber band fell to the floor, dead on impact.

Victor sat cross-legged in the corner of the living room designated for his use, playing with marbles and trying, incompetently, not to look at her. His eyes darted; he fought a smile. She stopped herself before she could rub her neck where the burn was fading. She hesitated to summon her mother, who was determinedly busy, walking through the apartment with a clipboard. She halted at each thing—a piece of furniture, a lamp, a picture—paused to contemplate it, and then wrote something on the clipboard. She was being very serious. Absent blood, she wouldn't have been impressed. This wasn't the right time. Viola was surprised by her own exercise of self-control, which felt like a physical exercise, stretching muscles and enlarging her body. She felt bigger already.

Victor later recovered the rubber band and examined it for damage. She expected to be hit again, but he seemed to have lost interest in her. He continued his investigations, first maneuvering the rubber band around bits of tinfoil and a blue glass marble. He seemed preoccupied with the challenge of wrapping small objects in it. He didn't know how to make a slingshot yet.

This went on for days. He found other toys and bounced them against the rubber band: a model soldier, a plastic doll shoe, a hardened wad of chewing gum. It was only a matter of time before he launched one. She observed as his babyish mind labored to grasp the rubber band's operating principles. Victor's world was composed of entirely random elements, and any connections they made were ephemeral and arbitrary. He pressed the shoe against a taut segment of rubber band, but he held his fingers in an awkward position behind the rubber band, preventing him from stretching it. Then the shoe slipped out and he found himself holding two unrelated objects.

Suddenly their parents were arguing with tremendous violence. She hadn't been paying attention and hadn't even noticed that they were, unusually, both in the living room. She couldn't distinguish the words they were flinging, shooting, spitting at each other, but her mother had become rigid and her father was jabbing his finger at the air. He said something and abruptly stormed away and her mother said something and he came rushing back, running halfway across the apartment to say something else. He walked away again and came back. They were shouting at once. The air in the apartment seemed hot enough to catch fire.

Her father grabbed the clipboard out of her mother's hands. Her mother screamed, one short, loud yelp. He pulled out the paper on which she'd been writing, threw the clipboard onto the carpet, and ripped the pages, first in halves, then in halves of halves, and so on. Viola wished he were making confetti but knew he wasn't. His jaw was clamped so that you could see the muscles straining against the side of his face. Her mother's eyes were set deep in their sockets. He worked intently on tearing the paper into small pieces and finally threw them, like confetti after all, into her face. She didn't blink and allowed it to fall into her hair and onto her shoulders and stick there.

He went into his bedroom and slammed the door. He opened and slammed it again, and again several more times. Afterward, with the door silenced, the glassware in the living room cabinet continued to chime and tinkle in a ringing angelic chorus.

Her mother walked away from the confetti and went to the chair by the window. Viola had been wrong in assuming that she didn't see anything from this window. She *was* seeing: not the city, but above the roof of the next building a slender slice of impeccably cloudless daylit sky. She contemplated the blue for some time as if it held some all-explaining vital secret.

The roaring of the atmosphere subsided to silence and then the rubber band made a new sound, a charged, humming, deep-bellied twang. From Victor's hand sprang the little pressed-tin airplane that had come with a board game they had never learned to play. The plane swiftly gained altitude as it crossed the living room. It flew steadily, without tumbling. The three of them watched it arc a few inches beneath the ceiling. The flight ended, bull's-eye, in the princess vase's midsection.

When the toy piece struck, the glass changed color top to bottom, from purple to a bright, pinkish white, and the vase iridesced before it crashed and returned to its original elements so that not a single piece of it could be recognized. Her heart leaped in the moment before it came down. There had been disorder in her analysis of what Victor was going to do, order in the vase's final fluent form, disorder in its dissolution, and a return to order in her comprehension of what had happened.

She had never seen anything as beautiful as this series of transformations.

"Oh!" her mother said, her cry feeble. She put her hand to her face.

Her father opened his door and took a half step from the bedroom. His face was drawn, its fire quenched. He saw the smashed vase at once. He peered at the debris for a while and turned, simultaneously with her mother and in a rare parallel orbit, to look at Victor. Victor wasn't trying to hide a smirk now as he struggled to appreciate the rubber band's cause and effect. Gaping, he seemed older now, no longer a baby or a toddler: hurled into full childhood. Her father and mother were both still. Viola expected them to hit him, but she was wrong—again. They studied the boy from a distance, as if asking themselves where he had come from and how he had gotten into the apartment.

And yet another mistake. Viola thought that the smashed vase had ended something, but no. Her parents swept it up together, her father on his knees with the dustpan, her mother with the broom. Either could have done the job alone. Something else was going on. They spoke to each other now in quiet, urgent tones—not exactly arguing, which, she realized from the absence of argument, was how they usually spoke. She couldn't understand what was being said. Both of them seemed tired. Her mother's face had gone soft and tender. Every few minutes they looked back at the children. They seemed to have come to an agreement. Viola wondered if tonight was the night.

"Kids," her father said, and then looked back at her mother, helplessly. She frowned and motioned that the children should sit on the couch. They stood stiffly at either end, tottering above them like two withered trees.

"Kids," her father repeated, but didn't say anything else.

"Kids," her mother said. "This is what we need to tell you.

This is what we need to say: we want you to know something and that is that we love you both very much. Really, you're the most important things in the world to us and always will be. Can you understand that? No matter what happens, I will always be your mommy and Daddy will always be your daddy."

Her mother paused, staring at them. Victor squirmed under her gaze. Viola met her stare and, aware of the occasion's gravity, assumed an attentive, adult expression. She asked, "Will Victor stay my brother?"

Her mother shot a queer, desperate look at her father, who was pinching the top of his nose between his fingers and looking at the floor.

"Yes, always," her mother said. "That's why it's important to be nice to him and take care of him, all right?"

Viola insisted, "It wasn't my fault!"

"Okay, okay, this isn't about you and Vic," her father said vehemently. "I mean, it *is* about you and Vic—this conversation, I mean—but Mommy and I have something to tell you."

"*He* broke the vase."

"Not on purpose!" Victor objected.

Her father said, "We don't care about the vase, it was an ugly vase. I hate the vase. Stop talking about the vase. Listen, Viola. Listen, Vic. Nothing's been settled yet, unfortunately. We're still working out the details, but this is what we need to tell you..."

For several minutes then, she stopped understanding what was being said. Her parents were talking at the same time, rushing out the words and damming them up and then yelling again to contradict each other. Her mother spoke about a happier family. Her father several times mumbled the words "new arrangements." They were told that in the new apartment they would have a second set of toys, but there would be no important changes in their lives. Her mother wept silently and did nothing to cover her face. Her father said that they didn't know when what would happen would happen. Her mother replied sharply that it could happen first thing tomorrow morning. The sound of their argument, as always, swirled around itself, entangling and accelerating. This went on for several minutes until she heard a single word that cut through the mists, a word she could comprehend immediately and completely. The word was this: divorce.

Forget Rachel and Maria. They had nothing to do with divorce. Elizabeth, Roxanne, and Keisha had to do with divorce. Viola knew what it meant: people talking about your parents being divorced; you were the kid with the divorced parents; divorce divorce divorce—as if you were a divorce yourself, which perhaps you were. She knew from Elizabeth, Roxanne, and Keisha what divorce was. They were watched by one parent at a time, never the complete set, and this made them incomplete too, either one half or the other, set adrift in the schoolyard.

But weren't Victor and Viola set adrift now? Their parents took turns with them every weekend, just as Elizabeth, Roxanne, and Keisha's parents did with them. Their parents never kissed each other like parents in normal families did on TV; never cuddled, never snuggled. And now they'd have two apartments. Their parents were getting divorced: wasn't *everything* in her life about this? Dr. Nancy, Mr. Peter, her mother sleeping on the couch, her father quiet in his bedroom, the tears, the shouting, the slammed doors... How could she have been so stupid? This had been going on forever. They had been plotting it. The realization was as transforming as Victor's transformation of the princess vase.

So she had been stupid. The evidence of the divorce had been around her all this time—lain there? hovered there? glittered there like a magic ring inside a coin machine?—waiting to be made sense of. The universe was an immense construction that rose from facts, an infinitesimal fraction of which could be apprehended in a single glance. Evidence about everything was around her, if only she could see it. But she couldn't even imagine what she was ignorant about. She was *still* stupid. What else was she missing?

JULY

MARSHALL PASSED THROUGH the vaulted, gleaming halls of granite and crystal and ascended in a cosseted whoosh to his lawyer's offices. The elevator emptied into a broad, lofty, wooded chamber, its carpentry sensuously turned, profoundly stained, and seamlessly joined—the last a rebuke to human couplings, Marshall thought. His shoes sank within the plush. His ears popped. The receptionist, posing dark and sultry behind a console, appraised him coolly. She was shrink-wrapped in a low-cut, bare-shouldered white shirt, and her high-boned face was a *salade composée* of that moment's every glamorous ethnicity, Balkan, Latin, Eritrean. She fixed him with lustrous brown eyes and a smile precisely calibrated to be outrageously wanton without inviting familiarity. She asked him his name. Those teeth. Marshall felt sick. Who was paying for this? He was paying for this.

Thorpe, his lawyer, didn't rise when Marshall entered his office. His eyes sparkling, the fat man preferred to watch Marshall's entrance from behind his desk's immense mahogany redoubt. The desk must have weighed as much as a car. Everything in this office was big: the furniture, the pen resting on the extra-large yellow legal pad, the de Kooning on the right wall.

In the immaculate wall-sized glass behind Thorpe the children of titans had arrayed the spires of other towers, every one of them different, each partitioned by windows, each window another office, each office another locus of powerful moneymaking. Thorpe glanced at his watch. Marshall had already seen the watch, which he presumed kept track of his billable hours. It was a Teslar chronograph. Marshall wondered what expectation of success, what desperate strategy, what optimism about his finances had led him to employ a lawyer who wore a Teslar chronograph.

Thorpe's smile was ugly: mocking, cruel, and carnivorous. Or was that just Marshall's imagination? As Marshall descended into an unsettlingly deep chair, the lawyer demanded: "My friend, how well do you think you know your wife?"

Marshall replied vacantly, "What do you mean?"

Thorpe chuckled, amused as always. Marshall was so easy to catch off guard, Thorpe probably confused him only to keep in practice. "You understand, of course, that we're reaching the end of a very complicated, very delicate legal conflict. The moment of decision draws near. And this decision depends on your best answer to the following question: Will Joyce settle or press the case to the bitter end?"

"It's bitter enough now. But I don't know what she wants to do."

"Please." Thorpe scowled. "You're not paying for idle conversation. Think. You lived with her how many years?"

"Nine. If you count this as living with her."

"So you should have some knowledge of her character." Thorpe tapped several sheets of fax paper before him. "She's made an offer, and the question, which is not for me to answer, is how badly do you think she wants to settle? Will she come down? In a situation like this, how desperate is she? Is she tired, disgusted, still vengeful? How much is she thinking of the children's welfare?"

"Mystery of mysteries."

"I submit that's why your marriage failed." He said severely, "Every legal move she's made for the past two years has been a surprise. How can we make strategy? You don't know her. Where have you been? The two of you shared a home and started a family, but did you ever consider this woman as an individual, with her own motivations? It's as if Joyce were no more than your reflection, to be judged by her responses to your maneuvers—not to mention your mistakes, neuroses, and ambitions. You don't *comprehend* her. But she comprehends you. So she holds the advantage."

This was absurd. From the beginning, when they met in college, Joyce had summoned the vast bulk of Marshall's attention and contemplation. Who could say what he studied in his senior-year classes? He hadn't cared to learn anything but the girl's thought and substance. She had been a strange girl, immature, he thought, as fresh and fragile as a newly independent nation liberated from colonial misrule. She was still composing her constitution, finding allies, striking new emotional coinage, and rediscovering and rewriting her past. Marshall had been required to learn her obscure language. Over the years, with every new development in their lives, like career changes and children, he had needed to reassess her. And since the regime had turned militant, he had intensified his scrutiny. At times when he was away his vision was obscured by the memory of her face, and his hearing was deafened by the recollection of her words. How could he not know her? But Marshall told Thorpe, "You're right," and believed that perhaps Thorpe was.

The lawyer leaned over and rested his elbows on his desk. His cuff links were gold. He asked, "Why is she so angry?"

"I don't know." Marshall flung out his hands. "I mean, I *do* know, I can tell you all the little things that happened over the years and sort of piled up. She has grievances, *I* have grievances...and the fact that I have the temerity to entertain a grievance is one of her grievances! I'm not perfect, but some of her complaints are crazy or wildly overstated, or her reaction is disproportionate to the actual harm inflicted." All the bitterness of the divorce suddenly returned to him, like something in the blood. "If you isolate each of our betrayals and self-indulgences, the mean things we've said to each other, the errors in judgment—on their own, they're quite heinous. Yet neither of us did anything to the other that wasn't in the context of something else. That's the problem! That's why I can't say she's entirely wrong. I *can* identify the causes of her anger, but once I do, even to myself, it's almost like justifying them— and that makes me weak." He sighed and asked, "Anyway, how bad is her proposal?"

Thorpe quickly grinned, pleased by the question, his countenance as bright as the day beyond the window. He caressed the faxes and announced, "You're fucked. She gets residential custody, the apartment, support, education expenses...You'll be broke. By the way, before I forget, your account's past due."

"That's if I *settle*? What if we keep her in court?"

"There's a difference between being fucked and being totally fucked." He chuckled. "The settlement gives you room to maneuver on joint debts and liabilities. I've seen worse. The support level could be worse. The point is, you're both taking a chance with the judge. Give Joyce a reasonable counteroffer, if you think she's likely to come down—but not if you think she won't. Lowball her if you think she's forlorn, or if you want to bluff or scare her, if she's scareable. We have options. What do you think? This is where I need you to tell me what she's like, *really*."

Marshall briefly looked at the ceiling, doubting that you could know another person without depending on her responses to your stimuli—it seemed unscientific. Who knew what the Arabs were like, really? Who the fuck cared? He wondered how

Thorpe's office was illuminated: the windows were the only visible light sources, but the lawyer's deeply tanned face seemed to radiate on its own. Marshall said, "I don't know…She just wants this over like I do, probably. I don't think she cares about the money. She was never very, you know, financially oriented. She hates me or thinks she hates me. It's the dynamics of the divorce. She once loved me, too. I'm the father of her kids…" he said, trailing off pathetically.

Thorpe was not a handsome man, but his muscular, veined nose, his smacking, swollen lips, and the massive pendulousness of his jaw gave his gaze a compellingly raw effect. Now he turned the full contemptuous force of it on Marshall. Remaining at his desk, he leaned toward his client, his blunt, bald head like a missile.

He asked, "What is she like in bed? Sort of passive, I imagine. Distracted, distant—"

"No, no, not at all," Marshall rushed to say. He could feel the heat pooling in his ears. "I mean, it's been a long time since, you know, but she was very active, very inventive. Passionate."

How passionate? Very passionate, he thought, defensively. When they were courting, he and Joyce had occupied entire weekends making love and even after they were married, before the children, there had been what seemed like hundreds of drag-you-down-on-the-floor, hot-and-dirty, sweaty, spermy, pungently sopping, let's-try-*this* afternoons, if only he could recall them. Those days had been buried in the debris.

"How did she give head?" Thorpe demanded. "Was it vigorous, intense, full-mouthed, like she meant it? And how hard did she work out her pubococcygeus? When you had sex, did you get the impression she *wanted* it?"

"Yes, everything was normal. That wasn't our problem."

"Nice breasts, I bet. But she's a bit heavy in the tush, no?"

"She's had two kids!" Marshall protested. His face was

inflamed and he was disoriented by the interrogation. Thorpe's questions were insulting, of course, but to each he found himself searching for an answer. "And she's thirty-six, works in an office, I don't expect—"

"How much would you pay to fuck her?"

"I don't know. I mean the going rate these days is apparently rather high...But that's not how I think of making love—"

"Yeah yeah yeah," Thorpe said, raising a hand and swatting at Marshall's objections. "You're a fool, Marshall, this proves it. You're still in love! You're seeing Joyce *romantically*! That's why you can never figure what she's going to do. Listen to me, Marshall, she wants to ruin your life. She wants to separate you from your kids. She wants to separate you from your *balls*. Your image of Joyce is false; *that* Joyce is not the person you're dealing with today. That Joyce is finished. That Joyce is gone. If you want to get out of this divorce with any money or self-respect, you're going to have to look for the first time at Joyce and see how she *is*, now."

Marshall dropped his face into his hands. Unbidden, a memory rose to the surface like steam from a street vent. Years ago, before they were married, they had gone to Wales for a hiking holiday, making love as a matter of course or principle in each bed-and-breakfast along the way. On an old Roman road between one unpronounceably multisyllabic place and the next, they had stopped for lunch on a grassy rise at the top of a long clovered meadow. Sheep congregated by the woods at the meadow's distant borders, their bells' arrhythmic clangor lifting high into the morning air. Marshall couldn't recall any of the week's lovemaking, but he remembered the lunch perfectly: cheddar cheese sandwiches on crusty hard brown rolls, green Sicilian olives, one plum apiece, and a bar of bittersweet chocolate for dessert. He lay with his head in her lap afterward, seeing nothing but sky. They had talked in a happy, anticipatory way—about what he couldn't say now, not for the life of him—and Joyce had absentmindedly wrapped and unwrapped around her finger the long hairs at the side of his head.

"Okay, you're right. She wants me dead. I don't think she's ready to come down. They're trying to draw us out. So what's our next move?"

Thorpe picked up the fax sheets from her lawyer and rolled them into a tight cylinder. He declared, "We say she can stick this up her ass and give it a twist. Let her think about that. We go back to court, judges are funny these days, she could get next to nothing. Her lawyer will tell her that. She'll come back with a better offer, and then we'll go to work on that."

"Right," Marshall said, pleased by the firmness in his own voice, as if he had been the one to plan the strategy. "Okay. Agreed."

Rising from the chair with his battered attaché in hand, he wondered how long he had been here—about fifteen minutes, he guessed—and went wobbly in the knees thinking of the money he had just spent. But the billable hours were worth the expense. He was paying for more than a strategy to defeat Joyce: this education in rigorous self-interest was an investment in his postdivorce future. This was why you had a lawyer. Thorpe gave him a confidence he would be capable of deploying every day, in every other aspect of his life.

"By the way, that's some attractive lady out there in the reception area," Marshall added, his grin hearty.

Thorpe's expression didn't change and his minimal nod of acknowledgment required hardly more muscular effort than respiration. He remained in his seat watching Marshall with hard black eyes. Marshall's giddy impulse to ask the lawyer if he was having sex with the receptionist was quickly suppressed. He had intended to use, ridiculously and uncharacteristically, the word *balling*. He let himself out of the office. He went through the reception area past her with his own eyes averted, except for a single reckless moment. In that moment he knew with total certainty that the lawyer was having sex with her.

LATER THAT MORNING his boss drummed his fingers softly on the carpeted wall by Marshall's desk. Marshall didn't hear him, entirely immersed in the data stream gushing from his computer monitor. Hudson had to say his name twice before he looked up.

"Sorry."

"No, no, it's okay, I didn't mean to disturb you," Hudson said, his palms raised. "Do you have a minute?"

"Of course, sure I do. Pull up a chair."

Hudson's moon face was cratered by a small, shy smile. He stepped in and took the seat, careful first to hitch up his pants. He leaned forward. Holding back his tie, he met Marshall's eyes and then looked away.

"How are you feeling?"

"Fine, Bill. And you?"

"How's the kids?"

"Good. Viola has preschool graduation tomorrow. Caps and gowns. Now she wants an allowance."

Hudson nodded, taking in the information as if to remember it forever. Perhaps he would. He didn't ask about Joyce; everyone in the office knew now that Marshall was getting divorced, and despite Marshall's restrained denials, they believed the action stemmed from 9/11. At his firm 9/11 was the alpha point from which history moved forward, the Big Bang, Genesis 1:1. The director of the New York office had been killed in the attack, along with all the others who had been at their desks that morning. As head of the midtown satellite office, Hudson had immediately thrown himself into the crisis. Though he himself didn't return home for three days, he made sure that his staff did that evening, or he found shelter for those who couldn't. He secured the company's records and documentation. He personally obtained and posted around town photos and descriptions of those whose fates were yet unknown, including, briefly, Marshall's. Hudson had been the first to call the families. Little did he know, as he moved with decisiveness and sterling judgment, that this was to be his finest hour. In the following weeks he was chosen to lead the unified New York office, an uneasy amalgamation of surviving WTC people like Marshall, the former midtown staff, and some new hires who couldn't shake the notion that ghosts roamed the hallways. Hudson had been given free rein by the company's board to restore the office to normal—"whatever normal is now," the CEO had whispered darkly.

Marshall smiled, still a bit distracted. "What's up?"

"Something on the wire," Hudson confided, speaking softly. "It's just speculation, totally unconfirmed, but...You haven't heard anything? It has to do with LuQre."

Marshall showed polite interest. "Oh really? What kind of speculation?"

"That they're filing for Chapter 11," said Hudson, wincing. "That's the report."

"No-o-o-o-o-o!" Marshall made a low moaning sound that strove to express disbelief and distress. His eyes went wide. He brought his hand to his face. Their company maintained a complicated web of financial dealings with LuQre, including joint assets and debts, most of them threaded through Marshall's department. He wished he could reattempt the moan, if only out of respect for Hudson.

"By end of business today," Hudson added.

Marshall let his mouth fall open and he shook his head as if it had just been splashed with cold water. "Are you sure?"

Hudson shrugged helplessly. "I called. No answer. I think they've closed their switchboard. Can you believe it?"

Compensating for his weak theatrics, Marshall declared, "I'm not surprised."

"You're not?" Now it was Hudson's turn to show shock, honest shock. His face folded into a wondering squint. Marshall realized that he had incriminated himself, falsely, since he *was* surprised. The announcement's import was still percolating through various strata of preoccupation. Now Hudson said, "You're not surprised?"

"Well, I *am* surprised," Marshall insisted, pausing as he forged his response. Although he didn't wish to suggest that he had withheld information, he didn't want to appear ignorant or inattentive either, when in fact, to be honest with himself as Thorpe had counseled, he had been completely ignorant and inattentive. He tried to put together a few stray facts. He began, "I mean, not that I knew anything, but you know, you didn't get the impression they were the best-managed company in America." He peered at Hudson, hoping that this would be enough, especially with the shift to the second person. But the troubled cast in Hudson's eye remained fixed as he waited for further explanation. Marshall went on, tentatively: "It's not like we didn't know they had huge accounts receivable with Enron. And now that I think of it, they were in pretty deep with both WorldCom and Qwest; there was some kind of joint venture in Argentina. Didn't you know? And of course they took a beating from energy deregulation in California. I *must* have sent you a memo about last quarter's earnings. Their accountant is Arthur Andersen by the way."

Hudson's gaze fell to his shoes. He was quiet for a minute. He had once been a handsome man, but the march of the last several months had left their tread on his face. With the company struggling to recover from its 9/11 losses, human and financial, he had refused to take any vacation beyond the company retreats that he organized and led. He looked exhausted. "I guess the speculation is correct then," he said blandly.

Marshall was thinking. "We should call Legal right away, to

see where we stand, what obligations we're stuck with. And we have to make a list of clients who are going to be impacted..." He started compiling the list in his head, electrifying neurons that had been on standby for months. It would be a long, costly list. "Wow, we're going to take a hit and a half."

Hudson sighed, gripped the tops of his thighs, and lifted himself to his feet with difficulty, as if fighting another planet's gravity. His face had gone slack. "That's all right. It's okay," he murmured, and shuffled back to his office.

Marshall watched him go. Then, swiveling back to his computer, he saw that he had neglected to shift windows when Hudson arrived. His individual retirement account was still displayed, an increasingly recurrent indiscretion. He had begun tracking his positions daily ever since the market went into reverse two years ago. This summer, however, as the market slide became an avalanche, the Dow Jones plunging past 10,000, 9,000, and 8,000 to sweep aside picturesque alpine villages inhabited by small and large investors alike, he had tended to keep the account up all day, while rigorously hunting in other browser windows the most clairvoyant market forecasts and the least damaging prospective investments. Hudson must have seen that it wasn't company business on his screen this morning. Well, at least it wasn't porn.

MARSHALL CLICKED his browser's Refresh button, keeping his eye on his total assets number. It shifted downward. He did the math on the scratch pad he kept next to his computer. In the time it had taken Hudson to tell him about LuQre's filthy collapse, Marshall had lost $8.47. Damn, the market was shooting itself in the head again. The past hour had cost him $45, real money. If he had cashed out an hour ago, he could have missed Hudson's visit, bought himself a New York strip steak and a glass of wine at Michael Jordan's, reinvested the remaining funds when he returned, and found himself in the exact same place. Except of course, Mr. Big Shot Investor and Eater of Steaks, all he had left in the market was his 401(k), the money locked in until his retirement.

There had been other funds once, brokerage accounts established for capital improvements and the children's education, as well as a rainy-day fund, back, back, back in the Age of Progress. In those years, the nineties, Marshall had hardly ever checked his portfolio, content to let it grow out of sight, like mushrooms. Every eighteen months, according to a well-known computing principle, microchip speed had been doubling, the Internet itself doubled in size every *month,* and this was concomitant with exponential growth in consumer appliances— cell phones, DVD players, digital cameras, Palm Pilots, all of which contributed, even if they were made in China, to America's world-beating, in-your-face, proof-that-we-were-right-about-everything productivity. Wal-Mart opened in-store espresso bars. High-end fusion restaurants replaced cheap ethnic ones. Snuffles' dog-walkers showed up in Manolo Blahniks. New York became safer than ever, muggings no longer as profitable as mutual funds. You didn't need to check your account. You could see your affluence reflected in the world around you.

Now everything was burning. His 401(k), which had once promised a lush, softly golden, seraphim-packed golf course retirement, had been diminished to $34,000, despite his weekly payroll contributions, frequent divestitures and reinvestments, his intense research, and the investment therapy sessions he had attended this past spring. As for the other accounts, almost everything that hadn't been consumed by the bear market had fallen into Thorpe's gaping maw. Time was money: the losses were like a journey into the past, shedding years of investment patience. A year ago his assets had declined to their value at Victor's birth in 1999. Now they had reached their value at the year of Viola's. He had already plotted the graph that foresaw, given current trends, when his holdings would be equivalent to what they had been on the day he married Joyce. That date might yet coincide with the day his divorce was finalized.

Had he sufficiently enjoyed the nineties bull market? At the time everyone had known that the run of market advances was extraordinary—yet this triumph was mitigated by the suspicion that growth was a normal function of economic activity, nothing to celebrate. It was recession, inflation, stagflation, and despair that flowed against the current of history. Unexceptional common sense had demanded that New York slums would be gentrified and that free markets would establish themselves around the world—dissent required a kind of neurotic, life-denying pessimism. It was expected that within a few years a 10,000 Dow would seem as puny and as antiquated as a microprocessor running at 20 megahertz, installed in a PC with a 1-megabyte hard drive. Knowing that the nineties market expansion was extraordinary had been like knowing that your simple human existence was extraordinary—while not walking around being thrilled by it. You took it (market growth, life) for granted, while feeling ashamed of taking it for granted. You even expected retribution for taking it for granted. Yet you couldn't operate in the quotidian world without taking it for granted.

Now that the nineties were being erased, he was unsure what to do with his dwindled assets. He trolled the Web looking for a break: the one stock about to be launched into the stratosphere by some reversal of market conditions, or some technological advance, or some government agency's action or inaction, innocent or not. At the same time he sourly contemplated that in the last year his portfolio had been outperformed by Viola's passbook savings account, opened for her by Joyce's parents in their village's independent, slumberous, ATM-less, one-bank bank. She had beat Merrill Lynch too. He considered a wholesale shift to bonds or even CDs. But Marshall possessed a morbid fear of being locked in, of knowing precisely how much an investment would be worth at a certain date. Thirty-four thousand dollars invested in a 4.5 percent thirty-year CD would return $130,821.73 in 2032—and he would be sixty-six years old. A fixed instrument served to recall that your own passage through time was fixed: that you were being run at a steady rate down an inflexible rail.

Market risk made you liquid within time; it gave you freedom to travel within the temporal continuum, leaping ahead twenty or thirty or a hundred years of typical investment growth and seizing the payout, without having to live and age through those years. You just had to be smart. For the past several months, Marshall had been practicing the use of sophisticated and esoteric market forecasting tools. These tools acknowledged that the market as a whole made no more sense than a screen of television static or a godless universe—yet if you examined the history of a single stock, fund, or index's price fluctuations, it was sometimes possible to discern certain patterns within them. These recurred often and distinctively enough to have been given names based on the silhouettes they showed when they were plotted on a graph, such as "Symmetrical Triangle" and "Flags & Pennants." Marshall delved deeply into their fanciful and poetic typology, learning to distinguish segments of indexes that, when plotted against volume and other factors, exhibited the classic "Heads & Shoulders" profile or "Inverted Heads & Shoulders," the "Parabolic Curve" or "Wedges Formation," or "Osama's Beard" or "Saddam's Mustache" or "Saddam's Mustache Ascending." If, through careful study of a certain stock or index, you discovered one of these known patterns in progress, you would gain the ability to predict what would occur next, according to the established pattern, and bet on it. Profit lay behind the static.

His eyes watering, Marshall abruptly pulled away from the

screen. He rose to stretch his legs and survey the office: his colleagues doing their jobs or checking their own brokerage accounts, similarly staring at computers and punching in numbers that added to the data already in the globally vast market stir. The problem was that the market was nearly omniscient and nearly perfectly rational and would compensate for nearly every advantage in knowledge or understanding that you acquired, nearly always. Billions were made only in the *nearly*, the momentary opening of the demon-guarded door to aberrations and lapses. You had to be there and ready to rush in.

Forget it. His true wish represented the most ordinary of desires: that God would whisper a company or fund name in his ear and so end his humiliating calculations and recalculations. The wish was desperate, but Marshall believed that there wasn't an investor alive who didn't pray in the privacy of his cubicle.

Marshall didn't want billions of dollars. Millions would do. He needed only enough to escape his marriage, only enough so that Joyce could have the apartment, whatever support she wanted, *more* than she wanted in fact. He'd buy her a fur coat, anything. All he required was a single stock. All he required was for its three- or four-letter New York Stock Exchange symbol to appear in a dream or fantasy. Sometimes he'd lie awake at night and try to force the vision, to summon the correct letters onto the velvety screen of his bedroom's lightlessness. Come, come you bastards, come, but the only characters that ever appeared in the murk were shimmering glyphs and runes from languages long lost, dead, or privately held.

THEY TOLD JOYCE to stick her proposal up her ass, and there, apparently, it remained. Weeks passed without a response from her lawyer and—this was most maddening—Marshall saw no indication that Joyce was walking around with anything more up her ass than usual. She made no reference to her settlement proposal and never spoke about the divorce. She and Marshall maintained their independent, tight-lipped domestic regime, more faithful to it than to any other routine in their previous life together, accepting it as normal nearly as much as the children did, though unlike the children, they dragged themselves through their daily lives muffled beneath blankets of suffocating pain. At Viola's day-care graduation they were stationed at opposite ends of the tiny playroom, as were all the divorced and divorcing parents, with the estranged husbands on one side and the wives on the other, just as their families had been seated at their weddings. Wearing a chiffon blouse and jeans tucked into high boots, Miss Naomi beamed at her charges and smiled shyly at a few parents, Marshall included—especially Marshall, he thought.

According to the precise, stringent, tacitly observed rules, Marshall and Joyce were prohibited from looking at each other directly, or from even recognizing the other's presence, even at home. When they were forced to speak, they modestly averted their gaze and adopted a conspicuously flat tone. They spoke with elegant concision, unless of course they were screaming. From the limited intelligence available and a few stolen glances, Marshall couldn't determine whether his refusal to negotiate her settlement proposal worried her, angered her, or amused her—or anything. He began to wonder if her lawyer had even communicated his refusal to her.

And another court date was approaching, perhaps with decisive force, and it occurred to Marshall that Joyce's silence reflected confidence in her legal position. Her settlement offer might not have been a feint—very possibly, given her utterly contrary interpretation of every fact that had ever come into their joint possession, she thought its terms were fair, even generous. She could believe that otherwise he would be defeated entirely and she had offered it to him as a sop to her conscience. Under intense questioning over the phone, Thorpe told him in good cheer how badly the case could go against him. Once Marshall put the phone back in its cradle he sensed that, beyond its other indignities, the call had somehow established that he had been the one to insist that they refuse Joyce's proposal, over Thorpe's objections.

Preoccupied with his divorce, Marshall was slow to recognize the cooling in the office temperature over the next several days. Hushed whispers ricocheted off the walls. The LuQre debacle had severely shaken the company, exposing fault lines in its own governance. Contracts were canceled; lawsuits were put forward; *subpoenas were being issued!;* the losses couldn't be fully tallied. Hudson seemed especially distracted at company meetings, restless, pained. He probably wished he could go back to putting up "Missing" posters. The CEO was compelled to fly up from Florida to declare that there wouldn't be layoffs. "This is a company of survivors," he declared. "And we're in this together."

Marshall's 401(k) continued to shrink, dwindling even more quickly than did his company's stock, remnants of which he discarded. He clicked through the brokerage site's performance, account history, and trading pages and tried to catch views of his assets from every possible angle before they departed completely.

This intense scrutiny of a Web site whose every feature he thought he knew finally paid off. On Friday afternoon at the end of another losing week, he noticed a link to "Associated Accounts," underlined in tiny red print, beneath the link to the start-up page's "Terms and Disclosures." He had never seen it before. Associated Accounts? More money? He moved his cursor and an outline of a hand appeared over the link, with its pointing finger extended. Or perhaps, he thought, the hand was turned the other way, with the finger slightly crooked, beckoning.

He clicked on the link and another screen opened to demand a new log-on name and password. Something clicked in his memory as well. He had been on this page before: several years ago, virtually at the dawn of the Internet, when he had set up the Web link to Joyce's 401(k). He had shown her how it was done. He had impressed her pants off, literally. Now quivering in anticipation, his fingers typed in *letshavesex* as the log-on. A row of asterisks immediately appeared in the password field. The network server was hiding the password, but recalled it deep within its cookies.

The screen went blank for several moments before the new page came up, and in that time Marshall found himself holding his breath. He let it out when he saw that there wasn't an error message or an admonition that he had typed in the wrong log-on. He had really accessed Joyce's account, the page set up exactly as his was. His eyes immediately made their long-practiced flick down to the total assets figure.

$522,987.50.

Marshall was astounded. His eyes darted back over these digits, so many of them, making sure the comma and decimal point were located where he first thought they were. More than half a million dollars?

He clicked through the account's history. Except for her employer's weekly contribution, automatically deducted from her paycheck, the account hadn't been touched since Marshall had established the Web link. The original investments had remained in place without a single trade. Actively uninterested in money matters, except when it came to his impoverishment, Joyce could have forgotten that she even *had* a 401(k), or didn't even know what those three numbers, the single letter, and the set of parentheses *meant*. That would have been just like her. In all their years together, she hadn't opened a single bank statement. She had always let him do their taxes. Her lack of interest in even the most general outlines of financial planning and tax minimization had once driven him nuts. These days she probably just dumped her earnings statements on a desk at H&R Block.

Marshall went through her account. The stocks and funds he had chosen for her, a much more diversified brew than his own, had performed very well. Although she owned no flashy breakout stocks and had lagged behind the Dow through some of the nineties, she had hardly slipped at all in the last year. He was not only astounded, he was disgusted.

THEY WERE BOTH HOME that weekend, requiring that every action taken and word spoken would have to be vetted. As usual. Waiting for her to say something about her settlement proposal or the impending court date, he armed himself with rejoinders to every conceivable remark, but she remained silent. He sensed smugness. He knew that she told herself with increasing persuasiveness that the whole situation was going to be over soon, and that she was going to come out of it winning big.

Meanwhile there was her 401(k) to think about. His impulse was to tell her about it, in order to shock her with his secret knowledge of her finances and also to taunt her for forgetting about the retirement account. But he held off. You couldn't inform people they had half a million dollars they didn't know about without giving them some kind of pleasure.

It was his turn that Saturday to take the kids for haircuts. Joyce alternately took them to a fifty-bucks-a-pop children's styling salon, but his place was considerably less expensive, located several steps beneath Atlantic Avenue, its fathomless realms overseen by a jowly, depressed, scissors-sceptered Poseidon named Dominic. Dominic was a man of very few words, apparently unimpressed by the costly remains of the kids' previous haircuts. After Viola's bangs were summarily straightened and he stuck a lollipop in her face, he put Victor in the chair. With Dominic you never had to have a styling conversation, but this time Marshall said, "What do you think, Dom? Can you give him a fade in the back, at the base of the hairline?"

Dominic didn't look up—couldn't, in fact. He had some sort of back problem that kept him in a perpetual stoop. He intoned gravely, "I can do that."

"Yeah? And, you know, what is it that I see around town, on black kids, fade cuts with the insignias shaved in the back? Is that a possibility? Could you carve in, say, a dollar sign?"

"I can do that," Dominic repeated.

"Daddy!" Viola protested, the lollipop still in her mouth. "Are you crazy? Doesn't Mommy hate you enough already?"

Of course she did. Marshall was nevertheless shaken every time it was confirmed—and even more so now that it was confirmed by Viola. All along he had believed, with Joyce, that the children remained oblivious to the situation and would accept the eventual divorce as a normal occurrence in an adult world composed of enigma and surprise. That was the plan, anyway. "Never mind," he said, and, feeling unsettled, brought them home.

Further unsettlement awaited their arrival. A new odor lingered in the apartment: his nostrils flared, his ear muscles tensed. The kids detected something too, sniffing. He stepped tentatively into the kitchen, where he discovered that their automatic-drip coffeemaker was missing. It had been replaced, as if in a puff of caffeinated smoke, by a gleaming, retro-futuristic apparatus, a piston-driven espresso machine. It was an elaborate thing, constructed around a brass water tank, to which were attached polished wood levers and knobs, plus a steam wand and a glass cylinder half filled with water. He could see his own astonished reflection in the dome. The machine's presence—anything new in the apartment—was like a slap in the face. The kids oohed.

Joyce was at the kitchen café table, sipping from a demi-tasse, one of a hand-painted set they had purchased in Italy and deployed only for guests, but they hadn't had guests in three years. Joyce was uncharacteristically relaxed, taking her pleasure from the coffee as if she occupied a table in the Piazza Navona. Before Marshall could speak she declared, without the least suggestion of defensiveness: "I was sick of Mr. Coffee."

Pending the divorce, major purchases for the home were supposed to be cleared through the lawyers. The espresso maker must have cost more than $700. By law every goddamned piece of chattel was still marital property. Joyce could have bought this thing only with the surpassing confidence that she was going to roll him over. She must have known for sure what he had always known in his gut: that she would get the apartment.

"Fine," Marshall said, nearly choking. "Just fine. I hope you have room for it in your next place."

"Can I do it?" cried Viola. "Can I? Can I make you coffee, Daddy?"

"No, not fair! I want to!" said Victor.

Marshall mumbled, "No, thanks, it'll keep me up."

He was so eager to get into work Monday that in the sprint up and down subway station stairs and across platforms he made earlier-than-usual connections and reached the office just as it was opening. A surprised colleague said good morning uncertainly. Marshall at once called up Joyce's account—*letshavesex*, he pounded into the keyboard—and all those hundreds of thousands of dollars came up again onto his screen, into his hands. He punched through her funds and stocks, selling every one of them. The dialogue box asked him each time, with rising incredulity, *Are you sure? Click OK to confirm.* Yes, yes, he muttered, and went to the purchase page, looking for those funds and stocks that were famous for being losers: the written-off, the faded, the infirm, the SEC-investigated, the collapsed, a mutual fund that unerringly chose hopeless IPOs. He bought them.

Then he sat back and looked at his handiwork, which had occupied most of the morning. What a mess. The larcenous thrill of it had left him famished and his armpits soaked. The prices had been so low that Joyce now owned thousands more shares, all of them crap. He resisted the urge of prudence to buy back the old investments.

Nothing happened to the account right away. The new stocks were dead in the water. After lunch Marshall had to leave his computer several times, repeatedly distracted by demands from the firm's Crisis Management Team, which was attempting to triage the LuQre situation. Some company honcho called from Florida to question him in detail, treating him with somewhat less delicacy than that to which he had become accustomed since 9/11. This was followed by a grim whole-office meeting in the conference center. In the recent past these events had been catered. Today there weren't even donuts. By the time he got back to his desk, after the close of trading, Marshall saw that Joyce's account had nudged down about $300.

Now he had something to be smug about as the court date approached. He studied her at home for signs that she knew what he had done to her 401(k). She remained stone-faced, an expression that, given her obliviousness to her own financial situation, now bordered on the fatuous.

But by Wednesday Joyce's account had done a small turnaround, actually advancing on where it had been when Marshall sold off her original investments. Marshall wondered if he had made a mistake buying stocks and funds that had nowhere to go but up. He Googled now for firms valued more highly on more precarious assumptions. While he worked, one of Joyce's new penny-stock companies announced that it had perfected a device that scanned for explosives hidden in running shoes. As its share price multiplied exponentially, Marshall rushed to dump the stock, but not before Joyce's account had earned several tens of thousands of dollars.

While Marshall's own assets continued to slide, not even taking part in the modest across-the-board rally at the end of the week, Joyce remained unaware of her good fortune, which would have been a consolation if her mood hadn't seemed to improve anyway. She was still unyielding with him, but her day-to-day maneuvering around the apartment became more light-footed, accomplished with more confidence, even grace. And the kids were suddenly pliable in her hands. Yes, Mommy, of course, with pleasure. When he arrived home one evening she was at the hall mirror, trying on shoes with what looked like a new skirt. He couldn't help noticing the shoes were recently bought too, with high, sharp heels. She promptly went into the bathroom to use the mirror there. Thorpe called to ask if *he* wanted to propose a last-minute settlement. "Won't that be taken as a sign of weakness?" Marshall whispered into the phone. "Sure," Thorpe agreed. Marshall heard her in the bathroom softly humming.

He sold off the previous week's stocks and bought expensive, go-go-years stocks, companies with storied histories and far-flung operations but no conceivable futures. Steel mills, a railroad. He bought into funds managed by twenty-six-year-old cokeheads and stocks issued by companies that owned huge pieces of Russian automobile factories. He bought free-falling shares of his own company. He thought he had done his research well—until the *Journal* reported that Dick Cheney had emerged from hiding to play a round of golf with the railroad's directors.

Marshall made more trades, his decisions based on his marketing forecasting tools and intelligence from online news sources and paid-subscription investor tip sheets, but Joyce's account only improved. He sold off her investments again and started purchasing stocks at random: first, poking his finger at

the newspaper's stock tables with his eyes closed, and then, after these stocks advanced, replacing them with shares of firms
whose New York Stock Exchange symbols were IHA, TEJ, and
YCE. Some of these did better than others, but they all performed well, quickly. Joyce's total assets passed $800,000. Mar-
shall recognized that he was living in a moment in which the
market had fluctuated out of its characteristic disorder, apparently in resonance with some factor hidden within his decision
making, or within his state of being. He was doing what was
not normally permitted by classical mechanics: diminishing the
entropic value of a closed system, effectively removing a measure of randomness from the cold, conscienceless, ignorantly
expanding universe. Even his sell-offs were timely: the company
with the shoe-explosive detector now announced that the device didn't work.

One evening at home Marshall was on the floor wrestling
Victor's inexplicably wet sneakers onto his feet so that he
could take the kids for pizza. Joyce passed them on her way
out, her heels clicking like a desktop mouse. Marshall stopped
to look up, Victor's foot still in his hands. She was in the new
skirt, brown suede wrapped tightly around the tops of her
legs, which was as far as it went. She wore a loose open
blouse and must have lost at least ten pounds. She had done
something with her hair too. He couldn't remember what it
had been like before, or ever, but this was cute, brief, and
razor-cut.

"Wow," he said, unable to stop himself. It was like something building and rushing up within him: a flood, a stampede,
a cloudburst, an eruption, an economic boom. "You look
nice."

Marshall watched mortified as the words emerged from his
lips and hung in the air between them. Joyce's mascaraed eyes
locked on his for the first time in months. Her exquisitely prepared face—he just noticed the makeup—crimsoned almost to

the color of her lipstick. She took a step back, almost tripping over her heels.

"Fuck you," she cried. "Fuck you. Just totally and completely and absolutely fuck you."

She rushed from the apartment, slamming the door. A moment later Marshall thought he heard anguished mutterings in the hall by the elevator.

"Mommy said a bad word," Victor observed.

Marshall groaned and fell back to the floor, Victor's sneaker in his hand. With their legal combat approaching resolution, with every weakness and misstep exploited to the max, this was the wrong moment to go off-message; at the same time, Joyce's breakdown represented for her a serious battlefield loss. Her upset was mysterious, emphasizing again his ignorance of everything that went on inside her mind. He turned to Viola. She knew more than he thought.

"The compliment," she explained.

Joyce had looked terrific, as young and as fresh as when they were courting. Marshall recalled a time when he thought he needed to be with her every moment of the day. He had once driven two hundred miles in the middle of the night only to walk her from dorm to class in the morning. When she had opened her door the light of her smile was like the sun coming up. He said now, "I see."

"And she's nervous. It's a first date."

"A date?"

Viola nodded somberly but then let go with a grin, delighted to know something her father didn't. Marshall was stunned. He and Joyce weren't divorced yet or even legally separated—she couldn't date. He was going to tell Thorpe. Meanwhile the sidewalks were swimming with adorable women who checked him out from the corners of their eyes, interested, available. Marshall had presumed that he would be the first to date.

"With an FIB agent," she said.

"A what?"

"They catch terrorists."

"FBI, and hardly ever. What do you know about FBI agents? What do you know about *dates*?"

"It took a while," she said. "But I figured it out. You have to pay attention."

MARSHALL WAS TORN by indecision the following morning. He could have aligned what was left of his investments with Joyce's, proportionately augmenting his tiny 401(k) while hers continued to balloon—but could he stand for her to retire a multimillionaire? The alternative was to simply sell off her investments and stick the cash in a money market, where it could sit and smolder and be eaten away by inflation for the next thirty years. As he came off the elevator he became aware of an unusual human hum within the office, with many of his colleagues outside the cubicles conferring with each other in low voices. He breezed past them and went right to his computer. But something was wrong with it: he couldn't log on to the local network.

"Hey. Marshall-man."

Marshall turned to look behind him. It was one of his co-workers, Eduardo, the young slacker guy who worked opposite Marshall in the new office just as he had in the World Trade Center. On the morning of September 11 he had been on the way to his dentist for root canal. Everyone knew that. The survivors were identified each by how they had survived.

"What's wrong with the system?" Marshall asked. "It's down?"

"Most certainly."

Marshall felt a prickling on the back of his neck. He looked around the room. Every computer screen was like his, the company logo dominating it like a test pattern. His colleagues

seemed relaxed about this, chatting amiably with each other. A
few shook hands, others kissed, others handed out cardboard
boxes.

"Where's Hudson?"

"Ah, Bill Hudson," said Eduardo ruminatively. "Dear sweet
Bill. Fired. Sacked. Defenestrated. Exiled. Sent to The
Hague."

"How could they fire him?" Marshall was so surprised he
could hardly keep from laughing. "Look what he did for the
company after 9/11—he pieced together our records, he established the new office, he brought us back from the dead. I
thought he was a company hero. Anyway, the CEO said no one
was going to lose their jobs."

"Yeah, he's fired too. Almost the entire management team is
gone, last I heard. The stock's up, though."

"Gee," said Marshall, thinking it through. He hardly knew
the people in Florida. The New York office's relationship with
the company headquarters had always been distant, corporate
command loosely directed by unseen deities detached from actual human labors. "Where does that leave us?"

Eduardo raised his arm majestically. "Go to the bulletin
board; it's over by the Eternal Flame. They've listed the times
for our exit interviews."

Marshall again surveyed the room, finding few signs of
emotional upset. His colleagues were quietly going through
their desks for their personal items and removing from their
cubicles photos, posters, and other wall ephemera he hadn't
noticed before. Within a few hours the physical evidence of
their careers would be gone forever, lost in the entropic mists.

"The stock's up?"

"Five points since the opening."

"And we can't log on?"

Eduardo smiled sadly. Something shifted within the spec-
trum of the office's visible light; Marshall heard in the ambient

office noise change in pitch as well. It was too late now, even if he went to an Internet café and accessed their accounts from there, even if he had Joyce's password. The market moment had passed and its departure continued to vibrate through his body. He became aware, his heart thumping as regularly as clockwork, that he was living in normal time again, the ordinary, nonfungible, consistently paced sequencing of events, consuming it as surely and as steadily as he consumed his remaining cash. Thorpe had sent him another bill. Marshall would pay it with a chunk from his stockpile and then stand back and watch, as everyone did, as the remaining days, hours, and minutes skittered away.

AUGUST

EWS OF JOYCE'S ESPRESSO MAKER made everyone at court angry: Joyce's lawyer as well as Marshall's, the judge, the stenographer. The two parties had been wrestling over the smallest trivialities for months, and the appliance represented yet another detail that would upset entirely every provisional calculation and agreement. The decisive court hearing earlier in the summer had turned out to be not decisive at all, with the judge wearily warning that a settlement negotiated by the parties would prove fairer and more workable than anything he would devise; in any case he was going on vacation. He sent them back into the increasingly warm and fetid conference room. It seemed to Joyce she had already spent a considerable fraction of her adult life in this room, its physical details indelibly scratched into her memory. Time halted within its confines, so that the third meeting between them and their lawyers perfectly coexisted with the eighteenth, preceding and succeeding it at once; the only evidence of nonsimultaneity was the accretion of billable hours. New points were raised about the most excruciatingly banal trifles of their household life—who made the kids' lunches, who bought the laundry detergent. Both Joyce and Marshall silently wondered if these issues hadn't already been resolved. When they left the court, taking care not to leave at the same moment or ride the same train home, they each sensed that they hadn't been in court at all, that they had only imagined it. About the espresso maker, Joyce had protested, embarrassed, "It was only $699.95!"

MEANWHILE, Thorpe was unimpressed and even contemptuous when Marshall told him about Joyce's date. "You want to prove adultery? Good luck, my friend. You're going to subpoena the kid? The G-man? This will go on for another two years, and I'd be glad to take your money but you don't have it—and what's the point? It's a common mistake, thinking that grounds will determine the terms of your judgment. She won't get less, if that's what you're thinking."

"Okay, okay. I just thought I should tell you."

Thorpe leaned his shiplike bulk forward over his desk and grinned. "Do you think they're fucking? Actually fucking? You know, she *looks* like she's had some sex. You, on the other hand…"

WITHIN THE INDUSTRY there was a certain amount of curiosity about meeting someone who had lived through 9/11 and his former company's famously abrupt restructuring. Marshall engaged in several employment-related conversations that started off mostly as convivial talks with middle managers who knew him by reputation and ended as slightly cooler, more formal dead-end interviews. He was presumed to be hireable, but when he arrived tieless, his shoes scuffed, his facial stubble a micrometer too long, he seemed to have brought with him more than his share of the world's anxieties. He sat on the edge of his chair, his eyes darting, and responded to questions with artless concision. The interview would conclude with a firm handshake.

Although he looked good on paper, with the economy in slow recovery no one felt compelled to offer him a position.

He went into Manhattan every day anyway, just as he had in the weeks after 9/11. When he asked himself what he would do when his cash ran out, he heard no reply: the future was an echoless void. He had no plans, no road map. In the meantime he lost himself in the swell of office-going humanity, walking fast as if he were late and idly humming to himself. Some of the tunes were religious hymns from his childhood. The days were warm and bright, Mediterranean; at the same time the sky seemed unnaturally close, at the scraping edges of the city's towers, a transparent glass bowl.

Or it was like a teardrop swelling before its fall. Or like a child's spinning top in its terminal wobble. Or like a blow before its pain was registered. One day when Marshall was walking east in the Twenties between Lexington and Third avenues the entire morning came down with an enormous crash.

This was the result of a heavy steel grille being slammed shut on the back of a truck parked in a loading zone, but in the three or four seconds required to identify the noise, Marshall found himself reeling, his limbs ripped from his body, his clothes bloody and torn. The impact was felt by other passersby as well. An elderly lady clutched her bosom. Two women office workers walking side by side grabbed each other by the hand. A man walking with a small child reflexively leaned over to protect her from something neither could see. Even the delivery-man who dropped the grille flinched.

Suicide bomb: this was the thought they held in common. Yesterday, seven time zones ahead, a Palestinian youth dressed as an Orthodox Jew had rushed past a guard into a Tel Aviv corner pizzeria, cried out in Arabic, "God is great!" and blown himself up along with nearly everyone inside. The total body count had come to seventeen and the pictures had been all over the news last night and this morning. The attack followed two others this week on public buses, each claiming diverse victims: Jews, Arabs, a Filipino woman, soldiers, civilians, schoolchildren, two nursing mothers and their infants. Dozens more had been hurt badly enough to suffer their injuries for the rest of their lives. Last week a bomb at Hebrew University had destroyed a cafeteria named in honor of Frank Sinatra, killing nine and wounding eighty-five.

The New York television news replayed the scenes of devastation every half hour, as often as the traffic reports. The pizzeria had been gutted, its walls scorched, its plastic checkered tablecloths, chairs, oregano shakers, and paper soda cups torn, smashed, and scattered, yet it remained as recognizable as any New York pizzeria. The camera slowly panned the wreckage. Thousands of New Yorkers knew that Tel Aviv intersection precisely, knew that pizzeria and could argue the merits of its crust relative to the crust produced by the pizzeria across the street. A cash register was upended. A charred pizza box lay closed on the floor, the same jolly, fat-faced chef declaring, as he did all over the world, "You've tried the rest, now try the best!" The faces and biographies of the dead were intimately familiar too: the piano tuner, the doctor and father of five stopping to pick up dinner, the truck driver, the babysitter, the electronics store clerk, the only child, the teacher, and the nurse whose salary was supporting her family in a Manila shanty. In a single moment these individuals were linked together for the rest of eternity by another ordinary person, some high school kid from Nablus, good with his hands. Marshall had just passed a newsstand whose papers screamed their grief and rage.

Here on East Twenty-fifth or Twenty-sixth Street the pedestrians who had been startled by the falling grille straightened their postures and stared at each other without embarrassment. They were about halfway between the two avenues, about nine or ten of them stationed like chess pieces on either side of the street, their powers of motion in check. Marshall studied them as they studied him, images of their faces, clothes, shoes, hair-cuts, and demeanors collected and carried into the lifeless fu-ture. Even the deliveryman who had brought down the grille remained where he was.

The pedestrians would each move again in their separate anonymous ways, but within this moment they lived the ter-ror as it had been experienced within the pizzeria, by the bomber and his victims together. The boy had probably been praying to a distinctly conceived God not to lose courage; he must have been simultaneously aware of the rush of time trans-porting him to the explosive instant; the patrons were sprinting along the lines of their own thoughts and personal dramas, their love affairs, their work conflicts, their sporting enthusi-asms; the youth probably found his field of vision tightly nar-rowing once he made it past the guard into the pizzeria; inside they must have known immediately why a youth dressed as an Orthodox Jew would be rushing past the guard; he shouted, *"Allahu Akbar!"* reported the wounded, failed, severely ques-tioned guard; they didn't see him press the trigger; the boy pressed the trigger (in his pocket, beneath his black coat?); this was followed by an ultima of total clarity in which the bomber and his victims saw every detail of every aspect of their envi-ronment crystallized into that minute and second of that day in the month of August in the year 2002. In a single lightning flash the unconnected parts of the world had been brought to-gether and made into sense. No, *sense* was not made. This was a world of heedless materialism, impiety, baseness, and divorce. Sense was not made, this was jihad: the unconnected parts of the world had been brought together and made *just*.

And then the survivors on East Twenty-seventh Street did proceed and the moment was shuffled into the deck alongside innumerable other moments lost to history. Most of the pedes-trians would forget the incident—it was not even an incident—before they reached the ends of the block.

———

JOYCE HAD WATCHED the television reports from Israel as well and, riding the train beneath the East River, she saw the *Post*s and *News*es on the other passengers' laps open to the atrocity. The photos ran across several pages, the pizzeria wreckage flanked by yearbook pictures of the victims and shots of emergency personnel carrying the wounded on stretchers to ambulances emblazoned with slanted, razor-edged Hebrew lettering. Looking up and down the subway car, hearing the ominous rapid thump of its wheels against the tracks, Joyce was riveted by the thought of a suicide bomb's spectacular effect here: the noise, the fire, the flying glass and shrapnel, the overcoming, roaring rush of water and estuary silt. The terrorists were on their way. It could happen before the next thump.

She closed her eyes to rest them. The journey under the river took hours, it seemed, but she was in no hurry to arrive at the hate-drenched apartment she shared with her not-yet-ex-husband. She despised the place. It was small and dark, everything in it was broken, she hated her neighbors, and she was sick of living in New York. For the same money she could buy a house in the suburbs with a backyard and a garden. A garden. She had never wanted one before, but now she ardently wished for a garden.

She wished she could start over—yes, with the kids, though not necessarily (as long as she was fantasizing about a new life). She fixed on the idea of leaving New York, this cramped, violent, bitterly competitive, small-minded city that had never been a real home, where she had become a victim. She wanted to start a vegetable garden somewhere and spend more time with her face in the sun, her bare arms plunged into the soil. She wanted to inhale deeply and smell moist, fecund, freshly dug earth. She would buy comfortable work boots, flattering in their rugged utility. Feeding herself with food grown from her own efforts, she thought, would change her entire character; it would make her more self-sufficient, more capable of standing up for herself. She opened her eyes. God, she was buried underwater in a fluorescent-lit steel tomb.

At last she arrived at Borough Hall and dragged her body through the streets, barely able to face another several hours of silent combat with Marshall. They had been alternating evenings minding the kids, but she couldn't afford to go out to a restaurant or movie every night he was home with them. To ignore him, to avoid getting involved with his haphazard parenting, she would have to sit by herself in the kitchen—when what she needed was to be alone in her own home, without a single artifact or residue or aroma or memory of his existence. She needed to be on her own before she could begin the process of self-repair or reinvention.

But Marshall wasn't home. When she opened the door, their babysitter Sonya was standing in the living room, wearing her coat and holding an oversized shopping bag. She had been staring at the door, waiting for it to open. Joyce saw at once that her eyes were moist.

"It's a quarter before seven!" Sonya cried. "My family needs me. My daughter has to go to work. She can't leave the baby!"

"Where's my husband?"

Sonya gave her a hopeless, grief-stricken, accusatory expression—he's *your* husband!—with which Joyce was already familiar. Sonya had been a high school physics teacher in Tashkent before immigrating to Israel right before the Gulf War. After a tumultuous decade she and her family had made it to the U.S. with their nerves shattered and their circumstances severely reduced. In Tashkent the Jewish faculty had been fired; in Israel a Scud had struck near their housing complex, and her son-in-law's army unit had suffered casualties in Gaza; in Brooklyn, after 9/11, she took to her bed for a week, convinced that world history was hot on her trail, about to rap its knuckles on her door. Victor and Viola loved her, but Joyce had once wondered if Sonya was simply too pessimistic an influence on their lives. Now she didn't find her pessimism extreme at all.

"He was supposed to be home by six!" Joyce protested, opening her bag and riffling through her purse. "That's what we arranged."

"My daughter will lose her job!"

"Okay, I'm sorry, I'm terribly sorry," said Joyce, thrusting a twenty at her. "Take a cab. I'm sorry, I don't know what happened."

Sonya raced from the apartment, not even saying good-bye. Joyce could hear her in the hall, punching repeatedly at the elevator call button.

The kids at once clamored for dinner. Joyce went to the kitchen, Sonya's lamentations still ringing in her ears. As they faded Joyce's own anger started to build. There had never been any question that Marshall was supposed to relieve Sonya at six today—no question at all! He was willfully negligent of his children's welfare. For a moment she was so blinded by fury that she couldn't see the contents of the refrigerator. She simply stood there, smoldering within a cloud of refrigerated air. Victor and Viola observed her hesitation and demanded to be taken for pizza.

"No, no pizza," she said, but the kids picked up on her weariness as well and she had to give in. Fuck it. She didn't want to cook. Once they made it to the street, she was sufficiently demoralized to be persuaded to bring them to Marshall's low-rent pizzeria on Court Street, instead of the brick-oven pizza restaurant on Montague, which served wine and excellent Atkins-sensitive salads.

Not until they had ordered the pie and taken a table did Joyce notice just how awful Marshall's pizzeria was: strewn with

wax paper and soda cups, overbright, flyblown, rank, and
hardly bigger than a walk-in closet. Part of the low dropped
ceiling had been removed to reveal bare fluorescents; the rest
of the tiles were water-stained. Travel posters from Italy were
carelessly fastened to the chipped paneling, though the swarthy,
unshaven men behind the counter appeared to have no connection to any indigenously pizza-making nation. They had
seemed wary when she gave them her order. The eyes of the
bearded man at the register watched her sadly from deep within
their sockets. The kids ran to claim a red Formica table. Joyce
saw the long, coruscating tomato sauce smear right before Viola dumped her sweater on it.

The kids shot straw wrappers at each other, further littering
the unswept floor as their pizza was being prepared. Joyce
looked away and tried to focus on some unsoiled, serene space
and time beyond the pizzeria, a green place unknown and un-
contested, and then she saw Marshall at the front of the shop,
by the register, waiting. He hadn't seen them. He was intently
watching one of the guys remove a slice from the oven. He had
his wallet out with a bill in his hand. She stood and advanced
on him.

"You were supposed to be home by six."

Marshall slowly revolved his head as if out of idle curiosity,
as if not surprised by her presence, as if he barely knew her, as
if she were some bag lady. It took enormous self-control. He
regarded her for less than a moment before turning back toward the oven.

"Where were you?" she demanded. "We had an agreement!
Sonya was nearly in tears. Why didn't you at least call?"

In fact, as Joyce would remember later, the week's child-care
arrangements had been altered to accommodate an appointment she had set for Friday. They had discussed it the day before yesterday. But Marshall, congratulating himself for the

maddening aplomb with which he had just brushed her off, didn't want to be drawn into an argument just now. He held the moral advantage. Let her stew. He told the bearded counterman, "Some extra napkins please."

"Marshall!" She could barely keep from screaming.

"Daddy!"

The kids had seen him and rushed to wrap their arms around his legs. "Eat with us, Daddy!" said Victor. "We're getting double cheese."

Marshall smiled weakly, disconcerted by Victor's plea. He thought the boy accepted that they never ate together. He pulled himself from the children's embraces. It was bad luck that they had gone to the same pizza place.

"No, not tonight, honey. I can't."

Joyce reached over and snatched the bill from his hand.

"You owe me," she said, seething. "I had to give Sonya cab fare."

He made a move to take back the bill, a twenty, but she was too fast. She pivoted on her heels and returned to the table. The children didn't go with her, standing uncertainly in the space between them.

"Joyce! Not now. Let's talk later."

"One dollar ninety cents," said the counterman grimly. He put the slice in a white paper bag and placed the bag on the counter.

"Actually," Marshall said, smiling at the counterman in a self-deprecating way. There was no response. He turned to Joyce. He hated talking across the pizzeria. Everyone was watching. "Joyce, really, please. That was all I had on me. I'll pay you back later."

She ignored him, her face very dark, her hands and arms on the table with her palms down.

"Joyce!" he insisted.

He turned back to the counterman. "Can I give you a credit card?"

"No credit," the man said, deeply offended.

"American Express? Visa? Come on, you know me, you see me here three times a week. After I eat I'll go to a cash machine and bring you the money. I'll eat on the way to the cash machine, how about that?"

But the counterman was already sliding Marshall's frugally plain pizza from the bag and returning it to the piles of other slices with assorted toppings beneath the glass, to be re-reheated at some future hour. He also put back the bag and napkins, folding them with care.

At that moment everything and everyone in the pizzeria became still. Even the children remained in place, Victor on tiptoe, unsure of what was being negotiated above their heads. Joyce's unfocused eyes watched something in an unseen world, on an unknown channel. At other tables several young men were hunched over their slices and sodas, but they had looked up when Joyce grabbed the money. Now they were in mid-chew or mid-sip, their Adam's apples in mid-bob. The three pizza guys stood behind the counter, one with a disk of raw pizza dough rising from his hands. Deep within the moist, throbbing folds of Marshall's brain tissue, something turned over: their crappy, disordered existences, these shameful skirmishes, this soiled money, this debasement, this cruelty, this insensitivity, this impiety had become intolerable to God. A black, egg-laden fly hovered, about to deposit its larvae on a Parmesan canister. God saw it all.

"Bitch!" he exploded, storming out.

EXACTLY HOW GREAT would sex with seventy-two virgins be? Thinking it over later, Marshall presumed that the lovemaking would not have to take place in a single night and that in Paradise the martyr would be allowed to work his way through the list over several months or years, if Paradise allowed for the counting of months and years or any passage of time at all—and without time, within a static, eternal Present, how could the sex act even be conceived? These considerations aside, he imagined that limiting your sexual partners to virgins would become as tedious as being married; well, nearly. In Marshall's experience, which encompassed a single virgin, a high school friend, sex with a virgin tended to be clumsy, frustrating, and humiliating (it had been his first time too). Even in the skillful hands of a martyr-lover you might expect those celestial houris of perfect virtue to be especially skittish and inexpert. And afterward, after those seventy-two ex-virgins were carted away, would the martyr ever be allowed to have sex again or would he spend the rest of eternity without it, consumed by the same foolish conceits and unrealistic, tormenting desires that had occupied his existence on earth?

No, the martyrs weren't in it for the sex.

Marshall worked at his bedroom desk diligently for the next week, spending hours at a time on the Internet. In the darkened room he searched through scores of news reports and commentary until he found a site that offered what he wanted. The site was in Arabic, but it contained a printable diagram. The Internet also directed him to a mining equipment company in Reading, Pennsylvania, where he bought a box of dynamite sticks and blasting caps on his credit card and took them home in a rented car.

The diagram called for a complicated detonation system built for concealment and quick use. At RadioShack he picked out two dry cells, wiring, alligator clips, and switches. When he went to pay, the clerk asked for his name and address.

"You don't need it," Marshall declared, annoyed.

He couldn't see the clerk's eyes beneath his flaxen bangs,

which hung over his face as he worked the register's computer. He had been plugged into an MP3 player. Now that he had removed the earpieces he still seemed to be listening to the music, conscious of Marshall's presence as the smallest distraction.

"Name and address," the youth mumbled.

"What do you need my name and address for? I'm paying cash! I don't want your junk mail, I don't want to get calls from telemarketers, I don't want you to know who I am. Aren't there enough assaults on our privacy as it is? Does every last piece of data about us have to go into a computer? It's bad enough the government is doing it."

The clerk looked up and winced at Marshall's speech. He was a good-looking boy, with gentle, clear blue eyes and an unblemished complexion. Marshall was surprised by the delicate little blond ringlets that spiraled down in front of his ears.

The youth said, almost plaintively, "You don't have to give me your real name. I just have to type something in."

Marshall was embarrassed that his objections were so easily met. He attempted to compose a made-up name. All he came up with was Yasir Arafat. That wouldn't work: Marshall understood that the deal the youth was offering, in order to permit him to purchase these few electrical parts, required a name that was not so obviously not his own. But who knew if another human eye would even see the form he was filling out? What was the point of this exercise? Marshall's annoyance compounded itself, yet he was unable to generate a name that was not already attached to a celebrity. Saddam Hussein, he wanted to say. Muammar Qaddafi. Rin Tin Tin.

At a complete loss, he gave the clerk his real name and address, including the zip code, made his purchase, and went home.

188 | KEN KALFUS

Their divorce negotiations had stalled again. Court dates were set and postponed, the lawyers continued to coo and bill, and then nothing would be decided. Still they lived together. Every once in a while an outside party would come up with a stratagem to break the deadlock—a simultaneous exchange of major concessions, a splitting of the differences—but Joyce and Marshall closed ranks against it. Their positions had shifted shape to exactly meet and oppose the contours of each other's interests. Meanwhile Marshall worked in his bedroom, his hands, a wire cutter, and a pair of pliers maneuvering in the spotlight cast by his halogen work lamp. He had taped the diagram to the wall in front of him. Joyce and the children stirred elsewhere in the apartment. Passing feet cast long shadows from beneath the door. The phone rang, the TV went on and off, pots were dropped, and drinking glasses broke. Each sound assaulted his nerves: it was dangerous, it was wrong, it was evil. Their apartment was the world of derangement and chaos.

Several days later Marshall finally emerged from his bedroom, the package wrapped around his chest beneath his gray bathrobe. He held the two alligator clips apart, one in each hand. The children were watching television. He stood behind them for several minutes, gazing on their delicate skulls. They were unaware as he reviewed their vulnerability to their parents' failings, as well as the tragic childhoods they had been bequeathed. He left and found Joyce in the kitchen preparing the kids' lunches for the next day, store-bought falafel balls. As always, she tried to ignore his presence.

He approached in slow, steady steps, his hands heavy with electrochemical potential. She had picked up a carrot and was peeling it over the sink.

"God is great," he announced. He took a moment to inhale and brought the clips together.

She looked up, annoyed that he had spoken to her, apparently without necessity. It was against their ground rules.

"Since when?" she snapped.

"God is great," he repeated, again touching the clips. He opened one and clipped it around the other, but it slipped off. He then squeezed both clips and snagged one in the other, jaw to jaw. They held.

"What are you doing? What is that?"

"A suicide bomb."

His bathrobe had opened and the explosives wrapped around his midsection were visible. She raised an eyebrow. "Really?"

"I made it myself. I have enough dynamite to blow up half the block. God is great."

He put the two clips between his thumb and forefinger, squeezing hard. He imagined, for a moment at least, that he could feel a tickle of a shock.

"Why doesn't it work then?"

"I don't know," he said, irritated. "The wiring is tricky."

"Did you follow the instructions?"

"They were in Arabic. But there was a diagram."

She put down the carrot and the peeler and sighed wearily. "Let me see."

"I can fix it myself," he declared.

"Don't be an asshole."

"Too late."

She said, "Do you want me to look at it or don't you?"

He grimaced and shook his head. But he said, "If you want to."

She thoroughly dried her hands on a dish towel and came over. He pulled back his robe to reveal the wires passing through the firing caps and leading to the two linked dry cells resting in the hollow of his back. The explosives carried an acrid odor, like leaves in late autumn.

"Where'd you get dynamite?"

"A mining supply factory. The electrical stuff comes from RadioShack."

"RadioShack," she said. "That's why they started sending junk mail. Hmm, the red wire's slipped off the terminal."

"Okay then. Would it be too much to ask you to re-attach it?"

The children had risen from their places by the television and had silently filed into the hallway next to the kitchen. Viola's expression was thoughtful as she assessed the situation. Victor probably had no memory of ever seeing his parents like this, nearly touching. Marshall felt self-conscious.

Joyce asked, "And then it's going to explode?"

"It should."

The four were in a tight space at the entrance to the kitchen, virtually huddled there. Victor squinted as if the overhead light had become unnaturally intense. Joyce hooked the loose wire around its terminal. She said, "There you go."

"God is great. Crap."

"Watch your language."

"It's not working."

"Let me check the other wiring," she said. He scowled and wriggled halfway out of his robe. The intertwining wires for the device looked about as logically ordered as a bowl of spaghetti. She ran her fingers along the black and red. Against his will his body grew warm. Her fragrances were like second nature to him, even now. He was breathing hard; he realized that she too had quickened her breath. A drop of perspiration trickled down his side. She murmured, "I've never seen dynamite sticks before. They look just like in the cartoons."

"What cartoons?" Viola asked, her interest sharpened. She was wearing the cute little navy sundress Joyce's mother had just sent her.

Joyce said, "Oh, you know, Road Runner. Powerpuff Girls. Dexter. All the cartoons, really."

"Uh-uh," Victor objected. "Not Arthur."

Viola told him, "You haven't seen every one."

Marshall said, "Can you fix it?"

"Hold your horses. I have to look at this. Don't move."

"Can I help?" Victor asked.

"Not now, sweetie." Joyce dropped to her knees to better examine the mechanism, her face at Marshall's hip. The kids crowded around their parents. Victor was resting against his father with one of his tiny hands on a dynamite cap. This was how the family once looked to the outside world, how it had once been: a compact unit, loving and intimate. Marshall was suddenly fatigued.

"Forget it," he said abruptly.

"Wait, I think I see the problem. I don't think this cap's plugged in."

"It doesn't matter."

"Just give me a minute."

"I said forget it."

Joyce was still on her knees, trying to force the cap. Viola's hands were on her back, completing the circuit: Joyce touched Marshall at the hip, Marshall touched Victor, Victor's shoulders made contact at Viola's arm. Joyce worked to fasten the cap as if success would resolve every single one of their problems. She said, "You don't follow through with anything. That's what's wrong with you."

"Oh, great, one more thing. I'm keeping a list."

He tore away, leaving her on her knees. Victor nearly lost his balance.

Marshall didn't look back. He went to his bedroom, closed the door, and stripped off the robe and bomb assembly. She was probably right about everything that was wrong with him:

he *should* keep a list. He tossed the dynamite onto the floor next to his unwashed laundry and fell on the bed. He could hear Joyce and the children move away from where they had been in the kitchen, and the machinery of the apartment's daily life eventually resumed operation: lunch being made, TV. He buried his face in his pillow and quietly sobbed until it was soaked.

FEBRUARY MARCH APRIL MAY JUNE

THAT WINTER BEFORE the war the snow was prodigious, inches piling upon inches that were already packed down and had turned to ice the week before, followed by sleet. School was canceled and offices were closed, further complicating Marshall and Joyce's efforts to stay out of each other's line of sight. A court date, promised to be the absolutely climactic hearing, was postponed; the next simultaneously available openings in the judge's and lawyers' calendars were foretold to occur in March. One weekend Marshall took the children to his parents, buying time away from Joyce. On Sunday afternoon he raced the next blizzard back to New York. In his rearview mirror he could see billowing, sparking black clouds gaining on him. By the time they reached the FDR Drive—not quite 5 p.m.—the storm had struck. Traffic slowly tunneled through a dense midnight obscurity. The children had fallen asleep, but Snuffles was awake and had begun to whine, probably needing another walk. Marshall felt immeasurably alone—and not only in the rented car; also in the cosmos. Behind the wheel he had been reduced to a simple organism, a pair of feverish, noctilucent eyes attached to a single foot that tapped the brake in response to the flickering of the taillights ahead of him. The lights eventually led him off the highway. He headed for a gas station, to fill up before he returned the vehicle.

The local streets were in even worse shape than the highway, with cars sliding out of their lanes and some intersections blocked. The children woke, groggily surprised by the storm, and announced that they had to go to the bathroom too. "Hold it in, we'll be home in a minute," Marshall said anxiously, aware that the mark of a great mind was the ability to entertain two competing ideas at once. In this case the first idea was the devout belief that they would be home in a minute, and the second was the certain knowledge that filling up, dropping off the car, and getting home in the blizzard with two small children, a dog, and a suitcase would occupy a full hour.

No, more than an hour: the Amoco station was a self-serve mess. Cars sucked at the pumps from every direction. Others milled behind them, tentatively forming and re-forming lines and blocking the exits. A single attendant brooded within a glass-walled bunker at the center of the lot, unable or unwilling to intervene. Drivers punched their horns; Marshall too, pointlessly, only because the others did. Snuffles barked. The public radio news came on but Marshall couldn't follow what was being said about terrorism and war any more than he could understand the crooked, wandering anecdote Victor had begun telling him, a complaint that Viola had tricked him into giving her his toy soldiers. For twenty minutes he rocked the car forward, on a line feeding into two pumps. When one of them finally cleared he darted in alongside it.

A red Nissan stopped with its bumper just inches from Marshall's. Marshall wasn't sure where it had come from, but the car hadn't been on any line that could reasonably have claimed his pump. Yet now a new line had somehow formed behind the Nissan, demanding priority. The swarthy, mustached driver made a face. Marshall jerked his head impassively: *up yours.*

"Kids, wait here."

He opened his door.

"But I have to make pee-pee!" Victor said.

Marshall stepped into the wind and oily New York ice blew down his neck. He would have remembered to put on his scarf if the other driver hadn't distracted him. The guy was still making a face and jabbing his finger in the direction of his car. Then he spun his finger around in a half circle, signaling something foreign and offensive. It was going to be another New York moment. What a fucking city. Marshall flicked his hand at him, like brushing away an insect.

He read the directions at the pump. He was just about to put his credit card into the slot when the other driver rapped hard at the inside of his windshield. Marshall wondered if they were going to fight. He almost hoped so: he needed to punch out someone tonight—something he had never done before, yet an action that seemed now like the most direct response to every irritation and frustration of his daily reality. He squeezed his right hand into a fist and even through the glove it felt strong. He wanted to lay the guy out across his hood. One punch. Unless of course the guy had a gun. Then it would take just one shot, to end Marshall's life and leave his kids alone in a driverless rented car on a frigid night on the Lower East Side. It could happen, anything could happen. Marshall grimaced to show that he was ready for him, but the man smiled as he pointed toward the back of Marshall's car, to the side near the pump. Marshall looked. There was no door to the gas tank. It was located on the other side.

Marshall returned to his car, glowering. The other driver
motioned that he should pull back and turn around to the
pump, demonstrating with complicated gestures how to maneuver between the other cars. Marshall made no sign that he
saw him. He would leave the kids and the dog home with Joyce
and come back in an hour, by which time this entire lunatic
population of the Amoco station would have been replaced,
but his vision was still misted by the anger that had coursed
through his blood moments earlier, soaking his brain tissue
with the specific mix of chemical compounds that produced
the thought processes characteristic of anger. He took a deep
breath and rested his head against the steering wheel for a
moment. He couldn't think straight anymore. His brain was
just a damned vat of tissue soaked in solution, his mood, mind,
and identity dependent on minute changes in the solution's
composition. The other motorists were waiting. Marshall was
still angry. The transformation from anger to non-anger lagged
behind the sequence of chemical ions passing through his nerve
cell membranes that had signaled the realization that he had
been wrong. You could be dead certain of something one moment and then sure of an entirely contradictory fact the next.
And still be mad. He put the car into gear and threaded his way
out of the gas station.

THORPE HAD BEEN WRONG about Nathan and Joyce. There
had been no romance or anything like a romance. They had
simply met for drinks that evening last summer, her mascara
not quite right despite some emergency repairs, her head spinning. *Wow, you look nice*—Marshall always knew how to fuck
with her head. Agent Robbins also seemed preoccupied, as if
Marshall had gotten to him too. He thanked her for coming
and hurried to say, "Mrs. Harriman, you understand, this isn't
part of the investigation."

"Of course," she said brightly, trying to regain the enthusiasm she had first expressed when he called her. They were in a quiet bar on the East Side, neither trendy nor romantic enough to be an obvious date spot. She had ordered red wine; he had taken an immediate gulp of his bourbon, not even making a toast. She added, "It's a social thing. Please, please call me Joyce. That's what you do when it's a social thing."

He nodded at his drink, avoiding her eyes. "Right, though in fact the bureau has certain procedures and prohibitions governing external social activities. Um, people you meet in the course of fieldwork..."

She smiled warmly. She knew she had a great smile and intended to use it tonight as often as possible. "Well," she said, trying to sound flirtatious, "I'm sure they're wise rules, but I'm glad you thought we could bend them a little."

He threw up his hands. "My therapist told me I should get out more."

Joyce was dismayed. He went to a therapist! Another loser, another broken personality, another midlife nutjob... This confirmed what she had heard, that the only men she'd meet now would have something wrong with them—just like she did, of course.

"Oh," she said, unable to summon another smile.

"He said I'm working too hard. It's true. The FBI's my whole life. I don't have a family, Joyce. I hardly have friends, only colleagues, all of them overworked. It's all 9/11 all the time—we're overwhelmed. We took thousands of Arabs into custody and can't even keep their names straight. We're months behind in translating intercepted communications, and half the time the translations don't make sense. I bring home files that aren't supposed to leave the building. I stare at them for hours, trying to figure out what they mean." He confessed, "We're just spinning our wheels. So I'm depressed. That's why I have a therapist. He tells me to get out more. He's also from the bureau."

"I'm sorry you're depressed," she said. "It's been a rocky couple of months for me too. Actually, years—"

"It's the interrogations," he interrupted, whispering. "We hold so many guys now—not only the prisoners in civilian custody, but also the CIA and military detainees—you have to figure at least one of them knows where bin Laden's hiding. That's the reasoning. So we take these guys and ask them, do you know where bin Laden's hiding? Simple as that, but not so simple. You have to ask them repeatedly, for example. In varying tones of voice. In varying circumstances, in varying environments. You have to take a man and break him. Do you get me?"

Nathan's dark eyes blazed now. He was hunched over his drink, looking up at Joyce as if from inside a well. She was frightened by his attention and his talk of terrorists, and also aroused. She nodded slightly.

He said, "The key to breaking a man is making him aware that you control his environment—everything in his environment. So we take a guy, we mislead him about the time of day and the day of the week. We mess up his sleep, meal, and toilet habits. His prayer routine too, so he can't remember whether he just did his noonday prayers or whether it's time for the morning ones. This takes a couple of weeks. After a while he doesn't know which season it is or even which year—and he depends on you to tell him. First you become his father and mother. Then you become his God."

"Does it work?"

"No, of course not. It's completely idiotic."

"You don't know where bin Laden is?"

Nathan forced out a sad laugh. "No one knows where bin Laden is. I'm not even sure he ever existed. We've had prisoners who swear that he doesn't. They swear it on the lives of their mothers, their fathers, their sons, and their daughters. They swear they'll gouge out their own eyes if they're proved lying. After a while you start to believe them..."

"But he was seen on TV!"

"Yeah, right," Nathan said, unconvinced. "I've been interrogating this one prisoner now for weeks, or maybe it's been months, I forget. Listen, we have sixteen interrogation techniques approved by the Department of Justice. I've tried every one of them. And guess what? He's not a terrorist, he has nothing to do with terrorism, even if he's broken just about every immigration law from here to Mars. But we found in his cab a video camera with pictures of the Brooklyn Bridge, the Lincoln Tunnel, Grand Central...Yet we know he's not a terrorist. He's a poor dope from Yemen who came to New York to drive a cab. In Yemen he dreamed of driving a cab in New York. That's all he ever wanted from life. In Yemen he studied the Koran and he studied how to get to LaGuardia during rush hour. He's a gentle, sweet man, ignorant as shit, no, *more* ignorant than shit, shit is a genius next to this guy, excuse my language. Yet when I say I *know* this, I don't really know this. I think I know it. Perhaps he's fooling me, manipulating *me* with his sixteen resistance techniques approved by al-Qaeda. Maybe I know he's innocent like he knows it's seven a.m."

"I don't understand. Do you want to free him? Can't you free him?"

He leaned over his drink, speaking in a near-whisper. "I think I have control over him. I regulate every aspect of his existence—his sleeping, his eating, his sobbing. And he knows that everything in his life revolves around me. But he's the one *I'm* thinking about day and night, the one who keeps me from eating and sleeping. And maybe he knows that. I think I'm controlling him but he may want me to think that. He may have the power to break *me,* Joyce. When I'm in the interrogation booth with this man, it's like we're the only two people in the world. He's on one side of a cheap Formica table and I'm on the other, and it's not obvious which of us is the prisoner."

Joyce smiled again. "Nathan, I don't know what to say. But I'm glad you feel you can confide in me."

He looked at her as if she were crazy. He said, "You're not the first person I've told. I've told everyone: the old woman who lives next door, the dry cleaner, the Chinese food delivery boy. Find me someone else to tell. I have to talk. I have to prove that there's a world outside the booth, outside the bureau. Something bigger than me and this guy."

After that night Joyce saw Nathan from time to time, usually in a bar or at a restaurant—and on one occasion at her prompting they went to the Guggenheim, where he stared at a Rothko for about ten minutes and said, "How do we know this isn't a con job?"—but so little romantic chemistry developed that she would have been embarrassed if he had tried to kiss her hello or good night, which he didn't. He continued to talk about the FBI probably beyond the bounds of bureau regulations and certainly beyond the limits of her interest. Once when she arrived five minutes late at P. J. Clarke's she found him half leaning over the bar and insisting to the bartender, "The less they know, the harder they are to crack." The bartender was trying to bring drinks to some other patrons. Nathan made her nervous.

THROUGH THAT WINTER diplomats convened, troops massed, and battleships steamed to their classified positions. A space shuttle broke apart over Texas. The world prepared to turn. Joyce was telephoned by her lawyer, who told her that the next hearing, now scheduled for late March, would resolve every outstanding issue in her favor. The lawyer sounded almost girlish on the phone, giddy with relief. "You'll get your bedroom back!" Joyce didn't understand how the lawyer could be so sure, but these days she welcomed anyone's optimism.

The ether was electrified that season as men and women in television studios prosecuted matters of fact and principle. Joyce was awed by the strength of their convictions. They spoke gravely in simple declarative sentences without hedging or equivocation, their faces hard. They *knew*, because they were smarter than she was or possessed greater moral clarity or had access to military intelligence. The strength of their contempt for the doubters—you *don't* believe Saddam has WMD? you *don't* think Saddam has links to al-Qaeda?— was a pro-war argument in itself. Joyce was stirred to encounter, even on television, anyone who had this certainty at his core. She remembered when Marshall had been like that, a young man driven by conviction. When he had issued a political or moral judgment, or simply a judgment about the way he and Joyce would conduct their lives, the declaration had reverberated down to her loins. And then at some point along the timeline, his convictions had become wrong, loony...

Colin Powell brought to the United Nations satellite pictures of weapons sites and intercepted transmissions between Iraqi officers intending to conceal banned weapons from UN inspectors. Britain issued a report warning that the Iraqi army could launch biological and chemical warheads within forty-five minutes of Saddam's order. Tony Blair said, "What I believe the assessed intelligence has established beyond doubt is that Saddam has continued to produce chemical and biological weapons, that he continues in his efforts to develop nuclear weapons, and that he has been able to extend the range of his ballistic missile program." Hillary Clinton agreed that Saddam had "given aid, comfort, and sanctuary to terrorists, including al-Qaeda members." David Letterman complained, "Even after Colin Powell's talk, France says it wants more evidence. The last time France wanted more evidence, it rolled through Paris with a German flag."

Smart people she had never heard of but knew were respectable, including outspoken liberals and Clinton administration alumni, argued for a war that would break the stranglehold dictatorship, ignorance, and poverty maintained on the people of the Middle East. The spread of democracy was the only way to halt the conflict between Islam and the West before it spawned terrorism far more catastrophic than anything that had happened on September 11. Writing in *The New Republic*—it was the first time Joyce had read the magazine; she never read political magazines, but now she found herself shopping for an opinion—Leon Wieseltier asked, "How can any liberal, any individual who associates himself with the party of humanity, not count himself in the coalition of the willing?"

You could poke holes in the pro-war arguments—why would a secularist regime make common cause with unpredictable religious zealots? do we have enough troops to occupy a country of 25 million people in a region of the world virulently opposed to us on historical, religious, and cultural grounds? won't regimes more reflective of popular opinion be even more anti-American?—but the arguments remained standing, their dread scenarios looming over everything you believed in and hoped for. Chemical weapons, nuclear bombs hidden in suitcases, smallpox, Ebola, something they didn't have a name for yet... *What if Bush was right?*

THAT FRIDAY EVENING Marshall needed a drink, specifically a vodka martini, but as soon as he walked into the anonymous bar on Atlantic Avenue he saw that it was the wrong place to ask for a vodka martini. The door slammed behind him, leaving him engulfed by cigarette smoke and head-banging rock. He shuffled to the bar anyway and ordered a Wild Turkey.

Most of the guys were in jeans and open-collar shirts or T-shirts. The women wore jeans too, their jeans below their hips, their shirts terminating well above their navels. The navels were pierced. Marshall was too old to drink in a place like this but he was exhausted by a difficult week at work—he had been hired recently by the Corporate Entity Formerly Known as LuQre to iron out its intricate dealings with the remnants of his previous company—and it was cold outside. He looked around, his eyes narrowed, taking note of the attractive, convivial women in the place, most of them in their twenties.

It had been more than a year since he had gone to a bar. That last time had been with Roger and Linda, before Roger and Linda had mysteriously gone underground, incommunicado. They had stopped returning his phone calls. He had heard they had broken up. Everyone was breaking up. It was like a virus, another sexually transmitted disease.

He gazed at the TV above the distant end of the bar. The screen was carved into pieces by flickering images he could barely resolve and text and logos he could not read. He sipped his whiskey under the flickering, abstract glow. Occasionally Marshall thought he saw something familiar, jet fighters taking off, Arab youths mobbing in a dusty street, soldiers stepping from a Humvee, a glamorous woman at an anchor console, an American flag unfurling in slo mo, but these apparitions escaped meaning. He found comfort in the emptiness of his vision. Let the light pour in.

This reverie lasted about two minutes.

"Go fuck yourself, you fucking fuckers!"

The imperative was shouted by a man two stools from

Marshall, a big man with long graying hair falling flat over his ears. He was fairly shit-faced. Marshall hadn't noticed the man when he had come in or wondered why the stools on either side of him were unoccupied. It was unclear what had provoked him. The shout had lowered some voices in the room for a moment and smirks and giggles sprouted around the bar. The man cried at the television again, "What do you know, you stupid miserable fucks!"

Marshall stealthily inched his stool away, but apparently not stealthily enough.

The guy wheeled, showing two tiny bloodshot eyes. He leaned over the vacant stool and growled, "What's your problem?"

Marshall smiled as disarmingly as he could. He raised his open, empty hands. "Hey, no problem at all."

The man demanded, "Do you support our troops?"

People were watching them, to see what the drunk would do. Marshall looked for a place to take his glass. No tables were free. Marshall tried to catch the bartender's eye, but he was busy at the other end of the bar, intensely smoking, apparently the only person in the room unaware of the confrontation. Marshall said, "Of course I do. I'm not so sure about going to war, but—"

"That's bullshit, the same old crap from the same old United Crap of America. If you say you support the troops, you have to support the mission. Otherwise it's an empty promise, an implication that their sacrifices mean nothing. Our troops serve our nation and we go to war as a nation. Those who oppose the war inevitably oppose the men who fight it." He shook his head bitterly. "It happens every time. We give up our lives, our limbs, and the best friends we'll ever have. When we come back you spit in our faces." The man drained his glass and challenged him. "You're not a vet, are you?"

"No," Marshall said apologetically. "I guess you are."

"Yeah." He spat on the floor. "A United States Army Ranger. Seventy-fifth Regiment, First Battalion."

Marshall tried to sound like a Democratic politician. "I honor your service, with pride. What, you were in Vietnam?"

"Grenada."

Marshall pushed a tiny parcel of air from one of his nostrils, an infinitesimal fraction of a chuckle. The guy saw it and took a swing at him.

The punch never connected, but Marshall jerked away from it, slipped off his stool, and sprawled onto the floor's wet saw-dust—*ooof!* he heard himself say—and then the stool fell on top of him. The other patrons scattered out of the way. It was very dramatic and totally ridiculous. He should have stayed in the Heights. From the floor he witnessed the guy being hustled off the premises.

Arms he didn't see elevated him to his feet and unknown hands brushed him off and somebody slapped him on his back once it was clear that he wasn't hurt. The stool was righted. People were laughing. The bar had come together over the incident—apparently the drunk was locally famous for picking fights. Another glass of Wild Turkey materialized at Marshall's side. For a moment he was the center of atten-tion. Some men good-naturedly congratulated him on his fall. He smiled and downed the whiskey. Women had arrived at his side too, two slender girls in jeans and snug pastel shirts, con-cerned that he might have been hurt. He rushed to introduce himself.

In a few moments the bar's patrons went back to where they had been but the two women lingered. Having survived his encounter with the vet, Marshall was inspired to act on impulse. He ordered a round for the women and a friend who had turned her back to say something to one of the guys at the bar. When the drinks came the third woman

206 | KEN KALFUS

took her drink and smiled and a little bomb went off in Marshall's gut.

The woman cried, "Victor's daddy!"

He wished he could hide. He had been caught fighting in a dive bar on Atlantic Avenue and buying drinks there for women he didn't know.

"Miss Naomi. Hello."

She was hardly recognizable from this morning, when he had dropped off Vic. Since then she had applied eyeliner and orange-brown lipstick, put on a pleated skirt, and exchanged her track shoes for knee-high boots. The only part of her ensemble that he recognized was her pink leotard top. She told her friends Dora and Alicia that he was one of her preschool parents, the father of Victor and Viola—and a 9/11 survivor. Alicia abruptly brought her hand to her face in a gesture of concern. "It's okay," he said quickly. "I'm fine. I got out."

"Still," Alicia said. "It must have been the worst thing that ever happened to you."

"I suppose," he replied, not wanting to disagree, not with such gorgeous sympathy drawn across her face. He paused to soak in the loveliness of the three young women. Alicia's face was lustrously rouged and her lips were moist and full. Dora's dense, matte-black hair corkscrewed down to her shoulders. All three women wore body-hugging tops. He took his time counting the six breasts between them. He raised his glass and they toasted his presence at the bar. He said, "Who knows. Tonight may be the best thing that ever happened to me."

Dora asked, "How'd you find this place anyway?"

"I was passing by," he said. "I needed a drink."

The women looked at him for further explanation. Their eyes were open wide as if to take in the whole of him.

"There was noise and light inside and I just wanted to be part of it. It's a cold night and I have nothing to do," he confessed. For a moment he thought he would confess further to just how wretchedly, shamefacedly lonely he was. Would they have pity on him? Would they embrace him? Should he tell them his 9/11 story?

"Unfortunately, we're just about to leave," Miss Naomi said.

Marshall's smile was brave. The girls had barely sipped the drinks he had ordered.

"We have to be someplace. A party," Miss Naomi explained. She looked to her friends. Dora flashed a half smile. Miss Naomi shrugged. "If you want to come..."

"Sure!" Marshall didn't try to hide his eagerness. "I mean, if it's okay. I'm not really dressed for a party..."

"It's in Nassau County, though. Do you mind? We have cars, you can ride with me."

Within minutes, less than a half hour after someone tried to hit him, Marshall was encased within a low-slung beat-up sports car with Miss Naomi, just the two of them leaning back side by side in the bucket seats. "My boyfriend's," she told him, nearly singing it. "He's going to meet us." Marshall didn't like hearing about the boyfriend, but the boyfriend was really only a momentary disappointment, a kind of abstraction. Miss Naomi was close by, her gin-rich exhalations mingling with his, her hand firmly on the stick shift. The city outside the car seemed as remote as another country.

She drove the car hard, grinding its gears as she weaved through traffic. She was high. He liked that. She slapped a cassette into the tape deck, early Courtney Love. Her eyes were still wide, her contact lenses visibly bobbing in the opposing cars' headlights. He would have liked to speak, to say something friendly or funny, with perhaps a hint of a come-on, but the music, the engine, and the road were too much in his ears. Instead he smiled and she smiled back. He liked that too. This morning she had looked up pleasantly when he brought Vic into her classroom. She had been on her knees, putting some pillows into a cubbyhole, her face slightly pink.

Just past the Nassau frontier they reached a raggedly illuminated boulevard of strip malls and small shuttered shops. Young men huddled on street corners, their hoods pulled over their heads against the cold. Marshall avoided eye contact. Instead of fleeing this nether region of trash-can fires and cratered, glass-strewn lots, Miss Naomi turned into a small street of small unattached homes. She had been here before. The house at which they arrived was halfway down the block, a simple two-story single-family house, with no driveway and a short untended lawn and a few lamps lit inside. As they came up the walk he heard the music. He wondered what the neighbors thought. "Whose house is this?"

"No one's. Dora has a friend in real estate. It's one of her listings."

The door opened to a blast of noise and cigarette smoke, and adjacent to the burning tobacco he detected the scent of marijuana. This was great; this was the kind of party he hadn't been invited to since before he was married. A dozen people were in the house already and some grinned and nodded at Miss Naomi when they entered, ignoring Marshall. Marshall nodded hello anyway. "He's coming later," Miss Naomi said. One of the women pulled her away to tell her something hilariously scandalous. Marshall folded his coat and laid it in the hangerless hall closet and backed toward the drinks table, where he picked up a bottle of vodka and poured it to the rim of a plastic cup. In the center of the living room a woman danced alone with her head down. Her long brown hair whipped back and forth.

Marshall stood off to the side of the room, which was generically furnished, presumably for renters. A few other men were by themselves, hands in their pockets. They were mostly younger than he was, big fellows, some of them already well paunched, blue-collar guys who possibly worked for heating companies or construction firms. Marshall might have been the only man present wearing dress slacks. One of the living room's corners was occupied by two men and a girl sitting against the wall, squared off around a joint.

The party had not quite started yet, he intuited; they had come too early. Marshall stayed near the drinks table. None of the women were as fetching as Miss Naomi, he decided, after the vodka sufficiently detached him from his surroundings. Some wore capris and tank tops, despite the weather. Were they also preschool teachers? Several wore butterfly tattoos at the base of their spines; a snake crawled from the top of one girl's blouse, its teeth bared. Marshall grinned at the girl. She didn't appear to see him.

He idled toward Miss Naomi, who turned to speak, but then the front door opened again and her motion was arrested by the entrance of a tall rangy man with hollow cheeks. The man was greeted by shouts: "Nick! Nick-o!" They were happy shouts, as if the guests had been actively waiting for him. Nick removed neither his sunglasses nor his leather jacket and maintained his place in the foyer, surveying the scene warily. He also examined Miss Naomi, who stood before him patient under his inspection. He said something indistinct, his voice a faraway rumble. She leaned forward to listen. Marshall remained in place, unsure whether to step away from the intimate conversation. When Miss Naomi finally noticed Marshall's presence she murmured, "This is Mr. Victor." Nick nodded, a cigarette dangling from his lips.

"You can call me Marshall." Nick didn't say whether he would or he wouldn't. To fill the silence Marshall added, "Nice party."

Nick stared. Marshall smiled under his scrutiny. Miss Naomi kept her eyes on Nick's weathered face, waiting for Nick's response. At last he said, "You think?"

Marshall looked at his watch: eleven-thirty.

"It beats *Nightline*."

Nick chuckled, an easy laugh that lit his entire face. Flooding into the crevasses of his cheeks, momentarily visible behind his eyes, the illuminant made his face strikingly handsome. Miss Naomi smiled at Marshall in gratitude for this transformation. Nick reached out and roughly squeezed Marshall by the shoulder. Marshall laughed too, feeling the warmth enter his arm. Nick glanced at the other guests and his scowl returned. Given his sudden connection to the man, it was obvious to Marshall what Nick saw: restraint. Hardly anyone danced. Nick muttered from the side of his mouth, "It beats meat." He looked at Marshall hard and said, his voice rough, "It's going to improve." He abruptly left the house.

Somebody guffawed. Miss Naomi giggled. "He's in corrections," she said, as if that would explain everything. Later it would. Marshall finished his vodka, possibly his second. After a while someone passed a pill into his hand. He swallowed it and took another drink. The party had subsided now to a low, nervous rumble. The dance music on the boom box had been replaced by something moody and indistinct.

Having passed some test of acceptance, he dropped heavily onto a couch next to a girl. "My name is Marshall!" he declared. The girl turned, appraised him for a few moments and offered him a joint. The smoke bubbled up through his cranium. The girl didn't say her name, or if she did he didn't hear it. He gave the joint back and she took a hit, sweetly pursing her lips where his had just been. He recalled that this was one of Miss Naomi's friends, Dora. "Nice party!" he said, and she just bobbed her head. He lost the moments in which they crossed the living room and climbed a stairway. When they reached the landing on the second floor he became aware that he was gazing into her face, wondering whether he should try to kiss her—her face was flushed, her curls splayed across her eyes—and then he lost her. He looked in at the open doors to the unlit rooms and saw a few people smoking as if in cells chained to their cigarettes. One guy was doing an abs set, squatting with his back and hands against the wall and straining to keep his position. Another guy was being dunked in the bath, with his clothes on, while his friends counted how many seconds he could hold his breath. Dora wasn't there. Perhaps she had never come up.

The front door opened downstairs, allowing into the house a nimbus of cold air that rose up the stairs accompanied by more shouts and hurrahs, rescuing Marshall, halfway at least, from the dreamy abyss in which he hadn't known he had fallen. Nick's name was called out again. This was followed by sharp barking laughter and then a kind of humming sound: news wordlessly telegraphed around the living room and the rest of the first floor. Marshall remained on the second floor for a while, but he didn't see any rooms in which he might have been welcome. One of the bedroom doors was closed. His head felt very warm and soft. He wondered whether this was a result of the alcohol, the pot, or the pill. He should at least have asked what kind of pill it was.

When he returned downstairs, fastidiously maintaining his grip on the banister, the dance music was up again, much louder now, and the living room seemed more congested. Nick stood by the drinks table with Miss Naomi, embracing her loosely with one arm as she buried her face in the shoulder of his jacket, her eyes closed. Nick surveyed the party from behind his sunglasses, unsmiling. Marshall tried to determine what had changed and saw at once that new guests had arrived, two young African American women at a party that up to now had been entirely white. Each held a drink in her hand and had drawn from the shadows several emboldened guests, including a few of the men. One of the women wore red short shorts and a loose silvery halter top that brought hoots from admirers every time she shifted position. Marshall saw another black, a young guy in a sweatshirt, his hood still up. He had stepped away from the women and hadn't taken a drink.

The party had been invigorated. Couples finally made their way to the floor to dance. A man was doing a shimmy with one of the black women. Nick must have picked them up nearby. Marshall presumed he had agreed to pay them somewhat less than would have been demanded by an incorporated escort service.

Another joint passed into his hands. He didn't know who gave it to him. He brought it to the couch, intending to smoke it thoroughly. He was embarrassed by the hookers—he was still too old for this crowd—but now in the early morning hours the party had reached the tipping point. Alicia had unbuttoned her shirt to reveal a red lace push-up bra and was doing a mock grind to the music, listening intently. She moved in slow, smoldering rotations and once in every orbit she faced Marshall. Marshall locked on her eyes, trying to arrest her spin. People were making out in the shadows and one of the black girls filed into the bathroom off the kitchen with one of the men. They were having sex in the bathroom. Marshall wanted to have sex in the bathroom. He felt himself being lifted now on an enormous swell of anticipation.

The black guy, still hooded, had taken a joint too. He retreated back to the wall, watching everything, the tip of his joint glowing steadily. Alicia had stripped down to her pink boy-shorts, across which was patterned a foreign alphabet of scimitarlike curves and swelling inky spots. Marshall wondered if the grind was for his benefit. He felt enormously benefited— she had smooth legs and taut, high buttocks; the shorts neatly squared them off—but he knew that right now he was unable to leave the couch.

Marshall must have dozed off, at least for a moment, because he didn't see the black guy take off his sweatshirt and reveal a head of cornrows. He was wearing a white T-shirt now and was performing some clumsy swing moves with Miss Naomi while Nick watched, his arms crossed. Miss Naomi was grinning, allowing herself to be spun, and at one point she was dipped halfway to the floor, her partner's hand on her leotard at the base of her spine, her back arched, her hair nearly grazing the parquet-tile floor. When they came up Alicia moved near them, hoping to get into the act. Nick reached over and whispered something into the black guy's ear. The guy shook him off.

Another girl had taken off her shoes and stripped down to jeans and a brassiere. She was heavyset and moved with little grace, unable to keep up with the driving music. Her face was feverishly mottled. Two guys sitting within a barricade of beer bottles at the edge of the dance floor made ribald catcalls and she turned and tried to shake her upper body at them.

"Come on, take it off," Nick said. Marshall realized that he had said this two or three times already; the demand now carried a searing urgency.

Marshall first thought he was talking to the fat girl in accord with her hecklers, but Nick was looking at Miss Naomi and her dance partner. Something thumped in Marshall's chest. Miss Naomi was still wearing her pink leotard top, her breasts smooth round scoops, her nipples hard little buttons rising beneath it. Yet Nick flicked his head at the guy's white shirt. It was an ordinary Fruit of the Loom T-shirt, not quite filled out except at his upper arms.

The man said, "Not here."

"Yes, here. Two benjamins."

Scowling, the man mumbled, "It's your party," and peeled off his T-shirt, revealing that he wasn't a man at all, but only a boy, perhaps fourteen or fifteen or two or three years younger than that, a thin boy whose ribs showed above a long hollow stomach, below a hairless chest. Only his sinewed arms looked strong. When his shirt came off it revealed glowing, silvered skin and the party buzz shut down as if it had been hit by a sledge-hammer.

Nick nodded that he should continue moving with the music. He didn't look at anyone as he danced; his movements were athletic and unsuggestive. He was being watched now by everyone in the living room. Miss Naomi had stepped back and the other girls had stopped dancing. Miss Naomi seemed dazed, not quite sure what was happening. Nick motioned at the boy's long baggy jeans. The boy shook his head, but the rebellion lasted only moments. He kicked off his running shoes and slid out of his pants. He kept his white cotton briefs. Nick suddenly grinned—the smile was death cold—and turned to the guests to see how the spectacle was playing out on their faces. Marshall sensed his contempt for them—for him—and for the pleasure they—and he, Marshall—were taking from this entertainment.

"The underwear too."

The boy resisted again and Nick repeated the command, his voice bearing down. It was a voice you might hear in your sleep. After a moment the boy complied, almost tripping when he pulled off the briefs and igniting a burst of titters in the audience. The black youth was entirely naked now, surrounded by white people. Marshall hated looking at undressed men, whether at the gym or in the movies, but he was sufficiently tranquilized now to allow himself to be fascinated. The boy's body was supple and unmarked, as fine as a piece of statuary. The youth maintained a fiercely sullen expression on his face, at odds with his private parts: his testicles had retracted and his uncircumcised dick was left hanging there, no more than a little hooded worm.

Nick had noticed the penis too. "You call that a cock?" He said to Miss Naomi, "I bet your preschoolers have bigger cocks than that."

She shook her head, her eyes cast down. "Nick, don't talk that way."

"He's shy," one of the prostitutes drawled protectively. "He hasn't done it before."

Nick ordered the boy, "Make it hard."

The defiance remained on his face, but Marshall saw through the youth's glassy eyes his consciousness withdraw somewhere safe and remote. He showed no sign that he heard Nick or that his unclothed body was chilled. He hardly seemed to breathe.

"Show us what you're made of, son. A few strokes. You know how to do that, don't you?"

The boy slowly raised his right hand to his penis and gave it some halfhearted tugs while staring into space. Nothing happened. Nick raised his own hand and made a fist, shaking it vigorously in front of the youth's eyes. "Come *on*!" The boy continued to rub the recalcitrant organ.

Nick was disgusted. "Look at these beautiful women here and you can't get it up?" He gestured to Alicia. She had half buttoned her shirt but remained in her shorts, absorbedly watching both men. Nick said, "What are you, a faggot?"

The boy pretended to ignore him, to be entirely self-composed despite his inability to make himself hard. He rocked back on the balls of his feet as he worked at himself. His feet were large, much paler than his legs.

One of the other men produced a Bloomingdale's shopping bag and placed it gently over the youth's head. The boy's square, brown, alien mask provoked a few chuckles and, from the back of the room, a mock-rebel yell.

Nick said, "Naomi, how about it?"

Miss Naomi grimaced and didn't move. Little creases appeared on her forehead, as if she were trying to solve a very difficult math problem. Her eyes had gone dull in the course of the night and her lipstick was smeared. Marshall recalculated her age downward: she was possibly just twenty.

"Give the fellow a hand."

She stared at Nick to gauge his seriousness. His eyes were still opaqued by his glasses, leaving her entirely on her own. Marshall wondered if she recognized the other guests any longer: their faces were shiny and distorted by alcohol, drugs, the lateness of the hour, and a raw, primitive appetite.

"It's not like you've never done it before."

She took a step forward to the boy and then a half step back, looking not at him but at Nick. She was standing on a knife's edge now. Her gaze implored and then faded. Around the room she found nothing but expectation. The boy had let go of his limp penis. She stooped toward it but didn't fully extend her hand. Marshall could see that both of them, Miss Naomi and the boy, were trembling.

The moments rushed by yet Marshall remained motionless with Miss Naomi and the boy in a vessel of timelessness as time swirled around them, Miss Naomi poised only inches from the boy's cock. Her head was still turned toward Nick, looking up. Marshall found words rising to the surface of his stoned, drunk, addled consciousness. He spoke:

"Nick, she doesn't want to."

The words echoed off the walls of the living room like the sound of a gunshot. The partygoers noticed Marshall for the first time. Nick's attention fell on him as well and Marshall saw himself reflected in his sunglasses: small, in a dim, smoky, low-rent living room. He turned away. Miss Naomi's eyes came into focus. She gave Marshall a stare expressing intense irritation. No, it was a look of disgust.

When she put her hand on the boy's penis the boy flinched and the Big Brown Bag made a brief rattling sound. This was met by general laughter, good, easygoing, unironic laughter, the kind of sweet laughter you might hear on a playground. The boy kept his fists clenched. Miss Naomi's examination of his penis was thoughtful, clinical. She seized the penis in two fingers and very gingerly pulled on it. Then she clasped it and the organ disappeared in her hand.

Marshall's few words of protest had sapped his spirit. It had been childish to think they would have made any difference. He sensed the other guests' enduring animosity. He wondered what fantasies of self-righteousness and power had motivated him. The gesture had been as ridiculous as the one he made on September 11, when he had gone back for Lloyd. Why had he done that? What good had it done? He regretted that too.

The youth's penis began to stir and take on weight, allowing Miss Naomi to make measured, regular strokes along its shaft. The organ gradually responded and every pulse of life ignited a round of laughter and whoops. The youth held his hands behind him and stood legs slightly apart, his back gently arched. You could hear his labored breathing now, amplified by the bag. When Miss Naomi went down to her knees she received further shouts of approval. She lifted the boy's penis into her mouth for a few moments and pulled away from it, leaving it glistening. She flicked her tongue against the squared-off sheath and then put the entire penis into her mouth again. She left it there, gently rolling it around her tongue. Now the youth's penis emerged nearly erect. She returned to it. Marshall felt his own dick stiffen.

A flash camera flamed beside him. As the photographer watched the picture come up on the digital monitor, he held the apparatus several inches in front of his face, the camera's silvery curves as smooth and tactile as a sexual surface. He was one of the guys who had been hanging back in the shadows. Poised to take the next shot, the man bent at the knees. His mouth was open like a gash. A blister of spittle floated at the edge of his lower lip. Marshall didn't need to see the monitor. The flash immobilized the image in his eyes: Miss Naomi's face closed around the youth's rigidity pushing against the inside of her mouth, its form shadowed on the outer surface of her cheek. Her eyes were open, staring at the camera and knowing exactly what it saw.

When she removed her mouth the boy was hard, his dick lifting well above the horizontal. This was met by raucous applause and laughter. More hoots and ribald remarks were directed at the kid: mock admiration for his good fortune, mock praise for his hardness, mock wonder that he hadn't already ejaculated, disdain for the size of his hard-on.

Miss Naomi laughed too, her eyes searching for Nick's sunglasses. She found them and pointed to the boy's cock with both hands. She said, "Mission accomplished."

More photographs were taken, each accompanied by yips and cries and bursts of dazzling, excavating, absolute illumination. In the intermittent glare Marshall found his coat in the hall closet, piled halfway down a pyramid of stacked outerwear. Carrying the coat in his arms and leaving the gloves and scarf that had separated from it, he pulled open the front door and passed into the early morning gloom as if through an air lock into interstellar space. The cold penetrated his clothes and made him as sober as he had ever been. He allowed it to reach every hollow and pore before he wrestled himself into the coat. Streetlamps up the block burned steadily under the indigo, overcast sky. Cheers indicated something great had just happened within the house, something amazing and earnestly hoped for. Marshall's soft footfalls took him down the cracked sidewalk past unlit homes onto the next street and then onto another, a mixed-use boulevard in which the shops had been abandoned for years. He walked for hours. Police cars and other vehicles glided by soundlessly, but in a night that would never end he didn't once see a bus or train that would carry him home, if home was still worth going back to.

EVEN WITH JOYCE'S DIVORCE IMMINENT, finally, this was the season of ashen foreboding. The first morning of February saw the *Columbia*'s destruction, after NASA's unequivocating, hard-faced experts ignored warnings that repeated damage to the shuttle's foam insulation made it unsafe to fly. A portent. The world waited for the invasion of Iraq in despair, warned of its consequences. Joyce received e-mail from her colleagues in Europe—stylish, well-read Belgians, Dutch, and Italians who always brought gifts when they visited the States and invited her into their homes and lives when she went abroad. They asked, Has America gone crazy? Are you bewitched by propaganda? Do you believe, with 69 percent of your fellow citizens, that Saddam was involved in 9/11? Can't we stop this rush to war?

As if they had no errands to perform on their days off, no hair that needed to be colored, and no kids who grew out of their winter boots with just one month left to winter, the Europeans demonstrated every weekend. Joyce watched on television as they surged through medieval landscapes that had suffered war and now knew the postnational, remunerative, touristic pleasures of peace. She too was moved to declare herself a woman who sought peace—a woman who could be reasonable, conciliatory, and kind. Although she had never before been politically active, and wasn't even sure that a war to disarm Saddam wasn't necessary, she understood that her new situation as a soon-to-be-divorced woman required a new mode of thought. She would have to break the restraints that had shaped her former, failed life. In the process of redefining her character, Joyce could no longer assume that she wasn't a woman who went to antiwar demonstrations. Perhaps she was.

Demonstrations had been called around the world for

February 15: in Berlin, Paris, Prague, Seoul, Cape Town, and even at the American research base in Antarctica. Joyce asked coworkers to join her at the protest in Manhattan (she no longer knew anyone she could honestly call a friend; she was waiting for Marshall to move out before embarking on anything, including new friendships), but they wouldn't ride the subway that weekend. The Department of Homeland Security had just raised the terrorism alert level to Code Orange, gravely advising Americans to stock up on duct tape and plastic sheeting as protection against a chemical or biological attack. Tom Ridge went on TV to say these were "the most significant set of warnings since prior to September 11. The threat is real." He repeated, "The threat is real." Officials speculated that a new Osama bin Laden tape contained coded messages to terrorist sleeper cells. CIA director George Tenet appeared midweek at a congressional hearing. Testifying under oath, Tenet said, "The intelligence is not idle chatter on the part of terrorists or their associates. It is the most specific we have seen."

When Joyce called Nathan to ask him how seriously to take these warnings, another man answered the phone. His flat, middle-of-the-country accent was immediately distinguishable from Nathan's. "Yeah," he said.

"Is this Nathaniel Robbins' office?"

The man asked sharply, "Who's calling?"

"I'm a friend."

The long pause that followed was accompanied by tiny electronic gurgles beneath the hum of the wires.

"Joyce Harriman," he announced, unable to subdue the note of triumph in his voice. Clipping his syllables, he went on to reveal that he knew the address of her apartment, or rather the house number of the adjacent building; her phone number, with the last two digits reversed; and the name of the company for which she had worked six years ago.

"Yes," she said, wondering if she should correct him. Hurriedly, she asked, "Is Agent Robbins there?"

"You have the wrong number."

She read him the number off Nathan's card.

He said forcefully, "There's no one here with that name."

Now Joyce paused so that she could consider the man's phrasing and his curt manner. He sounded much more like an FBI agent than Nathan ever had. She would have hung up the phone if she hadn't already been identified. "This is the FBI, right?"

"How can I help you, Mrs. Harriman?"

"I'm trying to reach Nathaniel Robbins."

"Why?"

"It's personal. Personal reasons. I'm a friend."

After a pause he spoke with cold deliberation. "There's no Nathaniel Robbins here." He added, "Mrs. Harriman."

"Okay, well, thank you then," she rushed to say.

"And how do you know Nathaniel Robbins?" he asked.

"From around."

"What was the nature of the relationship?"

"It wasn't a relationship. We were friends. Really, more like acquaintances."

"Did he ever speak of bureau matters?"

"You mean about the FBI?"

"Please answer carefully, as this may or may not be the subject of a federal investigation."

"Of course not. The FBI? He *never* talked about the FBI or anything about work. Thank you. It's been a pleasure speaking with you," she said. This time she did hang up and stared at the phone for a long time, expecting it to do something.

She had written Nathan's home phone on the back of his card but she was too discomposed to call it. She wondered if her name had just been fed into a computer, her name more data to be crunched before being placed into intimate conjunction with other pulverized identities. She sensed now that her calls were being monitored and perhaps had been listened to for some time.

She did not attend the demonstration after all. She remained home with the children, the three of them watching the news on TV, where the worldwide protesters were an image shrunk within the screen to make room for the "War on Terror" logo, the Homeland Security Threat Bar, and the news crawl. The crawl scurried: you had to have quick eyes to catch it—UN resolutions... troop movements... terrorist attacks—and still follow the stories being told by the live images. You could never catch it.

When Marshall arrived Joyce looked up and for a moment she believed that a dangerous stranger had broken into their apartment. Then she couldn't help staring. Marshall was un-shaven, his hair matted and uncombed and glinting with frost, and his coat was open to a sweater begrimed by ice that hadn't thawed in the elevator. He hadn't come home last night, not that she cared, not that she cared the single most infinitesimal jot, but still. He looked as if he were about to fall over. The children were frightened by the apparition, as if it were a prom-ise of their own futures. Their father was blind to them and stank of vomit. He staggered into his bedroom, leaving the odor behind him.

THAT DAY in the middle of February was gravid with immi-nent war, but weeks passed as diplomats clashed in the United Nations and alternate plans of action were proposed, debated, rejected, and revised. American and British troops dug in at Iraq's border with Kuwait. In a television interview with Dan-Rather, Saddam Hussein denied that he still held weapons of mass destruction and disavowed any links to al-Qaeda. Bush, Blair, and the Spanish prime minister met in the Azores.

Thousands of candlelight vigils were held throughout the world in mostly silent hopeless self-affirming protest. The Department of Homeland Security, having quietly dropped its terrorist threat assessment to Yellow, returned it to Orange. Every day seemed like the last before the first battle's onset, yet another day would pass, narrowing the distance to war by half again. Despite the bluffs and feints in the Security Council, the failure to get a pro-U.S. majority for a second resolution, and the last-minute antiwar appeals by the pope and other world leaders (which were rebutted by Elie Wiesel and Václav Havel), the war loomed as inevitably as a date of execution. You went through your daily life in a haze, knowing that fellow Americans were preparing to race across deserts and jump from planes and kill and die and elsewhere a man or woman just like you, with kids just like yours, was waiting for this violence to wreck the fabric of a life already as tenuous and complicated as yours. You could watch the TV with the sound off. By now the arguments for and against the war had been repeated so many times they could be inferred from the commentators' facial expressions and hand gestures.

In the same gathering moment, even though they remained unpersuaded by the administration's arguments, Joyce and Marshall secretly and impatiently wished for the invasion of Iraq to begin. They couldn't stand the increasingly repetitive, circular political debate: had anyone said anything new in weeks? The nation's military muscle tensed. After years of tantalizing America with the potential of war, Iraq had finally aroused the nation's patriotism, its fighting spirit, and the pleasure it took in the exercise of new technology. Now the nation was ready and even those who opposed the war tasted that longing. To their television screens they whispered, *Let's get it over with.* When the war finally did begin, with a surprise air strike at a bunker where Saddam was believed to be hiding and then the shocking, awesome air raid on Baghdad, broadcast live, Marshall and Joyce were visited with relief, watching from separate TVs in the same apartment.

The divorce was imminent too. Marshall knew the judgment would go against him, but he was eager for it. By the time the decision was mailed to their lawyers he was no longer capable of being surprised and he wasn't surprised when Thorpe announced merrily that he would have to give up all rights to the apartment whose mortgage he had paid for the past seven years. Marshall was given thirty days to Vacate the Marital Residence. Thirty days seemed unbearably long, an expanse of time on a cosmic scale: he was determined to get out in three.

The prospect of having the apartment to herself delighted Joyce, at least for a moment, until her lawyer fully explained the judge's decision. Joyce made her go over it again, from top to bottom, all sixty pages. It was evident that Marshall's stipulated support payments were more than he could afford, yet they would amount to nowhere as much as she would need. Flushed, her voice rising girlishly, the lawyer spoke as if she had won a big victory, a veritable *Brown v. Board of Ed.* When Joyce made a modest demurral, the lawyer said, tartly, that it could have gone much worse.

Marshall rented a studio apartment in Flatbush, on a street that was probably safe in strong, direct sunlight. Unable to pay movers, he rented a small van and took only what he could carry away in cartons. He told himself that he wanted to start over.

He made many trips up and down the elevator, wordlessly letting himself into what was now Joyce's apartment. In the living room Joyce and the kids watched the news, which that day was very good. After racing ahead of their supply lines, coalition military forces had seized Baghdad with hardly a fight. American forces were now consolidating their hold on the capital, met by grateful, celebrating Iraqis inhaling their first breaths of freedom. Today a forty-foot statue of Saddam in the center of the city had been pulled down. The networks repeated the film clip many times, each time in dramatic slow motion. Although the newscasters reported that U.S. marines had provided and operated the tank and cables that wrecked the monument, you couldn't see their equipment in the clip: it appeared that the jubilant Iraqis were toppling the statue themselves. The image was indelible.

Marshall stood behind the couch and watched for a moment, a box of CDs in his arms. The statue wobbled on its multistory pedestal, Saddam's stiff, outstretched arm trembling, while onlookers threw shoes at it, a gesture of disrespect. Suddenly the statue fell halfway off the pedestal, still attached by internal cording to the concrete. Now it looked like Saddam's arm was trying to brace his fall. After dangling for a few moments, he broke at the knees and crashed in pieces into the street. The crowd roared and swept over the figure. Then the clip ran again.

"I'm not Saddam Hussein," Marshall declared. "If that's what you think."

He could see only the backs of their heads. Joyce made no movement or sound to acknowledge that she heard him.

"That's what you think!" he cried. "You think it's symbolic, don't you? 'Another evil person removed!' Am I right? Tell me, am I right?"

He came around the couch and stationed himself directly in front of the television. The children scowled but Joyce only rolled her eyes toward the ceiling, as if appealing to the people in 9E for support. When he recalled this moment weeks later, however, Marshall would realize that her eyes had been wet.

"There's no analogy here!" Marshall insisted. "I haven't gassed any Kurds, I'm not threatening anyone with weapons of mass destruction. I'm a nice guy. In fact, I think a case can be made that I'm a *great* guy—okay? Maybe not a great husband or a great father, but I did my best, Joyce. I put more effort into this marriage than you did. I gave up more of my basic human rights than you did. *I* was the one who was oppressed! To compare me with Saddam is totally unjust."

"Dad," Viola complained, "we can't see! You're in the way!"

THE DOG. The kids had lost interest in the dog, and even if he hadn't lost interest in him as well, there would have been no room for him in the studio. Marshall felt like an idiot for buying the animal in the first place. He fed him one last time and brought him in the van to a park in East New York, a desolate, virtually treeless expanse strewn with garbage. Marshall told him, "You're going to be free, Snuff. No more having to wait for your walk, no more having to eat the same old Science Diet shit. Roll around in the dirt if you like, anytime you want." The park was rich in dirt and dirtlike substances, poor in grass, a bit of the Empty Quarter in Brooklyn. He parked the van as far as possible from a small assembly of youths that had gathered on the sidewalk near the park. They had stopped whatever they were doing—more precisely, buying and selling drugs—and were watching the van.

Marshall let the dog out and took just two steps, not wanting to put distance between himself and the vehicle. Stooping slightly, he removed Snuffles' leash and collar and stroked the damp fur that had been matted beneath the collar. "Hey, boy," he began. "Have fun. Life, liberty, the pursuit…" Snuffles tensed under his hand, seeing the pack of wild dogs before Marshall did. They were at the end of the field, by a stand of scrawny trees, observing Snuffles in return. He burst from Marshall's loose grasp so quickly that his fur scorched Marshall's hands. The dog took full strides across the litter-spotted terrain, running leashless as he had never run before. The other dogs yapped at his approach and once he reached them they sprinted into the woods together. Snuffles never once looked back.

That night Marshall lay down on his new single bed purchased with a fitted sheet and a light polyester quilt at Bed World, located far down Flatbush Avenue. He lay with his head on the too-pliable pillow and listened to the sounds of the building: drips, creaks, scurrying, random pings. At some point during the night he heard a series of rhythmic thumps somewhere. He wasn't sure whether they represented lovemaking or violence or which possibility was more disturbing. He couldn't imagine ever bringing a woman here and that was why he had purchased a single bed. That woman, no more than a potentiality, her features and contours unknown, the color of her hair and her scent and the tone of her laughter undetermined, would have to have her own apartment somewhere, preferably on the Upper East Side.

He bought a cheap portable TV and watched the remainder of the war without cable. Even through the static he could see the crowds dancing in the streets, waving Iraqi and American flags, the sane finally released from their asylums, knowing they had been sane all along. "No Saddam! No Saddam!" a young man shouted at the cameras, insistently, as if the viewers couldn't possibly understand what that meant. No, they couldn't. One of the broadcasts ended with a clip of a gaunt, unwashed GI striding through a narrow alleyway by himself, his helmet strapped tightly to his head, a rifle over his shoulder. His face showed the lines of fatigue and grim resolve. From unseen hands above, cut flowers rained upon his shoulders.

Marshall had been thoroughly screwed, thoroughly unexpectedly. This apartment, this bed, this crappy TV had never been foreseen when he and Joyce had embarked on the road to divorce. At the start, so long ago, once they had agreed that for the sake of the children and their own happiness—and really, had it been so wrong for them to seek happiness, or some small measure of contentment?—they would have to live apart, they had each been optimistic, predicting a good-natured, reasonable divorce. Without even beginning to do the math, Marshall had imagined some kind of lawyerless settlement that would leave them neighbors in Brooklyn Heights, celebrating Christmas and birthdays together, recalling old family stories and laughing ruefully over drinks about the rapidly receding past. At the same time he had expected that Joyce would be totally removed from his life, that even while sharing custody of the kids he would manage never to see her again. It was unclear now how he had secured simultaneously these two mutually contradictory and individually unrealistic visions.

ONLY DAYS AFTER Marshall had moved out, Joyce had nearly forgotten how terrible the past several years had been. The time with Marshall was only history now, to be summoned to mind at will, but oddly no longer part of her life. Her existence was defined by new, marriageless parameters. So that was that: she was no longer married.

She was no longer married. Sometimes the thought made her weak in the knees, and on several mysterious occasions, probably coinciding with the approach of her period, she was convulsed by sobs. She fell on the bed, smearing the new bedspread with her mascara. Marshall had been part of her life for the past fourteen years, most of her adult life. In all the years of intermediate maneuvers leading up to their final separation, she had never realistically imagined living without him.

If she were asked by a (hypothetical) close friend why she and Marshall had divorced, she would have been unable to respond. An answer would have required that she revive long-dead arguments and "issues," none of which seemed like just cause, or at least enough cause to justify their impoverishment and the intensely complicated arrangements they would now have to devise involving the kids. She wondered if she and Marshall had made a terrible mistake.

Meanwhile the Iraq war had been won with unprecedented speed and dexterity. A light coalition presence had swiftly established order around the country. Conservative television commentators crowed over Saddam's defeat and even more so at the rout of the antiwar liberals. The liberals had been proven wrong *again,* this time about the most elemental questions involving the nation's security, American military capability, and the moral obligation to oppose tyranny. Joyce was gratified by the victory of American troops, especially with such minimal losses, but she watched the news glumly, as if Bill O'Reilly and Ann Coulter were gloating about what was wrong with *her.*

Marshall took the children to his apartment in Flatbush as infrequently as possible and he always seemed relieved to bring them back. He was forlorn and haggard these days—finally middle-aged—and she wondered if the divorce had done that to him. Of course it had. They were each now in the postmarriage phase of their lives and, though neither was even forty, indisputably middle-aged. She stared at her face in the bathroom mirror to identify the creases and swollen jowls left by her ordeal. Once, nearly by chance, she found in her hands one of their honeymoon pictures from Antigua. In the photo taken on the hotel balcony, a spotless beach behind her, her eyes were bright and she was trying to stop laughing. Marshall had just said something hilarious. What? And look how thin she had been, nearly underfed.

Saddam's location was given up by his Tikrit cousins and he was run down by a unit of the Free Iraqi Forces in an orchard on the outskirts of the city. The Americans demanded his handover for an eventual trial, but rejoicing Iraqis who converged on the site refused. It was one of the Iraqis' few acts of defiance against the Velvet Occupation. In a scene broadcast globally, Saddam pleaded for his life, falling to his knees. A scaffolding was constructed in the orchard, where hundreds of men, women, and children raucously sang patriotic, pre-Saddam songs and, at one point, "The Star-Spangled Banner." Although the lyrics were mangled, the sentiment was explicit. Tears fell freely. Thousands of ordinary Iraqis arrived at the site to cheer the proceedings, and to sing and dance and embrace their fellow liberated citizens. Men and women gathered around TVs in New York and New Delhi, and in Tehran, Cairo, Beijing, and Havana. In these electrifying hours the Free Iraqis convened a revolutionary court in the orchard. A young bearded anti-Saddam fighter soberly read the verdict; his speech, promising death to terrorists and freedom for all, electrified billions. The dictator was hung from the high branches of an olive tree. The silhouetted image of the corpse, captured by an AP photographer as the sun went down, swiftly became iconic. Within a day it was screened onto millions of T-shirts that would be sold and distributed in every country of the world, in some of them by clandestine means.

MARSHALL BOUGHT a T-shirt for himself and for each of the children. Everyone was wearing them that week. He felt foolish buying souvenir T-shirts, since he was living off his credit cards, but the dictator's execution had made him optimistic even about his finances. The world was soaked in optimism that spring. "This is history," he told Victor and Viola, who were restlessly lying on his bed, with the TV positioned on a chair in front of them. That morning American investigators in Iraq had uncovered a vast cache of nuclear weapons, some of them already loaded on medium-range missiles. The cameras panned slowly through the underground vault. Victor was barely paying attention. He was still taking in the new apartment's details:

the peeling, yellow-stained wallpaper; the rumbling refrigerator; the low ceiling; this musty smell that never went away; the shirts hanging from the frame of the shower stall; the shower stall *in the kitchen;* the mousetrap set by the refrigerator, where there was a hole in the wall so black it suggested the innumerable horrors of war.

A new day. Marshall was single again, with time to himself at last, most of the week. Nearly any evening he could ask himself what he wanted to do: go to a movie, eat Chinese food out of the carton, scratch his balls? Go ahead. He could think in practical terms of dating women now. True, he was dead broke...But even that regime might be overturned in this season of change. Meanwhile he bought top-of-the-line running shoes and stylish track shorts to match his "Death to Terrorists!" T-shirt. Without having to assemble the kids for school or wait for Joyce to complete her toilet, he ran in the mornings before work, sprinting down the fractured and pitted sidewalks of Utica Avenue as if he had just knocked over an all-night liquor store. A varsity outfielder in high school, he had forgotten how well he ran: his legs were light, they kicked high, and the storefront security grilles went by in a blur.

Marshall's new company, now called CeFKal and under new, unsullied management, which had recently adopted a logo that in no way recalled the firm's previous corporate identity, leased part of a hulking prewar building on lower Broadway. It was attempting to revive. Marshall was attempting to revive too. He threw himself into every assignment and soon won a promotion and a pay raise (that subtracted about $50 in take-home from his $600 monthly income shortfall). Partly to avoid sleeping in Flatbush, he took every opportunity to travel on business, visiting the remote, exotic sites at which the company's dwindled assets were hunkered behind elaborate creditor-protection devices.

Late one afternoon he flew in from a lab in the California

desert, brooding over what he had seen there. In the taxi on the way from Newark, he called to ask for an immediate appointment with Eduardo, his colleague at their former company who now headed the CeFKal division for which Marshall worked.

Eduardo was watching MSNBC when Marshall came in. Grinning, he apologized for the TV but pointed at the flat screen mounted in the wall to show Marshall what he had missed while he had been airborne: today, after weeks of peaceful demonstrations in Damascus—the police had refused to make arrests; the Army had declined to step in—Bashar al-Assad and several of his ministers had fled the country. A caretaker government swiftly assumed power that afternoon and promised freedom of speech, freedom of assembly, peace with Syria's neighbors, and autumn elections. The public squares and mosque courtyards were thronged.

"Amazing, huh, Marshall?"

"Yes, it is," he murmured, momentarily transfixed by the spectacle. A pert, apple-cheeked American correspondent in a flak jacket was surrounded by demonstrators waving Syrian flags at the camera. "This is history!" she shouted, and then someone produced the Stars and Stripes and she laughed. Now the crowd picked up the chant: "USA! USA!"

Eduardo said, "Bush is a Bible Belt moron who can't put together a coherent sentence, but, wow, look . . ."

"I guess." Marshall couldn't keep his eyes off the screen. Every second person in the crowd wore a "Death to Terrorists!" T-shirt just like his, except the words were in Arabic. Just last week Assad had outlawed the shirts.

"What's up? How was California?"

Marshall opened his briefcase and removed a sheaf of papers. "There's a problem with the rollout."

Eduardo turned from the TV and gave him his full, wary attention. Marshall was talking about the company's most viable new product. He eyed the papers but made no motion to take them. "What kind of problem?"

"Well, the phase three tests haven't been conclusive. But if you look at the partial sampling, you'll see results that are more consistent with phase one. Here, let me show you something that's suggestive of where this is going—"

"Come on, Marshall-man, give it to me straight. I don't do nuance."

Eduardo had joined the company shortly after it had been reorganized, and he had taken on responsibilities vital to getting it back on track. There had been setbacks. He still wore his hair long and affected a laid-back disposition, but the strain showed in his face and in occasional outbursts of testiness. Also, he was breaking up with his wife.

Marshall said, "It doesn't work. At least not now, not in the current config."

"They had a demo for the board last month. I was there. It worked fine."

"In a very controlled environment, and even then only sixty-three percent of the time. The lab thinks we should hold off—"

"Nah, nah, nah," Eduardo said vehemently. "It's too late for that. The board's seen it, the banks have seen it. We have an equity deal in two weeks. If we don't recapitalize now, the company's finished."

"But if it doesn't work—"

"It'll work. Have faith, Marshall."

Marshall nodded in agreement, but perhaps not as vigorously as he could have. Eduardo tightened his lips and stared at him for a moment.

"Marshall, have faith. Have faith in the people who sweat blood every day to keep this company alive. They come in weekends, they come in nights, they don't take vacations. They don't do this for me or for the shareholders. They do it for their families, to put bread on the table. And they do it because they're optimists. They believe we can overcome these challenges. They're people who believe in the future. We need people like that. Do you understand me?"

"Yes, of course," Marshall said, now fully earnest. He put the papers back in his briefcase, trying to dismiss their ill tidings. As if toward the nurturing warm light of the sun, both he and Eduardo turned back to the TV, where MSNBC had just gone to Tehran. The Iranians had rushed into the streets to cheer the news from Syria. Some of the women were flinging off their chadors.

THAT SPRING no one wanted to turn away from his television set. The handsome Wharton-trained freedom fighter who had captured Saddam took leadership of a provisional Iraqi government that won broad support from Sunnis, Shiites, and Kurds. At Wharton he had dated Jewish girls. Nearly all the coalition troops left Iraq, seen off by cheering flag-waving Iraqis who lined the thoroughfares to Baghdad Airport. The Israelis and the PLO reached a territorial settlement and an agreement to share sovereignty in Jerusalem. And then, just as summer was about to begin, Osama bin Laden was found huddled on a filthy rug in a cave located in the lawless, mountainous tribal lands on the Iraqi-Afghan border.

"They got him!" Eduardo's secretary shrieked, running out into the cubicle area where most of the division's employees worked. She stood in the center of the room, pumping her fists above her head, and shouted again, "They got him!"

Everyone knew who she meant. Marshall and his colleagues rushed to the windows, crying gleefully. Across the way in other offices people cheered and raised their arms too. Shouts rose from the street ten stories below, and cars and taxis sounded their horns all at once.

In Marshall's office his co-workers were hugging and slapping high fives, with grins on every face. A young woman in a light summer dress embraced Marshall and kissed him. She knew he had been at the twin towers. "You must be thrilled," she said, leaving the imprint of her body on his as she pulled away. It was the first time in years that he had been kissed by a woman who was not, say, his mother.

Abandoning their briefcases, his colleagues left the office in a hurry. Marshall followed them out, and once they encountered congestion in the elevator lobby, they went down the stairs. The stairwell was jammed too, everyone patient while they congratulated each other and shook hands. They filed out onto Broadway. Already the crowds had spilled into the street. Marshall knew exactly where they were going.

This time they headed downtown, this time with their shoes on their feet. Broadway had been cleared of traffic except for a line of fire trucks, the firemen blowing kisses to women and men. Some of the firemen wept as they waved placarded pictures of their fallen comrades. People in the street pounded the sides of the vehicles, cheering, and reached up to squeeze the firemen's hands and forearms. An American flag flew from nearly every operable window of every office tower. Just-shredded confetti fell in a multicolored blizzard. The mob kicked it up again.

They passed City Hall, slowing as the streets around Ground Zero filled with people coming from every direction, up from the Battery and along Park Row, overflowing into City Hall Park. At Vesey they pushed toward the construction site, shuffling down the block to Church Street, stopping at the intersection to gaze at the infinite vacancy that rose to the heavens from the pit that went down to bedrock. Humanity rebounded against him and gradually spread out around the sixteen acres' perimeter, flush against the chain-link fence.

News helicopters sliced the air overhead. Air horns tooted

while American anthems were sung by men and women who had come to New York from every country of the world. Marshall sang too, "God Bless America" and "O Beautiful for Spacious Skies" and "My Country, 'Tis of Thee," squeezed between a young sari-wrapped woman and a tall man in dreads. All around him schoolchildren bumped each other with their backpacks, giggling. They sang and so did these suited businessmen and this gaggle of big-haired young women in heels and an old guy in a bomber jacket and another guy and another guy and an elderly woman who had come out with a walker. Marshall felt a huge emotion surging within him: it was relief at bin Laden's capture, of course, but also sudden love for his country, at that moment an honest, unalloyed, uncompromised white-hot passion. He hadn't realized that he knew so many words to so many patriotic songs. His face was wet, soaked.

"Daddy!"

It was Victor, just a few feet away. He broke out of Joyce's grip and rushed to embrace his father at the knees. Joyce had both kids with her, both of them wearing their "Death to Terrorists!" shirts. They held chocolate ice cream cones. Surprised and embarrassed, Joyce nearly stumbled; Marshall nearly reached out to catch her. "Hi," he said. They eyed each other without actually making eye contact.

She replied, "Hi."

Victor said, "They captured Osama bin Laden."

"I know, honey, that's wonderful."

Viola offered him a bite of her ice cream cone. The crowd was halted now, too packed for anyone to move farther, too packed for Marshall and Joyce to separate. He felt her body against his, warmed by the sentiments of the day. New Yorkers occupied the streets in all directions as far as the eye could see, faces and bodies scintillating blocks away like the skin of a snake, leaves in a windblown tree, ticker tape. Their songs thundered against the high walls of the boulevards. Strangers embraced. Others patted backs and squeezed shoulders. Someone drummed on bongos. In the distance: the report of firecrackers. Marshall bit into the ice cream. The late-afternoon light was golden, molten now, pouring across the glass and stone buildings arrayed around the site, every surface incandescent. Before him the vastness of the emptiness of the hole in the city was inflamed with human noise and aspiration. An arrow's point of sparrows lifted from a nearby roof and wheeled into the deepening blue unopposed. The moment would last forever, or until everything contained within it was completely destroyed.